The Printed Adventures

JAMES VAN HISE

Cover art by Morris Scott Dollens

Library of Congress Cataloging-in-Publication Data
James Van Hise

    Trek: The Printed Adventures

    1. Trek: The Printed Adventures (television, popular culture)
I. Title

Published by Pioneer Books, Inc., 5715 N. Balsam Rd., Las Vegas, NV, 89130.

First Printing, 1993

DEDICATION:
To dreamers who not only talk the talk but walk the walk....

Publisher and Designer: Hal Schuster   Editor: David Lessnick

CONTENTS

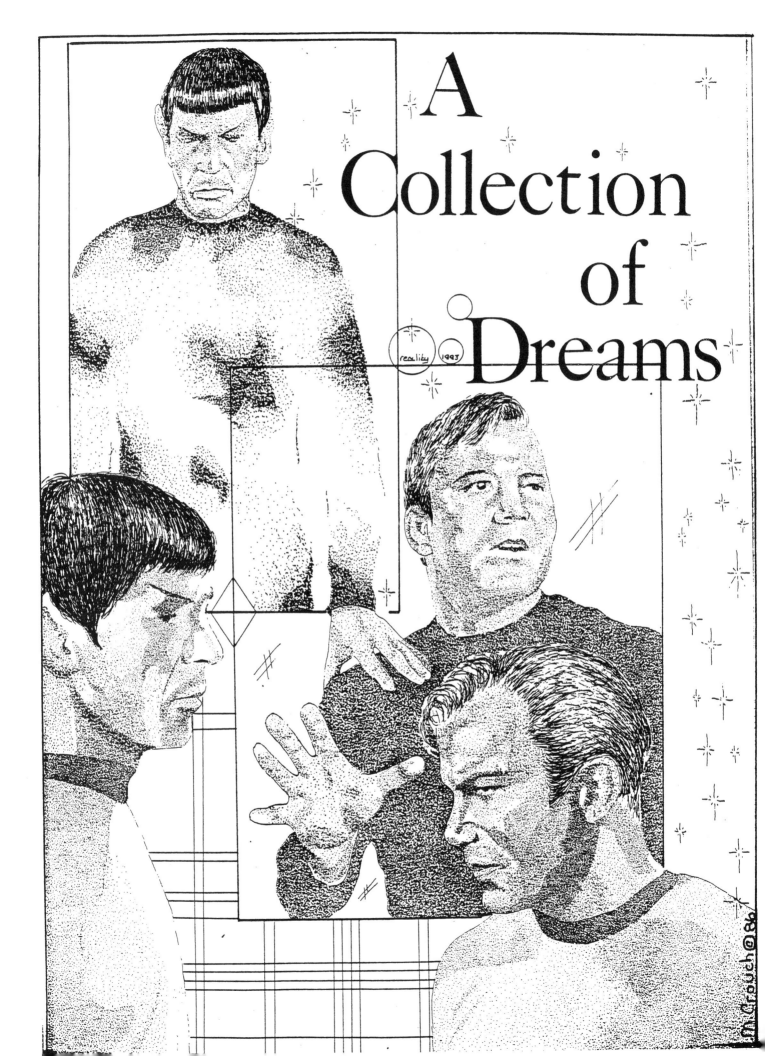

TREK

The Printed Adventures

Introduction

20TH CENTURY ODYSSEY

Jean Hinson is a fan writer/publisher and is well acquainted with the various forms of Trek fiction, both fan and pro.

After a couple thousand years, Homer's Odyssey is still a rousing good adventure yarn, although Homer could have done with a good editor—ever try to wade through The Iliad and keep your mind on the central storyline? But aside from his tendency to use ten words where one would have done better, Homer told a good tale in the Odyssey. And his hero is one of the Immortals of classic literature.

And speaking of Immortals. . . James T. Kirk as Odysseus? Yeah, I can buy that.

STAR TREK literature is part of our culture now; it has given us words that were not a part of our language before. Concepts that were "lunatic fringe" twenty years ago are commonplace and accepted today. For those of you who thought It presumptuous of me to compare STAR TREK to the Odyssey, I submit the Thorndyke-Barnhart Dictionary definition:

Odyssey: Any long series of wanderings and adventures.

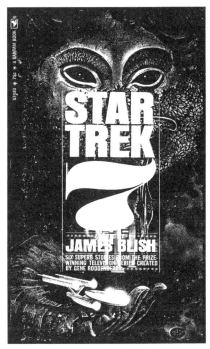

Above: James Blish series adapting televised episodes.
Opposite: Art by Gary Kato for the cover of the February 1976 of the fanzine 273 DEGREES CENTRIGRADE

A LONG SHORE LEAVE

The mystique of Classic STAR TREK has grown out of the long starvation of the 1970's, and has spawned an unprecedented body of literature, both professional and amateur. The classic Trek reader-

BY JEAN HINSON

ship grew out of what has come to be known in fandom as the "Long Drought," when the written stories were the only new STAR TREK adventures available. Only a handful of these are memorable, but to a Trekker, bad Trek is better than no Trek.

I suppose every Trek reader has his own Top Ten list. No two lists will contain the same novels since reading is a totally subjective experience. In putting together my own list of Most Memorable Trek novels, I made the surprising discovery that all but one of my favorite pro novels were written by women (no, really, I was surprised to make the discovery).

In pursuit of why I seemed to find the novels written by women more memorable, I found that, without exception, those authors appeared to view the STAR TREK universe in the context of the characters, keeping them true to the characterizations in the series. Men appear to see STAR TREK in terms of hardware and space opera—which it never really was. On the most basic level, what it really was—and this from Gene Roddenberry himself—was a series of contemporary social parables within the framework of the future.

HIDDEN HISTORY

In this vein, one of the most memorable of the pro novels on my personal list has to be STRANGERS FROM THE SKY by Margaret Wander Bonnano. To begin with, the theme blends present and future in a plausible plot. What if history was wrong about the date of First Contact with Vulcan? What if, by mischance, a Vulcan ship arrived on Terra 20 years earlier, and all evidence of their presence was suppressed by the military establishment (sound familiar?), necessitating a mission to the past by Kirk, Spock, and several others of the Enterprise crew.

The characterizations are quite good, including a welcome view of another side of Gary Mitchell, and the additional characters are also well-defined and believable. The action builds to a

cliff-hanging suspense as Kirk fights to save the lives of the Vulcan mother and son who survived the crash of their ship only to be captured by Navy Intelligence. He must also convince the Vulcans, by their own logic, not to self-destruct (per their standing order) to avoid Terra's discovery of Vulcan before our society is ready for contact.

This tale was both fascinating and believable to me because it has probably already happened. Oh, not Vulcans. . . but someone. . . from somewhere. If this sounds far-fetched, go to the library and look up the Roswell Incident, circa 1947 or so. The incident took place in New Mexico nearly 50 years ago; there were a number of witnesses who were intimidated into silence by the government.

THE FIRST STARSHIP

Among the pro novels, however, my personal favorite is FINAL FRONTIER by Diane Carey. Ironically, I was doubtful about this one when I first heard of it since it deals with a time before James T. Kirk and his intrepid crew. In a framework of Classic Trek present time, James Kirk is on leave at his childhood home in Iowa. At a low point, he is considering leaving Starfleet and spends his leave time re-reading letters he received from his father when he was a boy.

There are many unforgettable characters here, such as Spirit Claw Sanawey, the utterly serene and extremely dangerous Mescalero Apache, as well as a high-ranking renegade Romulan ship commander named T'Cael Kilyle who will make you take a new look at Romulans.

But the real heroine of this fascinating tale is the ship herself: the yet-to-be-named starship prototype that was to become the immortal Enterprise. This is one you'll want to re-read from time to time.

THE ROMULAN TOUCH

Two others on my most-read list are THE WOUNDED SKY and MY ENEMY, MY ALLY, both by Diane Duane. I find her concept of the warp field through which the Enterprise travels more believable than the sheer velocity of some authors. Her obvious love of the STAR TREK universe shows in the accurate portrayal of the well-known characters, and her aliens are always unforgettable personalities. The Hamalki engineer of THE WOUNDED SKY, a crystal spider, is a charmer (I couldn't help but love her, and I'm a devout arachniphobe), and the alien crewmembers on the Enterprise lend a dimension that was missing in the TV series.

Of all the many Trek novels now in print, Duane's MY ENEMY, MY ALLY is among the best of the lot. The plot is true to the highest ideals of STAR TREK, and Duane's writing style gives her imagery an almost poetic drama without sacrificing the moments of wry humor that endeared the series to so many of us. Kirk's antagonist is Commander General Ael t'Rllaillieu. This wily old Romulan she-wolf is possibly the most indomitable, intriguing character to turn up in a pro novel to date.

It is through Ael's thoughts that we get a glimpse of Romulan philosophy and customs, among them the concept of mnhei'sahe: ". . . not quite honor, and not quite loyalty. . . It can be a form of hatred that requires you to give your last drop of water to a thirsty enemy—or an act of love that requires you to kill a friend."

I found the final passage of this novel to be almost unbearably poignant. Kirk, acting for the exiled Ael who has lost everything, places her name pennon in a remote wilderness area in California so that she will be remembered by the elements after her death.

If you read only one STAR TREK novel, let it be this one.

DISCONTINUITY

Early on in the world of Trek novels, however, there were some which were eminently forgettable: a couple that come immediately to mind are THE STARLESS WORLD and DEVIL WORLD, both (coincidentally?) by Gordon Eklund. I figure they sold more than one or two copies only because, at that time, they were the Only Game In Town.

Another misfire was ENTERPRISE: THE FIRST ADVENTURE by Vonda McIntyre. She completely disregarded Trek history. The discontinuity from the series was so jarring that the entire novel was simply unbelievable. My final quibble with Ms. McIntyre lies in her insistent error (in all her novels) of referring to the Enterprise as a Constellation class starship; I wish someone would inform her that Enterprise is a Constitution class ship.

THE NEXT GENERATION GAP

Speaking of errors, one of the most recent novels, SHELL GAME by Melissa Crandall, contains some real gems: imagine reading along, happily immersed in the Trek universe, only to have Kirk say to Sulu: "Engage." If you're a Classic Trekker, it hits you like a cold shower.

Then, about the time you get over that faux pas, Kirk puts together his Away Team. At that point I put the book down. If I want Jean-Luc Picard, I'll tune in Channel 13.

In spite of all attempts to integrate Classic Trek with THE NEXT GENERATION, as in McCoy's appearance in "Encounter At Farpoint" and Spock in "Unification" (to say nothing of killing off Sarek in the same episode), I fear the effort is doomed to failure for a simple reason: in relation to Classic Trek, THE NEXT GENERATION hasn't happened yet. The two are not really interchangeable—or perhaps they are only interchangeable in one direction: forward. That is to say, THE NEXT GENERATION can build upon Classic Trek, use its history, terminology, etc., but to use terms from TNG in Classic Trek novels, as noted above, is simply a blatant error. The two frameworks are 75 years apart in time. If you think that doesn't make a large difference, compare 1900 and 1975.

KEEPING TREK ALIVE

As an admitted Classic Trek aficionado, I find I have developed no interest in reading the NEXT GENERATION novels, even though I will usually read anything that presents words in a row (to quote the late Robert Heinlein). This was a surprise to me, since I appreciate THE NEXT GENERATION as a natural development of the ongoing legend of STAR TREK; a necessary continuation, as not even James T. Kirk is immortal (neither was Odysseus, come to think of it).

An analysis of my disinterest in TNG novels brought to light an interesting psychological phenomenon: my fascination with written STAR TREK developed during the Long Drought of the '70s. There was no STAR TREK available except the novels, since there was no videotape until the '80s. Quite simply, I acquired the habit through deprivation of the TV series; the visual mode of images was transmuted (through necessity) to the visual mode of words, which generated "new" episodes of STAR TREK in my imagination.

All Classic Trek fans endured the Long Drought and will know what I mean, but neofans (pure NEXT GEN fans, that is) will not. Since the premiere of THE NEXT GENERATION in 1987, there has been constant availability of the series through TV and videotapes. No deprivation. No hunger. That is the true NEXT GENERATION gap.

Quick as the novelizations of THE NEXT GENERATION were to hit the bookstands (in comparison to the lag before Classic Trek novels ever began), I'm heartened by the fact that DEEP SPACE NINE novels were even speedier to appear; the continuity is taking root, and will endure, and the end seems to be nowhere in sight.

More Missions

15

More Myths

FIRST TIME IN PAPERBACK

STAR TREK 12

™

BY
JAMES BLISH
WITH
J.A. LAWRENCE

FIVE MIND-DAZZLING ADVENTURES
FROM THE AWARD-WINNING
TELEVISION SERIES CREATED BY
GENE RODDENBERRY.

11382.8 ★ $1.75 ★ A BANTAM BOOK

SP8401 ★ 75c ★ A BANTAM BOOK

STAR TREK 10

ADAPTED BY
JAMES BLISH

SIX FASCINATING NEW EPISODES FROM
THE AWARD-WINNING TELEVISION
SERIES CREATED BY GENE RODDENBERRY.

FIRST TIME IN PAPERBACK

PROZINES

THE MAINSTREAM

SIDEBAR
STAR TREK: SUBMISSION GUIDELINES

The following are the current submission guidelines Pocket Books has issued for their STAR TREK, STAR TREK: THE NEXT GENERATION, and STAR TREK: DEEP SPACE NINE novels.

First and foremost, Pocket Books will only read manuscripts submitted through an agent. This is because a certain number, perhaps even a great number of manuscripts, are filtered out by this process as an agent will only submit a manuscript which they feel is good and that they can stand behind. A good agent will not submit a manuscript that an editor will find to be sloppy and amateurish. This eliminates the slush pile submission stage which other companies go through who publish original novels.

There is a format which most publishers prefer for a manuscript. In the case of Pocket Books they require that manuscripts be submitted typed, double-spaced on one side of non-erasable typing paper. The page number and author's name should appear at the top of each page. I know of one agent who thinks this is unnecessary but manuscripts get shuffled around at publishing companies and it is not at all unusual for half a manuscript to be in one room and the other half in another room. The author's full name and address should appear on the first and last page of the manuscript, including your phone number.

PROCEDURE

Submit the first three chapters with a detailed synopsis (four to six pages) of the entire plot. Due to the large volume of submissions received, the publisher's reply can take anywhere from one to four months. If they are interested in publishing your novel the publisher will contact your agent. They may ask to see the completed novel before reaching a decision.

CONTENTS

Pocket Books is only interested in full-length adventure novels of roughly 70,000 words (which is about 250-300 manuscript pages). They are not interested in short stories, poetry, biographies, romances, encyclopedias, dictionaries, concordances, compendiums, blueprints or trivia books.

In a one sentence description they are looking for exciting science fiction stories featuring the STAR TREK characters we all know and love. All material is subject to the approval of Paramount Pictures, who are very concerned about maintaining the integrity of the characters and the STAR TREK universe. Absolute consistency is a practical impossibility, but some major themes which Pocket Books suggest be avoided include:

1) Traveling in time to change history or learn something, rescue someone, etc. (Such as has been done in such published Pocket STAR TREK novels as THE ENTROPY EFFECT and KILLING TIME. But like they said, "absolute consistency is a practical impossibility.")

2) Having a tear in the fabric of reality which could destroy the universe.

3) Pon farr in Spock.

4) Death of a major, established crewmember.

5) Any plot which hinges on or describes in detail sexual relations (normal, abnormal, and so on). They are not interested in books which suggest anything other than friendship among the Enterprise crewmembers. (What Pocket's guidelines don't mention is that if Spock and Kirk mind-meld, Spock is not allowed to touch Kirk as Paramount finds this "suggestive" in spite of the fact that it was done throughout the television series.

6) Any plot that mixes THE NEXT GENERATION and the original crews. (Those novelizations of official episodes which did this were assigned to writers to do based on the TV scripts, such as REUNIFICATION and RELICS.)

7) Any story primarily about a guest star or non-STAR TREK regular. This means no stories about other crews, ships or people that become the focus of the story. The novels should always "star" Kirk, Spock, McCoy or Picard, Riker, Troi, et al.

CLASSIC TREK

Plot elements to avoid with respect to specific characters.

Kirk: No offspring or close relations not already established. Also, no childhood or current sweethearts; though you can create temporary love interests.

Spock: No sisters, brothers, half siblings (beyond Sybok), offspring, sudden reversions to emotion or sex. The Vulcan mind-meld has also been seriously overused of late. No explanations of the "Vulcan way" beyond what has already been done in the TV series or movies.

McCoy: No offspring or close relations not already established.

Other crewmembers: In general, avoid trying to definitively map out a character's history much beyond what has already been done in the movies or television episodes. Of course, these are guidelines. Disobey them at your own peril if necessary to your story—but remember, you were warned.

STAR TREK: THE NEXT GENERATION

Plot elements to avoid with respect to specific characters.

Data becoming human.

You cannot use castmembers who have left the show (no Tasha Yar or Dr. Pulaski).

There's only one updated difference not reflected on these guidelines—Pocket Books has decided they only want to buy STAR TREK novels from published writers who already have 6 novels to their credit. Anyone remember what the Bantam STAR TREK novels of the '70s were like which were written by known science fiction writers? Need I say more?

Chapter 1
STAR TREK NOVELS

While the '60s saw STAR TREK novels produced for children in inexpensive hardback versions, the first mass market novel was SPOCK MUST DIE! by James Blish in 1970. Blish had been writing the popular condensations of ST episodes into short stories for Bantam Books. Oddly enough this novel was released about six months after STAR TREK left network airing and began appearing in syndication. This may have just been inadvertently poor timing since novels are scheduled a full year before they appear, but there was a market for it and the book remained in print.

No new novels appeared from Bantam until 1976 when merchandisers seemed to simultaneously discover that STAR TREK wasn't dead after all. Bantam continued issuing new novels until 1980, when Pocket Books outbid them at contract renewal time.

Pocket has issued about 30 novels in its series. Two other concurrent series of novels generated by STAR TREK were added to their output in the last year.

Although it is not always apparent (and the cover art sometimes creates deliberate confusion), the new novels are all set at the time of the original five year mission of the Enterprise under Captain Kirk. The movie adaptations occur at a later period. While the TV episodes dealt with a variety of story types, the novels deal with a cosmic menace threatening the safety of the Federation. Some might call this a cliché.

SPOCK MUST DIE! is a Bantam novel by James Blish.

BANTAM PAPERBACKS

Bantam's STAR TREK 1 through 12 by James Blish adapt the original 79 television episodes. Blish boiled the TV scripts down into short stories attempting to make them interesting by including elements from the original scripts which didn't make it into the aired version. Volume 12, also titled MUDD'S ANGELS, was written by J.A. Lawrence, the wife of the late James Blish. This last volume includes the two Harry Mudd stories and one original. It was not well received by fans.

Other Bantam paperback novels are SPOCK MUST DIE! by James Blish, SPOCK, MESSIAH! by Theodore R. Cogswell and Charles A. Spano, Jr., THE PRICE OF THE PHOENIX by Sondra Marshak & Myrna Culbreath, PLANET OF JUDGMENT by Joe Haldeman, VULCAN! by Kathleen Sky, THE STARLESS WORLD by Gordon Eklund, TREK TO MADWORLD by Stephen Goldin, WORLD WITHOUT END by Joe Haldeman, THE FATE OF THE PHOENIX by Marshak & Culbreath, DEVIL WORLD by Gordon Eklund, PERRY'S PLANET by Jack C. Haldeman II, THE GALACTIC WHIRLPOOL by David Gerrold and DEATH'S ANGEL by Kathleen Sky. Bantam also published STAR TREK: THE NEW VOYAGES Volumes 1 and 2, featuring short stories.

Mandala/Bantam published FOTONOVELS in the late '70s when most people in the business, including Paramount, didn't see STAR TREK as having much of a licensing future. These dozen books used high quality 35mm full color frame enlargements from the actual episodes to retell the stories. They sold so well that Paramount demanded a huge fee to license more books in the series. Due to the huge expense in producing 100 page plus books comprised of full color photos on every page, no new agreement was ever arrived at.

The FOTONOVELS included CITY ON THE EDGE OF FOREVER - Fotonovel #1 (1977), WHERE NO MAN HAS GONE BEFORE - Fotonovel #2 (1977), THE TROUBLE WITH TRIBBLES- Fotonovel #3 (1977), A TASTE OF ARMAGEDDON - Fotonovel #4 (1978), METAMORPHOSIS - Fotonovel #5 (1978), ALL OUR YESTERDAYS - Fotonovel #6 (1978), GALILEO 7 - Fotonovel #7 (1978), DAY OF THE DOVE - Fotonovel #8 (1978), DEVIL IN THE DARK - Fotonovel #9 (1978), A PIECE OF THE ACTION - Fotonovel #10 (1978), DEADLY YEARS - Fotonovel #11 (1978) and AMOK TIME - Fotonovel #12 (1978).

DEL REY PAPERBACKS

STAR TREK LOGs 1 through 10 by Alan Dean Foster adapt the 22 episodes of the STAR TREK animated series. Foster expanded on the scripts to produce some very interesting stories, particularly his adaptation of D.C. Fontana's "Yesteryear."

POCKET BOOKS PAPERBACKS

Pocket Books published a series of novels including (1) STAR TREK: THE MOTION PICTURE by Gene Roddenberry, (2) THE ENTROPY EFFECT by Vonda N. McIntyre, (3) THE KLINGON GAMBIT by Robert E. Vardeman, (4) THE COVENANT OF THE CROWN by Howard Weinstein, (5) THE PROMETHEUS DESIGN by Sondra Marshak & Myrna Culbreath, (6) THE ABODE OF LIFE by Lee Corey, (7) STAR TREK II: THE WRATH OF KHAN by Vonda McIntyre, (8) BLACK FIRE by Soni Cooper, (9) TRIANGLE by Sondra Marshak & Myrna Culbreath, (10) WEB OF THE ROMULANS by M.S. Murdock, (11) YESTERDAY'S SON by A.C. Crispin, (12) MUTINY ON THE ENTERPRISE by Robert Vardeman, (13) THE WOUNDED SKY by Diane Duane, (14) THE TRELLISANE CONFRONTATION by David Dvorkin, (15) CORONA by Greg Bear, (16) THE FINAL REFLECTION by John M. Ford, (17) STAR TREK III: THE SEARCH FOR SPOCK by Vonda McIntyre, (18) MY ENEMY, MY ALLY by Diane Duane, (19) THE TEARS OF THE SINGERS by Melinda Snodgrass, (20) THE VULCAN ACADEMY MURDERS by Jean Lorrah, (21) UHURA'S SONG by Jean Kagen, (22) SHADOW LORD by Laurence Yep, (23) ISHMAEL by Barbara Hambly, (24) KILLING TIME by Della Van Hise, (25) DWELLERS IN THE CRUCIBLE by Margaret Wander Bonanno, (26)

PAWNS AND SYMBOLS by Majliss Larson, (27) MINDSHADOW by J.M. Dillard, (28) CRISIS ON CENTAURUS by Brad Ferguson , (29) DREADNOUGHT! by Diane Carey, (30) DEMONS by J.M. Dillard, (31) BATTLESTATIONS! by Diane Carey , (32) CHAIN OF ATTACK by Gene deWeese , (33) DEEP DOMAIN by Howard Weinstein , (34) DREAMS OF THE RAVEN by Carmen Carter , (35) ROMULAN WAY by Diane Duane , (36) HOW MUCH FOR JUST THE PLANET by John Ford , (37) BLOODTHIRST by J.M. Dillard , (38) THE IDIC EPIDEMIC by Jean Lorrah , (39) TIME FOR YESTERDAY by A.C. Crispin , (40) TIMETRAP by David Dvorkin , (41) THE THREE-MINUTE UNIVERSE by Barbara Paul, (42) MEMORY PRIME by Gar and Judith Reeves-Stevens, (43) THE FINAL NEXUS by Gene deWeese , (44) VULCAN'S GLORY by D.C. Fontana, (45) DOUBLE, DOUBLE by Michael Jan Friedman, (46) THE CRY OF THE ONLIES by Judy Klass, (47) THE KOBAYASHI MARU by Julia Ecklar, (48) RULES OF ENGAGEMENT by Peter Morwood, (49) THE PANDORA PRINCIPLE by Carolyn Clowes, (50) DOCTOR'S ORDERS by Diane Duane, (51) THE ENEMY UNSEEN by V.E. Mitchell, (52) HOME IS THE HUNTER by Dana Kramer Rolls, (53) GHOST WALKER by Barbara Hambly, (54) A FLAG FULL OF STARS by Brad Ferguson, (55) RENEGADE by Gene deWeese, (56) LEGACY by Michael Jan Friedman, (57) THE RIFT by Peter David, (58) FACES OF FIRE by Michael Jan Friedman, (59) THE DISINHERITED by Robert Greenberger, (60) ICE TRAP by L.A. Graf, (61) SANCTUARY by John Vornholt, (62) DEATH COUNT by L.A. Graf, (63) SHELL GAME by Melissa Crandell, (64) THE STARSHIP TRAP by Mel Gilden and (65) WINDOWS ON A LOST WORLD by V.E. Mitchell. Pocket Books also published a series of larger novels not in the numbered series, including BEST DESTINY by Diane Carey, THE DEVIL'S HEART by Carmen Carter, ENCOUNTER AT FARPOINT by David Gerrold , ENTERPRISE: THE FIRST ADVENTURE by Vonda McIntyre, FINAL FRONTIER by Diane Carey , IMZADI by Peter David, THE LOST YEARS by J.M. Dillard, METAMORPHOSIS by Jean Lorrah, PRIME DIRECTIVE by Garfield and Judith Reeves-Stevens, PROBE by Margaret Wander Bonanno, RELICS by Michael Jan Friedman, REUNION by Michael Jan Friedman, SPOCK'S WORLD by Diane Duane , STAR TREK IV: THE VOYAGE HOME by Vonda McIntyre , STAR TREK V: THE FINAL FRONTIER by J.M. Dillard, STAR TREK VI: THE UNDISCOVERED COUNTRY by J.M. Dillard, STRANGERS FROM THE SKY by Margaret Bonanno , UNIFICATION by Jeri Taylor and VENDETTA by Peter David.

THE NEXT GENERATION AND DEEP SPACE NINE

In addition to novels featuring characters and situations from CLASSIC TREK, Pocket Books has also created a series for THE NEXT GENERATION. The novels include (1) GHOST SHIP by Diane Carey , (2) THE PEACEKEEPERS by Gene deWeese, (3) THE CHILDREN OF HAMLIN by Carmen Carter, (4) SURVIVORS by Jean Lorrah, (5) STRIKE ZONE by Peter David, (6) POWER HUNGRY by Howard Weinstein, (7) MASKS by John Vornholt, (8) THE CAPTAIN'S HONOR by David and Daniel Dvorkin, (9) A CALL TO DARKNESS by Michael Jan Friedman, (10) A ROCK AND A HARD PLACE by Peter David, (11) GULLIVER'S FUGITIVES by Keith Sharee, (12) DOOMSDAY WORLD by Carmen Carter, Peter David, Michael Jan Friedman and Bob Greenberger, (13) THE EYES OF THE BEHOLDERS by Ann Crispin, (14) EXILES by Howard Weinstein, (15) FORTUNE'S LIGHT by Michael Jan Friedman, (16) CONTAMINATION by John Vornholt, (17) BOOGEYMEN by Mel Gilden, (18) Q-IN-LAW by Peter David, (19) PERCHANCE TO DREAM by Howard Weinstein, (20) SPARTACUS by T.L. Mancour, (21) CHAINS OF COMMAND by Bill McCay, (22) IMBALANCE by V.E. Mitchell, (23) WAR DRUMS by John Vornholt, (24) NIGHTSHADE by Laurell K. Hamilton, (25) GROUNDED by

David Bishoff and (26) THE ROMULAN PRIZE
by Simon Hawke.

       To date, Pocket Books has released
two novels in a new series related to STAR
TREK: DEEP SPACE NINE. These are (1) EMIS-
SARY by J.M. Dillard and (2) THE SIEGE by
Peter David.

The first of a series of
books adapting the tele-
vised episodes, by James
Blish.

SIDEBAR:
A HANDY LIST OF STAR TREK FICTION BETWEEN HARD COVERS

With the exception of a couple of the "juvenile" titles listed here, all of the following books appeared first (or simultaneously) in paperback.

Gregg Press, Boston/G.K. Hall

STAR TREK II: THE WRATH OF KHAN by Vonda N. McIntyre
1984, 223 pages, 5 1/8" X 8"
Black cloth binding, Silver title, Dust jacket

THE ENTROPY EFFECT by Vonda N. McIntyre
1984, 224 pages, 5 1/8 X 8"
Black cloth binding, Silver title, Dust jacket

YESTERDAY'S SON by A.C. Crispin
1984, 1191 pages text plus one page bio. 5 1/8" X 8 "
Black cloth binding, Silver title, Dust jacket

WEB OF THE ROMULANS by M.S. Murdock C.
1984, 220 pages, 5 1/8 X 8"
Black cloth binding, Silver title, Dust jacket

THE KLINGON GAMBIT by Robert E. Vardeman
1984, 158 pages, 5 1/8" X 8"
Black cloth binding, Silver title, Dust jacket

THE FINAL REFLECTION by John M. Ford
1985, 253 pages, 5 3/8" X 8 1/2"
Black cloth binding, Silver title, Dust jacket

UHURA'S SONG by Janet Kagan
1985, 373 pages, 5 3/8" X 8 1/2"
Black cloth binding, Silver title, Dust jacket

MUTINY ON THE ENTERPRISE by Robert E. Vardeman
189 pages 1985 5 3/8" X 8 1/2"
Black cloth binding, Silver title, Dust jacket

CORONA by Greg Bear
1984, 192 pages, 5 3/8" X 8 1/2"
Black cloth binding, Silver title on Spine, Dust jacket

COVENANT OF THE CROWN by Howard Weinstein
1985, 191 pages, 5 3/8 X 8 1/2
Black cloth binding, Silver title, Dust jacket

STAR TREK III: THE SEARCH FOR SPOCK by Vonda N. McIntyre
1986, 297 pages, 5 3/8" X 8 1/2"
Black cloth binding, Silver title, Dust jacket

THE WOUNDED SKY by Diane Duane
1986, 255 pages plus one bibliography, 5 3/8" X 8 1/2"
Black cloth binding, Silver title, Dust jacket

THE TEARS OF THE SINGERS by Melinda Snodgrass
1986, 244 pages, 5 3/8" X 8 1/2
Black cloth binding, Silver title, Dust jacket

BLACK FIRE by Sonni Cooper
1986, 220 pages, 5 3/8" X 8 1/2"
Black cloth binding, Silver title, Dust jacket

THE ABODE OF LIFE by Lee Corey
1986, 207 pages, 5 3/8" X 8 1/2"
Black cloth binding, Silver title, Dust jacket

TRIANGLE by Sandra Marshak and Myrna Culbreath
1986, 188 pages, 5 3/8 X 8 1/2"
Black cloth binding, Silver title, Dust jacket

THE PROMETHEUS DESIGN by Sandra Marshak and Myrna Culbreath
1986, 190 pages, 5 3/8" X 8 1/2"
Black cloth binding, Silver title, Dust jacket

WHITMAN PUBLISHING

STAR TREK—MISSION TO HORATIUS by Mack Reynolds / Illustrated by Sparky Moore
1968, 210 pages, 5 1/8 X 7 3/4
No dust jacket, Glossy color bindings
(Juvenile novel)

POCKET BOOK/ SCIENCE FICTION BOOK CLUB

THE COVENANT OF THE CROWN by Howard Weinstein
1981, 184 pages text and 1 page bio, 5 3/4 X 8 1/2
Yellow paper binding, Black title, Dust jacket

STAR TREK II: THE WRATH OF KHAN by Vonda N. McIntyre
1982, 186 pages, 5 3/4 X 8 1/2
Red paper binding, Black title, Dust jacket

YESTERDAY'S SON by A.C. Crispin
1983, 141 text & 1 page bio, 5 3/4 X 8 1/2
Blue paper binding, Gold title, Dust jacket

THE WOUNDED SKY by Diane Duane
1983, 179 text & 1 bio page, 5 3/4 X 8 1/2
Black paper binding, Blue title, Dust jacket

STAR TREK III: THE SEARCH FOR SPOCK by Vonda N. McIntyre
1984, 219 pages, 5 3/4 x 8 1/2
Blue paper binding, Black title, Dust jacket

MY ENEMY, MY ALLY by Diane Duane
1984, 210 pages, 5 3/4 X 8 1/2
Tan paper binding, Black title, Dust jacket

THE VULCAN ACADEMY MURDERS by Jean Lorrah
1984, 214 pages, 5 3/4 x 8 1/2
Black paper binding, Red title, Dust jacket

CRISIS ON CENTAURUS by Brad Ferguson
1986, 184 pages, 5 3/4 X 8 1/2
Red paper binding, Blue title, Dust jacket

ENTERPRISE, THE FIRST ADVENTURE by Vonda N. McIntyre
1987, 340 pages, 5 3/4 X 8 1/2
Yellow end boards, Black cloth spine, Blue title, Dust jacket

STRANGERS FROM THE SKY by Margaret Wanderer Bonanno
1987, 310 pages, 5 3/4 X 8 1/2
Blue end boards, Black cloth spine, Gold title, Dust jacket

HOW MUCH FOR JUST THE PLANET by John M. Ford
1988, 5 3/4 X 8 1/2
Dust jacket

THE FINAL FRONTIER by Diane Carey
1988, 5 3/4 x 8 1/2
Dust jacket

SPOCK'S WORLD by Diane Duane
1988, 5 3/4 X 8 1/2
Dust jacket

STAR TREK V—THE FINAL FRONTIER by J.M. Dillard
1989, 5 3/4 X 8 1/2
Dust jacket

IMZADI by Peter David
1992, 5 3/4 X 8 1/2
Dust jacket

PROBE by Margaret Wander Bonanno
5 3/4 X 8 1/2
Dust jacket

THE LOST YEARS by J.M. Dillard
5 3/4 X 8 1/2
Dust jacket

THE VULCAN ACADEMY MURDERS by Jean Lorrah
5 3/4 X 8 1/2
Dust jacket

SIMON AND SCHUSTER

STAR TREK: THE MOTION PICTURE by Gene Roddenberry
1979, 252 pages text plus 1 page bio, 5 3/4 X 8 5/8
Blue paper end board, Dark blue cloth spineM Gold title, Dust jacket

AEONIAN/AMERON
(all 5 3/4 X 8 3/4, no dust jacket)

STAR TREK LOG ONE by Alan Dean Foster
1975, 184 pages
Ppurple cloth binding, Gold title on spine

STAR TREK LOG TWO by Alan Dean Foster
1975, 176 pages
Purple cloth binding, Gold title

STAR TREK LOG THREE by Alan Dean Foster
1975, 215 pages
Purple cloth binding, Gold title

STAR TREK LOG FOUR by Alan Dean Foster
1975, 215 pages
Ourple cloth binding, Gold title

STAR TREK LOG FIVE by Alan Dean Foster
1976, 195 pages
Purple cloth binding, Gold title

STAR TREK LOG SIX by Alan Dean Foster
1976, 195 pages
Purple cloth binding, Gold title

STAR TREK LOG SEVEN by Alan Dean Foster
1977, 182 pages
Purple cloth binding, Gold title

STAR TREK LOG EIGHT by Alan Dean Foster
1976, 183 pages
Dark purple cloth binding, Gold title

STAR TREK LOG NINE by Alan Dean Foster
1976, 183 pages
Gray cloth binding, Gold title

STAR TREK LOG TEN by Alan Dean Foster
1978, 250 pages
Gray cloth binding, Gold title

E.P. DUTTON

STAR TREK READER I by James Blish
1976, 422 pages, 5 3/8 x 8 1/2
Light blue paper end board, Black cloth spine, Blue title, Dust jacket

STAR TREK READER II by James Blish
1977, 374 pages, 5 3/8 X 8 1/2
Black binding, Red title, Dust jacket

STAR TREK READER III by James Blish
1977, 374 pages
Black paper binding, Light blue title, Dust jacket

STAR TREK READER IV by James Blish
1978, 4409 pages text & 1 bio page, 5 3/8 X 8 1/2
Black paper binding, Light blue title, Dust jacket

LITTLE SIMON

STAR TREK III: THE SEARCH FOR SPOCK STORYBOOK by Lawrence Weinberg
1984, color photos illustrating text, 8 1/4 X 11 1/4
Glossy color photo binding

RANDOM HOUSE

STAR TREK - THE PRISONER OF VEGA by Sharon Lerner & Christopher Cerf
illustrated by Robert Swanson, 1977, 6 3/4 X 9 1/4
Glossy printing bonding
(Juvenile)

STAR TREK - THE TRUTH MACHINE by Christopher Cerf & Sharon Lerner/illustrated by Jane Clark
1977, 6 3/4 X 9 1/4
Glossy printed binding
(Juvenile)

STAR TREK POP-UP - GIANT IN THE UNIVERSE
1977, 8 pages, 8 1/4 x 10 1/2
Glossy printed binding
(Juvenile)

STAR TREK POP-UP - TRILLIONS OF TRILLIGS
1977, 8 pages, 8 1/4 X 10 1/2
Glossy printed binding
(Juvenile)

Chapter 2

THE BANTAM STAR TREK

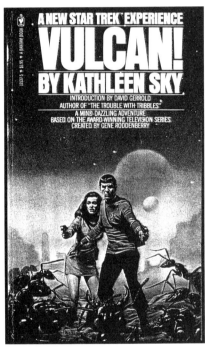

The Bantam novel, VULCAN! by Kathleen Sky.

The following review of the original Bantam STAR TREK novels of the Seventies explains why some readers turned to fandom for their new adventures of Kirk and Spock; they just weren't getting what they wanted in the professional STAR TREK novels.

Following are reviews of the fifteen original STAR TREK novels published by Bantam, including the two short story collections. In most cases these books remain in print, often redressed with new covers to make them look new and attractive to the casual reader.

Nearly all of the Bantam STAR TREK novels were originally published in the '70s, beginning with SPOCK MUST DIE which appeared in 1970. A couple, notably THE GALACTIC WHIRLPOOL and DEATH'S ANGEL, squeaked out in 1980 after Pocket had published their first novel; Gene Roddenberry's adaptation of STAR TREK: THE MOTION PICTURE. Pocket had to wait for Bantam to issue the remaining books on their contract before proceeding with their new series.

Only original novels are examined here, not the TV series adaptations done by James Blish.

Bantam Books novels published in the Seventies and early Eighties are some of the weakest released by a major publisher. Things didn't look up until Pocket Books picked up the contract.

The Bantam covers claim they contain adventures never before encountered. In truth, they presents incidents the Enterprise and its crew encountered plenty of times. The crew challenge several

BY WENDY RATHBONE

[THE GALACTIC WHIRLPOOL review by James Van Hise]

"most powerful forces in the universe," experience instrument failure in just about every story and discover black holes galore. Lack of imagination places many of these books in the ten-to-sixteen age bracket or in the category of beginning science fiction.

SPOCK MUST DIE!

SPOCK MUST DIE! by James Blish is the first original professional novel to come out of the STAR TREK universe. It isn't too bad considering that the TV series only started showing in Great Britain in mid-1969 and James Blish hadn't seen many episodes before he wrote this book.

The plot is average. The Klingons have broken the Organian Peace Treaty and Organia does not seem to be answering its phone calls. In fact, the entire planet of Organia has disappeared.

The logical conclusion our crew comes to is that Organia has been destroyed, possibly by the Klingons, if that is even possible. Spock is elected to be sent via a faster-than-light tachyon Transporter to Organia. It doesn't work and, instead, a replicate Spock is accidentally created.

Both are identical and no one can tell the difference. Both insist they are the real thing.

If we could have seen any part of the story from Spock's point of view it may very well have saved the book. As it stands, SPOCK MUST DIE! gives McCoy the brains, makes Sulu temporary First Officer and allows Scotty to tamper with the Transporter more in 118 pages than in any nine Trek episodes.

SPOCK, MESSIAH!

The title of SPOCK, MESSIAH! by Theodore R. Cogswell and Charles A. Spano, Jr. is enough to make anyone scream in despair. Gene Roddenberry is said to have done just that.

Afterwards, he set the standard all original STAR TREK novels must meet.

Spock makes only short appearances as Kirk, McCoy and one Ensign Sara George try to locate him and stop him from taking over a planet and ruling as a divine messiah sent from the gods. Spock's mind is mixed up with a native's highly emotional brain and the native has figured out how to control Spock.

He uses Spock as an image to attract followers into his cult. The plot is a typical "let's rescue Spock" mission where the rescuers get into so much trouble it's a wonder they're still alive at the end.

STAR TREK: THE NEW VOYAGES

STAR TREK: THE NEW VOYAGES edited by Sondra Marshak and Myrna Culbreath is highlighted with introductions by the STAR TREK actors. William Shatner, Leonard Nimoy, DeForest Kelley, James Doohan, Nichelle Nichols, Majel Barrett Roddenberry and George Takei all add their opinions to the stories. Walter Koenig was left out.

The first story, "Ni Var," by Claire Gabriel is well written for the characterization of Kirk and Spock. Spock is split into two people, an idea explored often in Trek fiction. One half is entirely human; the other, entirely Vulcan. The most interesting aspect of the story is the understanding Kirk and Spock have of each other.

That same mental link is touched upon in "The Mind Sifter," by Shirley S. Maiewski. Kirk, who has been kidnapped by Klingons, undergoes pain and torture and inadvertently cries out for Spock. Strangely enough, Spock, asleep aboard the Enterprise, awakens in horror. It is an effective flashback in the best story in the anthology.

STAR TREK: THE NEW VOYAGES has six more original Trek stories making it one of the best fiction books Bantam published in the series.

STAR TREK: THE NEW VOYAGES II

The best page in the follow-up STAR TREK: THE NEW VOYAGES II edited by Sondra Marshak and Myrna Culbreath is 247. The poem, "Elegy for Charly," is worth the price of the book. Antonia Vallario has taken an eerie theme and written a very moving poem that haunts the STAR TREK universe, "where dark is incredibly far."

NEW VOYAGES II is not as enjoyable as the first volume. "Surprise!" by Nichelle Nichols is the most memorable and humorous tale in the book. The stories are, for the most part, strange, sometimes violent or repulsive and often difficult to understand. Volume II contains eight stories and two poems.

VULCAN!

The cover of VULCAN! by Kathleen Sky shows Spock and a human woman surrounded by giant ants. However, I try never to judge a book by its cover, sometimes a very hard rule to stand by.

The female on the cover is Dr. Katalya Tremain, an expert biologist and a woman plagued with a prejudice toward the Vulcan race. In the beginning, Tremain pleads with Commodore Stone not to force her to "ship out with a Vulcan," and whimpers, "you know how I fell about Vulcans; how could you be so cruel?" She sounds like a two-year-old and doesn't get much better.

By page 21 she has had her first good cry. Kirk seems to be the only smart character on the ship. He logs an official protest at having Tremain on board, insisting she is a disgrace to Star Fleet. She is.

Unfortunately, Kirk does not appear often in the plot. The focus is on Spock and Tremain.

McCoy acts like an adolescent teenager doing everything short of throwing himself at Tremain. Falling for a woman who exhibits disgusting bigotry seems inconsistent for the doctor. McCoy's character begins to disintegrate. The others follow suit soon after.

VULCAN! also has several bothersome details to its discredit. The author appears to have little respect for the STAR TREK characters or the universe they live in.

The Enterprise personnel act like childish fools. Spock is set in his opinions and turns out wrong about life on the planet Arachnae being intelligent. Spock even gets his mind mixed up with an ant being's hive brain.

DEATH'S ANGEL

Though the idea for DEATH'S ANGEL by Kathleen Sky is better than the plot of VULCAN!, the writing is worse. It is poorly executed pace opera, embarrassing to read. The characters say and do things no real person would consider.

Kathleen Sky does not seem to understand STAR TREK or its characters.

THE PRICE OF THE PHOENIX

THE PRICE OF THE PHOENIX by Sondra Marshak and Myrna Culbreath does everything SPOCK MUST DIE! fails to do. The plot runs along the same lines but is more complex and memorable.

This time Kirk gets twinned. His twin, James, becomes the tragic hero to top all tragic heroes. The villain, a part Vulcan/part Romulan/part devil giant named Omne is the backbone of the story; the perfect villain.

He is nearly indestructible with a mighty Transporter that reconstructs an image to utter perfection, indefinitely. Omne may well be immortal.

The plot hinges on the battle between Kirk and Omne. Omne is obsessed with feeling superior to any man. He cannot stand the thought of "his match" freely roaming the stars.

To prove his superiority, Omne must own Kirk, thereby possessing his "other half." Kirk says he is everything Omne is not. Omne replies, "No, Captain. You are everything I might have been."

A few lines later, Omne adds, "I want to own you, to own the other half of my soul."

They fight, but the real battle has not yet begun. "You will cry and then you will beg," Omne threatens. "You will know the real right of the man who can best you and master you."

"I'll see you in Hell first," Kirk responds, to which Omne replies, "Captain, this is Hell."

The bantering is common throughout the novel and though it sometimes seems as if the characters speak with riddled tongues, there is a smoothness and intelligence behind their words which enhances the story and makes it fun to read.

None of the characters in PRICE OF THE PHOENIX are the bumbling idiots of SPOCK, MESSIAH!. The authors delve deeply, creating well-rounded, three-dimensional human (or Vulcan or Romulan) beings. They exhibit feelings, with varying strengths and weaknesses adding to the fascination of a good plot.

THE FATE
OF THE PHOENIX

THE FATE OF THE PHOENIX by Marshak and Culbreath is the sequel to PRICE OF THE PHOENIX. It is best to read FATE after reading PRICE.

Though FATE can stand on its own, it may be difficult to follow without having read the previous novel. PRICE introduces the Romulan Commander Di'on, James (Kirk's double), and Omne.

The sequel is as good as its predecessor. It has some new Romulan characters: a female Doyan and her male "princeling," Trevanian. The "princeling" is the role James plays as it is the only way he can be a Romulan without anyone finding out he is human with artificially green-tinted blood and clever plastic surgery to disguise his rounded ears.

The "princeling" always covers his face in public. He is considered a cut above most men and cannot be touched or fought by any male or female (except Di'on).

On board the Enterprise both Kirk and Spock are psychically burned out and virtually psi-null. This makes both more vulnerable to Omne, who could show up at any time unannounced.

It also affects the way the ship is run. Kirk no longer has hunches to save the ship.

The plot gets more complicated. The reader is guaranteed not to be bored.

TREK TO MADWORLD

TREK TO MADWORLD by Stephen Goldin is full of twisting surprises and eminently better than Kathleen Sky's VULCAN!. His novel is simple but clever with details worked out perfectly so everything falls into place from beginning to end.

The plot is slightly reminiscent of CHARLIE AND THE CHOCOLATE FACTORY by Roald Dahl. Enowil, a little gnome the Enterprise runs into in a bubble just outside the universe, claims to have been an Organian gone sour. He is a perfectly harmless fellow who speaks and acts with the same mannerisms as Willy Wonka in Dahl's book.

He has a problem and brings the Enterprise, a Klingon ship and a Romulan ship into his bubble to enlist their help. Whoever succeeds will be granted the reward of anything they want.

The Enterprise, on a mission to evacuate colonists from a planet where the sun's radiation has proven lethal, has a choice to stay or continue its mission. Kirk elects to stay because if the Klingons or Romulans solve Enowil's problem their reward may be deadly.

THE STARLESS WORLD by Gordon Eklund.

If the problem is not solvable Enowil will deposit the starship in orbit above the colonists' planet with no time wasted. They have nothing to lose.

The characters are straight forward. Kirk is given ample opportunity to exercise his genius and comes across as a gentleman.

TREK TO MAD WORLD is fun. It is light reading complete with a familiar moral at the end that most people will probably guess before finishing the book. Roald the Invisible makes an appearance as fitting tribute to Roald Dahl.

THE STARLESS WORLD

The world inside a sphere is the starless world of THE STARLESS WORLD by Gordon Eklund. The Enterprise is drawn into the world called Lyra where a Klingon starship has already been trapped.

They have to figure out a way to escape quickly because Lyra is on a collision course with a black hole. They have about four days.

This STAR TREK novel does not include a young, beautiful female for Kirk, McCoy or even (horrors!) Spock. Instead a young, waist-high, furry chimp creature becomes a major character.

The creature, Ola begins helping Kirk and the crew after Kirk saves her life. She ends up saving Kirk's life and is their main source of information about Lyra and its inhabitants.

Surprisingly, Uhura has a large role and is depicted as an intelligent officer. Never once does she say, "Captain, I'm frightened!"

She is captured by strangers on the planet's surface. When Kirk finds her, she is possessed. They are told she will be all right, but the plot never follows up on her condition.

In a flashback scene, Uhura and Kirk first meet as she tells him her name in Swahili means "truth." Actually uhuru means "freedom," a fact that escaped author Eklund's mind.

Spock and McCoy appear in brief scenes. Kirk is in charge of the whole show. At the beginning and end of the novel, Kirk is found flat on his bunk in his quarters reading Tolstoy's WAR AND PEACE as recommended to him by Chekov.

This is Kirk's third time through the book, one of the longest novels ever written on Earth. This is a comical way of illustrating the long stretch between planets and missions.

THE STARLESS WORLD is average. It reads fast but borders on boring.

DEVIL WORLD

Eklund's second STAR TREK book, DEVIL WORLD, is not as good as the first. It involves little aliens, Danons, who look like miniature naked devils.

The story involves a challenge by "an awesome disembodied intelligence, more powerful than any other force in the universe!" Sounds like Vejur.

It also involves a pretty young girl named Gilla whom Kirk falls in love with. Ho-hum.

Get the picture? DEVIL WORLD is as unimaginative and dull.

PLANET OF JUDGEMENT

PLANET OF JUDGEMENT by Joe Haldeman puts the Enterprise on a weird planet they appropriately call Anomaly. Anomaly is orbited by a black hole.

Five shuttles with various crew specialists, including Kirk, McCoy and Spock are trapped on the surface. The laws of physics do not apply on this strange world. The story is the survival tale of the trapped officers while the Enterprise runs to a nearby Starbase to get help.

Interesting scenes portray the inhabitants of Anomaly making Spock, McCoy and four other officers relive painful memories. Spock relives his "Amok Time" and an incident involving a visit with his mother to his human cousin's house when he was ten years old. McCoy relives the time he and his wife split up and another time when he was almost knifed to death while on shore leave.

The characters are well written, with no noticeable flaws. PLANET OF JUDGEMENT is a better adventure story than most Bantam novels, but lacks imagination.

WORLD WITHOUT END

Haldeman's second Trek book, WORLD WITHOUT END, is more technical than the first. The Enterprise passes through a magnetic field generated by a space vessel the size of a large asteroid.

Some of the crew members, including Kirk and McCoy, beam over to investigate. They are captured and cannot beam out because an anomaly affects their instruments. Eventually this power source captures the Enterprise and slowly drains it of energy while pulling it toward the surface of the asteroid ship.

Our heroes also have to contend with Klingons. This all sounds quite exciting but, unfortunately, is tedious and uneventful.

The characterizations of Kirk, Spock and McCoy are shallow. Haldeman adds nothing new. Some scenes have excellent potential for exposing inner feelings, but Haldeman glosses over emotions.

PERRY'S PLANET

PERRY'S PLANET by Jack C. Haldeman II is written by Joe's older brother. The cover shows a silhouette of Captain Kirk entering a room where a strange guy with wires stuck all over his body is lying under a glass bubble. Kirk is wearing his uniform from the movie, not the series. Since this is Bantam's only post-movie book, it's a mark in their favor that they tried to maintain continuity.

The movie left Trek open-ended so more adventures could follow. PERRY'S PLANET could take place after the movie.

The plot involves a peaceful planet, Perry, which a tired and overworked Enterprise crew must convince to join the Federation. Unfortunately, Perry's peace is maintained by a virus which forces a person to collapse any time they want to get violent.

The virus is highly contagious and infects the crew. When a Klingon ship comes into range, they can do nothing to defend themselves besides raising the shields.

Kirk has a tough time. The Klingon commander is the brother of a man Kirk previously battled. Kirk won, and when the Klingon's brother died, the commander swore revenge.

It is disconcerting to Kirk to learn he has unintentionally made a formidable enemy of the Klingon since he never asked for a fight with either him or his brother. It haunts him throughout the novel.

Spock lacks definition in the story. He doesn't have much of a role other than reciting computer-like theories on the condition of Perry and its population. In fact, Spock is hardly in the story until Kirk and company beam down to Perry.

Still, PERRY'S PLANET is better than most Bantam Trek novels. The plot is imaginative, Haldeman makes an effort to write about the characters' feelings and adds new characters to make it a good book.

THE GALACTIC WHIRLPOOL

There is an unfortunate tendency among authors who write series novels to approach them in a completely different manner than they would a book unconnected with any continuing set of stories. Nowhere has this been more evident than in the STAR TREK novels, particularly those published by Bantam. When David Gerrold announced he had written a STAR TREK book "for the fans," most expected something more than a routine adventure.

Gerrold has demonstrated a clear and undeniable capacity to write original mature science fiction novels including DEATHBEAST, WHEN HARLIE WAS ONE and THE MAN WHO FOLDED HIMSELF. For twenty years he produced an impressive body work. Unfortunately THE GALACTIC WHIRLPOOL does not live up to his standards.

There is one test a series novel must pass. It must be interesting as a story even if the main characters are perfect strangers. THE GALACTIC WHIRLPOOL fails.

The problems with this book are numerous. The plot is old, lifted bodily from a Robert Heinlein novel.

A great deal of background is laid, but THE GALACTIC WHIRLPOOL fails because it slips out of focus and fades off into questionable interest.

IT'S A WRAP

The Bantam STAR TREK novels were a disappointment. None match the Trek episodes and few are as good as much of the fan fiction being published. Thankfully the history of the STAR TREK novels does not end there.

Profile:

GREG BEAR

Greg Bear has had a distinguished career as a science fiction novelist, but in the early '80s he satisfied one of his creative longings when he wrote the novel CORONA (Trek Classic #15—Pocket Books). That book marked the first actual STAR TREK writing he'd ever done although he's been a fan of the series for years. Bear is the author of PSYCHLONE, THE STRENGTH OF STONES and many other books.

"In high school I did a sort of Mort Drucker [MAD magazine] style satire, but I hadn't actually written about STAR TREK before," Bear recalled. "I did do artwork for the STAR TREK CONCORDANCE, though, and I was one of those chosen to end up in the STAR TREK coloring book of illustrations."

His interest in STAR TREK dates right back to 1966. "From the very first episode when it was sneaked on KNBC in Los Angeles. That was the George Clayton Johnson episode with the salt-sucker. I've been a Trekkie ever since," he stated.

THE INFLUENCE OF STAR TREK

He continued, "I'm not sure it's influenced my writing as much as it's influenced all of science fiction by making it apparent what could be transferred from prose to television without a great deal of loss. Roddenberry really kept a tight rein on it and they had good writers working for them; it was good television besides being pretty good science fiction. It still sticks in my head. It's not something that I'm going to forget like a lot of things that pass away."

The odyssey of CORONA from premise to printed page actually began 5 years before it was published. He said, "My agent called me and told me that Timescape wanted STAR TREK ideas because they were going to expand the STAR TREK book series. I submitted three ideas. Some of these were based on a story

BY JAMES VAN HISE

conference that I held with Alan Brennert in 1977 at Paramount. I almost sold them an idea, although not the one which ended up becoming CORONA. But then they decided not to go with the TV show and went with the movie instead, so my STAR TREK script idea was never bought or produced.

.　"I converted these concepts into book ideas and added a couple of others, handed them over to Pocket Books and they picked out one. Then they took three years to get back to me about writing it!"

Greg Bear's CORONA.

WHAT MAKES STAR TREK POPULAR?

Asked what attracts him to STAR TREK and what it is about the show that he feels causes it to transcend other TV science fiction, Bear answered, "Character. They really spent a lot of time making it clear who the people on STAR TREK were. They took a lot of care with the character development and on finding actors who could carry out the roles professionally and consistently. Roddenberry had a distinct idea of what he wanted the future to be. He wanted it to be benevolent. He wanted human beings to have developed and he wanted them to still face challenges and live in adventurous situations. That's an almost ideal combination.

"Of course STAR TREK was not a successful TV show at first," he continued. "It may have been a little ahead of its time. It was before 2001 came out. So STAR TREK was really starting what would be the big wave of science fiction which would lead through 2001 and ultimately to STAR WARS."

Just like any Trek fan, Bear has opinions about how STAR TREK has fared as a wide screen revival. "The first motion picture had some problems," he admitted. "It was an impressive effort, but the second one was a little more faithful to the TV show idea, with more emphasis on character than on spectacle. I think that's what the STAR TREK fans want. They don't want all of the cosmic stuff so much as they want to see what happens to Kirk, Spock and the others."

#24

ENTER SECOND HISTORY—
AND A GALAXY GONE MAD!

THE NEW
STAR TREK® NOVEL

KILLING TIME

DELLA VAN HISE

POCKET
52488-7
$3.50

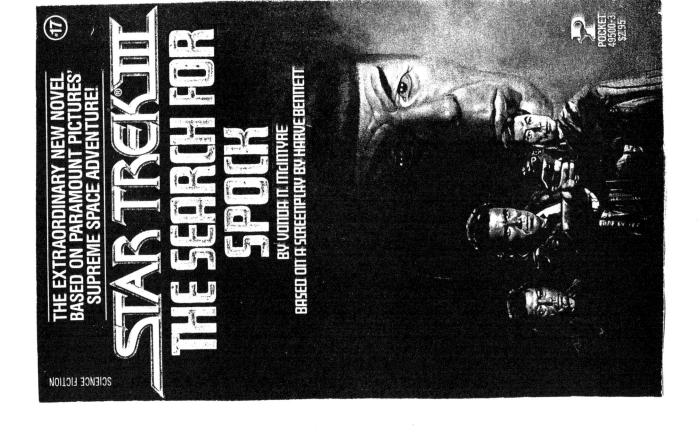

#17

THE EXTRAORDINARY NEW NOVEL
BASED ON PARAMOUNT PICTURES'
SUPREME SPACE ADVENTURE!

STAR TREK III®

THE SEARCH FOR SPOCK

BY VONDA N. McINTYRE

BASED ON A SCREENPLAY BY HARVE BENNETT

POCKET
49500-3
$2.95

Chapter 3
THE POCKET BOOKS

When Pocket Books took over publication of new STAR TREK fiction in 1979 with Gene Roddenberry's STAR TREK: THE MOTION PICTURE, it ushered in a new era. The novels finally began to reflect what the fans were looking for.

Pocket Books output already dwarfs Bantam's STAR TREK line. This chapter examines most of the 60 plus Trek Classic books. Separate chapters cover THE NEXT GENERATION novels, DEEP SPACE NINE and the special series STAR TREK novels Pocket has issued. While the vast majority of the 100 plus STAR TREK novels Pocket has published are covered in these related chapters, there wouldn't be room for anything else in this volume if we covered every one in detail. No one anywhere has attempted to review even this many in one place before. Since this volume covers more than 80, very little is left out.

Those who would like to be selective in their reading may find this an excellent guide.

STAR TREK: THE MOTION PICTURE

The Great Bird of the Galaxy retells the story of the first STAR TREK film in STAR TREK: THE MOTION PICTURE. The foreword by Roddenberry and Captain James T. Kirk is outstanding.

Opposite page: The adaptation of the third STAR TREK film, THE SEARCH FOR SPOCK by Vonda N. McIntyre and an original novel by Della Van Hise, KILLING TIME.

Roddenberry adds emotion to the death in the Transporter by making the victim Admiral Lori Cianna, Kirk's former wife. Gene uses a telepathic signal to Kirk to good effect.

The romance between Ilya and Decker is explained, as is Spock's return to Vulcan for the Kolinar discipline. The dialogue in the

BY ALEX BURLESON
(unless otherwise noted)

book occasionally deviates from the film, yet that is to be expected.

Roddenberry adds depth to his characters, exposing their thoughts as well as words and deeds. Gene sets the stage for the highly successful Pocket Books line retelling the story of the film which signaled STAR TREK's rebirth, based on the screenplay by Harold Livingston and the story by Alan Dean Foster. By expanding on the movie script, Roddenberry established the tradition followed in subsequent movie novelizations.

THE ENTROPY EFFECT

(Reviewed by James Van Hise)

Although die-hard fans of STAR TREK understand the subtext of the series and respond to the characters as human beings, novelists often take a different view. In most cases, until Pocket Books took over from Bantam the STAR TREK novelists did not understand the series itself but merely its superficial structure. They treated STAR TREK the same way they would an adventure of Flash Gordon or Buck Rogers. The characters are shallow archetypes starring in an adventure of no human consequence.

Gene Roddenberry showed that the characters deserved better treatment in his movie novelization. This left many fans to wonder if Gene Roddenberry was the only professional writer who really understood what a good STAR TREK story needed, because his novelization was more of a human adventure than the film.

When David Gerrold's novel appeared from Bantam, fans were sure they were in store for another treat. Gerrold had written two thoughtful books on STAR TREK, but he dropped the ball.

Pocket Book's second STAR TREK novel received some ballyhoo because Kirk died in the course of the story. The novel tells a human story. Why was this so difficult for so many STAR TREK novelists until this novel appeared?

Why could Leslie Fish write a fan fiction story populated with real human beings while Kathleen Sky produced only clumsy attempts? Why did Gene Roddenberry make something appear easy which David Gerrold found impossible? It's because Leslie Fish and Gene Roddenberry felt for what they were writing, and that makes THE ENTROPY EFFECT by Vonda McIntyre so successful—we feel it.

This story sweeps us into the lives of the characters and the locale of the story. Three hundred years in the future becomes now. Sulu's soul-searching is sensitive and real in subtle and powerful ways that Riley's introspection in THE GALACTIC WHIRLPOOL was not. Kirk is not just given a floor plan to walk after being identified, but we learn a new point of background in his character.

Vonda McIntyre spends the first third of the book setting up the characters, and pays as much attention to the old familiars as she does to the new people she brings aboard. The plot doesn't advance a great deal over those eighty pages, but it seems like it does. And that's the trick, isn't it?

Characterization can be boring when it's ham-fisted and unimaginative, but when genuine human insight and understanding is brought to bear by a skilled writer, a book becomes more than a story. It becomes a human adventure in which the reader is bettered by the experience, rather than merely passing time.

An applicable quote from Stephen King appeared on page 306 of DANSE MACABRE: "If you want to know how the rockets are going to work in any hypothetical future, turn to Larry Niven or Robert Heinlein; if you want literature about what the future might hold, you must go to Ray Bradbury or perhaps to Kurt Vonnegut. What powers the rockets is POPULAR MECHANICS stuff. The province of the writer is what powers the people."

That explains why THE ENTROPY EFFECT is superior to every STAR TREK book published under the Bantam imprint and clearly signaled that Pocket Books was taking the novels in a new direction. Vonda McIntyre clearly cares about the people she is writing about, and makes us care as well. When Captain Kirk dies, we do not just twitch as we would at a simple plot device, but experience his death along with the shocked and disbelieving crew. When Mr. Spock pieces together what has happened and begins his almost hopeless and increasingly complex quest across time, we live it along with him.

THE ENTROPY EFFECT is an excellent science fiction book which could stand on its own even if it weren't STAR TREK. A strong story is strong no matter what the main characters' names are. In this case those characters are part of STAR TREK and their humanity is part of us.

THE PROMETHEUS DESIGN
(Reviewed by Wendy Rathbone)

The most interesting thing about THE PROMETHEUS DESIGN by Sondra Marshak and Myrna Culbreath is that it is consistent with the events of the novel STAR TREK: THE MOTION PICTURE and recalls situations from STAR TREK episodes. The novel makes use of past episodes referring to them as a matter of record for the Enterprise crew.

This reference to the past makes the book stronger and the characters more well-rounded and three dimensional. If an idea resembles something done before in STAR TREK, Marshak and Culbreath do not ignore that. They use it to their, and their character's, advantage.

The story takes place some time after the V'ger incident. It begins with the landing party, consisting of Kirk, Spock, McCoy, Uhura and Chekov, in the middle of a crisis on the planet Helvan. Kirk is missing and Spock can't even register a life presence on the tricorder.

Spock collapses when he mentally hears a cry for help from Kirk. They search intensively but cannot find him anywhere until he finally shows up in the middle of a Helvan mob, half conscious and looking as though he may have just visited Hell itself.

It turns out that everyone on that landing party, except Spock, has experienced missing time. No one can remember what happened during the time lapses. All Kirk remembers is feeling shame, disgust and pure horror.

As usual, Marshak and Culbreath's characterization is strong. This description from Spock's point of view in Sick Bay shows the use of past events from both the episodes and the movies to further character development and depth:

It was here in Sick Bay that Spock had come back from deep shock after his mind-link with Vejur, and in that unguarded moment he had taken Kirk's hand, suddenly grasping through that 'simple feeling' the sterility of Vejur's vast and terrible logic—and the sterility of Spock's own attempt at the total non-emotion of Kolinahr.

Yet the Vulcan who had sought Kolinahr as an antidote to his pain still remained, maintaining long meditations, silences—stiff with the disciplines of the desert and the cause they had not cured. Whatever cause had sent Spock away from Kirk, McCoy and the Enterprise. (Page 17)

That "cause" that was not cured on Vulcan is only hinted at in this book yet is one of the main subplots of the subsequent novel TRIANGLE, also by Marshak and Culbreath. It is Spock's greatest fear, the pon farr.

He is not the same Vulcan from the series and certainly not the same Vulcan from these authors' other two novels, THE PRICE OF THE PHOENIX and THE FATE OF THE PHOENIX. When he goes into Vulcan command mode after taking charge of the Enterprise, he becomes very harsh and, if possible, even colder than a Vulcan. He is extremely hard on Kirk who seems to be the greatest loser in this book, and an admirable good sport about it.

The idea that highly superior beings are using the galaxy for the purpose of experimentation, like rats in a maze, is not the most original one, but this is carried out in unique, exciting and very intellectual ways. This was one of the most complicated STAR TREK books.

The concentration on Vulcan characterization and culture is excellent, though the book puts down humans a lot. The characterization and writing style is, as usual with these authors, excellent.

THE ABODE OF LIFE

In THE ABODE OF LIFE by Lee Correy, the Enterprise is caught in a gravity disturbance hurling the starship into a remote area of the Sagittarius arm. A planet and its star are the only objects in this section of the galaxy. The Enterprise crew must contact the aliens to repair their ship and return home; the planet holds material Scott needs to fix his engines.

A landing party encounters three groups of aliens. They are very polite because everyone is armed with an "Old West" style of firearm.

When Kirk and company refuse the weapons, they are warned this will make them objects of ridicule, in danger of attack. Even McCoy reluctantly straps on a sidearm.

Spock's hand is shattered by a bullet during an attempt to free Kirk. The Vulcan disobeys the Prime Directive to save the ship.

The unstable star has led to a government based on one group's ability to shield the population from the stellar activity. Spock stabilizes the star to save the Enterprise and Kirk must work out an equitable compromise since they've changed the society on the planet. Knowledge of other life in the galaxy succeeds in forcing change.

STAR TREK II: THE WRATH OF KHAN

The rediscovery of the crew of the Botany Bay is mixed with the intricacy of the psyches of two men in STAR TREK II: THE WRATH OF KHAN, Vonda N. McIntyre's adaptation of the movie. The pair discover that vengeance is the only thing they can agree on after years of neglect.

The history of the team who built the Genesis Device is a highlight of the novel. The film gives the team short shrift, but the book reveals the story behind each of the men and women who die at the hands of Khan.

Carol and David Marcus are given detail, as is the depth of emotion Kirk feels upon the death of Spock. Spock's relationship with Saavik is presented in far more detail.

Peter Preston, Scotty's nephew who dies in the attack, is a more defined character. Peter's portrayal as Spock and Saavik's student, and his attempt to prove his worth to the uncle who can't let up on his engineers for a second, move this book to a very emotional conclusion.

Also of note are the reactions aboard the Reliant to Khan's assumption of power. McIntyre's novel is based on the screenplay by Jack B. Sowards and the story by Harve Bennett and Sowards.

BLACKFIRE
(Reviewed by Wendy Rathbone)

An explosion rips through the Enterprise bridge, seriously injuring Captain Kirk, Spock, Sulu, Uhura and Chekov and killing all the cadet trainees. The entire saucer section is jettisoned due to severe damage.

Kirk is near death and a badly injured Spock desperately tries to piece together what happened. He believes the blast was sabotage and won't allow his body time to heal until he figures out the mystery.

This leads Spock on a bizarre journey for over a year. Events take drastic turns. In chapter seven, three-fourths of the way through the book, "Black Fire" is finally revealed as Spock's pirate name which he shares with his Romulan friend, Desus. Together they become legends and

Black Fire earns the reputation of a hero saving "damsels in distress." He goes from being First Officer of the Enterprise to legendary pirate consorting with Romulans — a bizarre journey.

Sonni Cooper adopts a narrative writing style from the omniscient point of view to delineate the passage of a year. The story unfolds at such an accelerated rate necessary information is told to the reader instead of shown. If everything in this novel was shown it would fill five or more volumes.

The reader is distanced from the events, reading about what has already taken place. There is no central theme to this book and none of the characters grow as a result of the story.

The flavor of STAR TREK is captured with Kirk, Scott and McCoy true to the series. The novel is plausible within the Roddenberry universe.

TRIANGLE
(Reviewed by Wendy Rathbone)

TRIANGLE by Sondra Marshak and Myrna Culbreath involves new, interesting conflicts between Kirk and Spock, adding unusual insight. The story revolves around the fight for power between two collective consciousnesses, groups of people mentally bonded as one.

The collectives are known as the Oneness and the Totality. They come from the New Human movement where the eventual goal is a galactic bonding—total oneness. They believe individuality is just a fad rapidly going out of style.

People such as the fiercely independent Kirk are considered amoebas with ideas as outdated as dinosaurs.

The collectives aren't bad. Live and let live is a standard most star explorers hold when they seek out strange new worlds and life forms. Kirk, Spock and the Enterprise crew hold few exceptions to this rule, unless they are denied the same consideration.

These two collectives are becoming so big and powerful it is virtually impossible to fight them. They are forcing people to bond with them, adding to their numbers. Kirk and Spock find this immoral, possibly worse than murder.

TRIANGLE holds interest from beginning to end, combining high adventure and drama with character development. The story happens in two days; the novel is fast paced and very realistic in its portrayal of Kirk, Spock and others. This one ranks up there with THE ENTROPY EFFECT.

YESTERDAY'S SON

Ann Crispin's YESTERDAY'S SON is a masterwork, combining the Classic Trek episodes "The City On The Edge of Forever" and "All Our Yesterdays." Soon after returning from Sarpeidon, Spock is going over the records recovered before the supernova claimed Bela Niobe.

The Atoz files reveal a cave painting of a Vulcan child and he realizes Zarabeth bore him a son. The child was unable to develop due to the lack of a Vulcan to teach him the mental disciplines. Spock gets T'Pau to allow him to use the Guardian of Forever to rescue his son.

After passing through, Spock, Kirk and McCoy create a way to allow Zarabeth and the child to return with them. Yet when they arrive, Zarabeth has been dead for years and the "child", Zar, is 28 years old.

Zar returns to the Enterprise and helps defend the Guardian from a Romulan attack. He realizes he must return to the past after seeing a painting he made of the Enterprise 5,000 years ago.

At first Spock and Zar are tense, but Crispin slowly and very realistically brings the two together. The final mind-meld allows Spock to show what he can't put into words.

This story provides perfect background for the next masterwork from Ann—TIME FOR YESTERDAY. The novels combine to give Zar a more powerful story than any guest character in

Classic Trek history. This novel stands on its own.

MUTINY ON THE ENTERPRISE

Kirk is surprisingly slow to catch on to what is happening on his ship in MUTINY ON THE ENTERPRISE by Robert E. Vardeman. Spock is unable to convince his captain until far too late. This is only part of Kirk's problem.

He must deal with the betrayal of his crew before realizing they are under mental control. It takes Kirk forever to figure out the obvious solution to the civil war.

He finally sees what most readers figured out 100 pages before. The Tellarite ambassador is atypical, but no other characters take more abuse than Tellarites and ambassadors. The mutiny is similar to that in STAR TREK V: THE FINAL FRONTIER.

THE WOUNDED SKY

THE WOUNDED SKY by Diane Duane combines an intimate knowledge of cutting edge theoretical physics with the mental state of the Enterprise crew to produce one of the finest STAR TREK novels ever put to paper. The Enterprise is selected to be the test ship for a new device allowing intergalactic travel. A glass spider is the theorist.

At first Scott is outraged by her new type of physics, but the warmth between alien and human grows into beautiful love that transcends their species.

Kirk's spacewalk while viewing the Milky Way from afar is spectacular prose, as is the scene when the crew of the Enterprise guides the building of a new universe using the best qualities drawn from each crewman. The image of Kirk leading his crew across the Rubicon into a world where mind and physics meet is not to be missed.

Sulu gets a great turn. At one point the Klingon pursuers suggest Kirk kill his helmsman to warn the Black Fleet. Kirk points out to Sulu the compliment he has received.

Kirk has an interesting encounter with the spider in his cabin and the reception the Enterprise receives is heartwarming. Kirk and crew save the entire universe and found a separate one as well. Quite a day's work.

CORONA

In CORONA by Greg Bear, Vulcan children fall under the influence of a being preparing to wipe out our universe to produce conditions wherein intelligent energy forms can develop. Spock must teach the Vulcan children mental disciplines to ward off the being.

Chekov is taken over. He is conscious of his actions but can't do anything about them. This novel features one of the few positive portrayals of a reporter in modern literature.

The female observer overcomes her racism and the xenophobia of her culture to help the alien understand that the organic pests are truly alive. She never divulges secrets, harasses victims or behaves as most reporters do in popular fiction.

She overcomes the adversity of prejudice imparted by her planet. Uhura helps her overcome her dislike of Spock and the other "little green men". Once again the universe is saved by the Enterprise.

STAR TREK III: THE SEARCH FOR SPOCK

The relationship between the ill-fated son of Kirk and the half-Romulan protegé of Spock is spelled out in STAR TREK III: THE SEARCH FOR SPOCK by Vonda N. McIntyre. Also of note is a return to the Genesis cave before the Grissom visits the Genesis planet.

How Spock's body is reconstituted by the Genesis wave is explained in detail. The commander, Kruge becomes more than the stereotypical Klingon. Kirk's failure to understand Kruge gives the Klingon the advantage until Kirk turns the tables. The theft of the Enterprise is well handled, and Nyota Uhura is given a much more prominent role than in the film.

The novel explains how she scrambled communications until the Enterprise got away. For Kirk, the loss of his ship, on top of his son, was offset by the rebirth of Spock. McCoy kept the Vulcan's katra until T'Lar merged the body and mind.

The book goes into the detail of the katra swap that saved Spock. McIntyre's novel is based on the screenplay by Harve Bennett.

MY ENEMY, MY ALLY

Ael debuts in MY ENEMY, MY ALLY by Diane Duane. Romulans conspire in an intricate plot to regain the mind-powers left behind when they fled Vulcan. The second USS Intrepid is taken from under the noses of a Federation fleet commanded by James T. Kirk. The Romulans intend to use the Vulcans' brains to gain mental powers.

Ael feels the Romulans will lose their honor as telepathy sweeps intrigue to unprecedented levels. Senators kill each other with thought after reading unwelcome thoughts. She devises an elaborate ruse to win Kirk's permission to capture his ship.

Ael's reaction to Spock's sword seems puzzling; the significance of the sword's maker is not spelled out until Diane and Peter Norwood's THE ROMULAN WAY. This novel stands on its own offering one of the most positive portrayals of a Romulan ever seen combined with a rich understanding of Romulan culture.

Of special note are the chess moves McCoy uses against Spock and how the Romulan commander reacts to her allies on the Enterprise crew. When Kirk agrees to honor the Romulan

with her secret name, it forever changes his perception of Romulans.

Enterprise Recreation Chief Herb Tanzer makes a key appearance. Herb is also featured in some of Duane's other novels such as THE WOUNDED SKY, SPOCK'S WORLD and DOCTOR'S ORDERS.

THE VULCAN ACADEMY MURDERS

The title of THE VULCAN ACADEMY MURDERS by Jean Lorrah seems to be an oxymoron. A murderer in a society that has no police official higher than a meter maid is an intriguing concept. Lorrah evokes emotion by placing Spock's beloved mother, Amanda at risk from an unknown killer.

Kirk investigates a series of murders, and attempted murders, finding his own life at risk as he battles Vulcan plants and animals. Despite the cover illustration, it is Kirk, not Spock, who faces the thrall.

Terran doctor Corrigan and his Vulcan healer partner, Sorel are well drawn out, as is the role of the healer's daughter and the doctor's wife. Lorrah portrays vivid characters, using symbolism to great effect.

McCoy's reaction to Vulcan heat and Spock and Sarek's emotional response to Amanda's condition open new facets of each character. McCoy springs to action to operate on that Vulcan body he had cut open so many times. Kirk questions Sarek and T'Pau as murder suspects. The novel also features a mind-meld between Sarek and Spock that the Vulcan fails to remember in THE NEXT GENERATION's "Unification."

The entire surviving cast returns for the sequel—THE IDIC EPIDEMIC. Sorel and Corrigan are also mentioned in TIME FOR YESTERDAY, when their nerve regeneration technique is used to repair the leg of Spock's son, Zar.

SHADOW LORD

Spock and Sulu are left behind on a primitive world in SHADOW LORD by Laurence Yep. Spock is supposed to update star charts for a superstitious society to use in astrology. McCoy is convinced Spock will be burned at the stake for renouncing the illogic of their wars.

He never gets the chance. The prince the two escort is immediately targeted for assassination, forcing Spock and Sulu to use swords to defend the ruler and help him escape from the castle as the entire household is butchered.

The escape brings them into a dungeon full of carnivorous insects intent on eating the interlopers. The death at their mandibles is unnecessary, although it serves to strengthen the prince's resolve. Spock's words are ineffective, but risking his life to save a young relative of the prince proves his point.

Sulu plays the real-life Dartanian of the Three Musketeers Spock said he was at heart in the Trek Classic episode "The Naked Time." When the prince is injured in battle, Sulu leads the troops during a key point in the battle.

Spock and Kirk later give him hell over the Prime Directive violations. Spock will later do the very same thing in TIME FOR YESTERDAY.

The Prince grows as he comes back to his primitive world with a Federation education and sees life with blinders removed. His odyssey with Sulu forges him into a leader.

The milk nurse is a true prize. One woman saves the prince's revolution. As a momento, Sulu is given the pistol he uses to change the course of the planet's history.

KILLING TIME
(Reviewed by Alayne Gelfand)

Welcome to the 'Second History' of KILLING TIME where Spock states, somewhat late in the game (and quite erroneously as it turns out), "Sometimes illusions are far more enduring and pleasant than reality." Reality is the name of the game in KILLING TIME by Della Van Hise, a page-turning smorgasbord of delightful twists, turns and paradoxes which take the reader through the dissolution of 'First History' (that of what we've come to know as 'The Federation') into the slipping sanity of 'Second History' (that of which we are introduced to as 'The Alliance').

Aboard the USS Enterprise, crewmembers dream of different lives from those they now lead. A shared theme runs through many of the dreams.

Kirk and Spock recall a slightly altered Enterprise, commanded by Captain Spock. Both see a reluctant Ensign Kirk dodging in and out of this altered reality. This theme isn't confined to the captain and first officer, but lives in the dreams of Lieutenant Jerry Richardson, and others.

Just as Captain Kirk and Commander Spock begin to realize something is amiss, Captain Spock and a drafted Ensign Kirk find themselves serving aboard the VSS ShiKahr, a ship in the fleet of the Vulcan-based Alliance. The Alliance seems to begin to crumble around them.

Insane orders to take aggressive action against the Romulans come from Fleet Command. Normally reliable crewmembers become homicidal. Spock enters the early stages of pon farr. Reports of irrational actions begin to filter in from other starships, proving that insanity is spreading throughout Alliance territory.

Meanwhile, the reader learns time disruption is the direct result of Romulan tampering. The book reveals the inner workings of the Romulan Empire.

Romulan agents have entered the past and prevented Terra from organizing The United Federation of Planets. The scheme is discovered and attempts are made to right the situation.

KILLING TIME is one of the series of "galactic menace" books the editors of Pocket Books felt readers wanted. Yet this "galactic menace" isn't a giant space-going amoebae or anonymous rip in the fabric of the universe. It is in each person's history, making the menace compelling and personally threatening. The KILLING TIME is refreshing.

While the plot is unique, the strong bond between Kirk and Spock rivets attention. This friendship, the essence of legend, holds the plot together. Without that friendship there would be no glue to cement the strange pieces of the puzzle into a whole. The instinctive trust between Kirk and Spock, who in 'Second History' are strangers, brings each to the difficult understanding of their destiny.

DWELLERS IN THE CRUCIBLE

DWELLERS IN THE CRUCIBLE by Margaret Wander Bonnano is a cautionary tale of abuse of prisoners not easy to read. It is well-written and worth your time yet disturbing. The love story between two women prisoners rises above the subject matter to transform the novel into a complex look at the way being a prisoner can affect judgment. The Vulcan and Terran women survive while watching their Andorian friend cut down quickly and their Deltan friends die slow, painful deaths of isolation and cruelty.

The Deltans form a trio and the female saves the Terran from rape by seducing the attempted rapists. Deltans are sexual creatures from birth and travel in groups for mutual support. That is why Deltan Starfleet officers must take a vow of celibacy. The emotional, sensual impact overpowers most other races.

After the Deltans' deaths, the Vulcan endures pon farr without her mate, whom she knows will die, due to her captivity. Her human friend helps her as does the Romulan commander from the Classic Trek episode "The Enterprise Incident."

She uses the Vulcan as a pawn to attack Spock, but learns Spock already carries the guilt without the spur from the injured Vulcan. The two are rescued at the very end by Kirk and

Spock who serve as a role model in Vulcan/human relationships.

MINDSHADOW

In MINDSHADOW by J.M. Dillard, Spock is severely injured and Romulans slice Starfleet security at every turn for inexplicable reasons. McCoy acts in interesting ways when he thinks Kirk is putting the moves on his new love interest.

She is not what she seems and her attempt to rectify her crimes is too little, too late. It is painful to see Spock in this condition. The underlying commentary suggests social policy in which so-called "nuthouse tranks" like Thorazine and Stellazine, are used to control patients, producing chemical lobotomies.

Kirk takes forever to figure out what the Romulans are doing. Security is terrible. Someone finally sees the obvious clues they stumble over for page after page.

Dillard's later novels are far more detailed and characters are given a better chance to develop. This story is reminiscent of the Classic Trek episode "The Alternative Factor," in which an obvious security risk is given free run of the ship.

BATTLESTATIONS!

BATTLESTATIONS! by Diane Carey is a very unusual Trek novel, a sequel to her earlier DREADNAUGHT!. The story is told first person by a female commander.

She narrates the tale of serving with Kirk on his wooden ship, The Edith Keeler, named after the love Kirk was forced to let die to save the proper time-line in the Classic Trek episode "The City On The Edge Of Forever." The female protagonist fights her way through a Starfleet security squad to her first space command, which Kirk has arranged.

Kirk is arrested on his sailing ship and Bones assists her in taking both ships. Her starship, The Banana Republic, a.k.a. Tyrannosaurus Rex has to fend off a threat to the Federation by her colleagues whom she betrayed to fend off a similar attack in DREADNAUGHT!.

She must struggle to maintain her dignity, performing undercover as a dancing girl. When she finds one of her shipmates playing a holograph of her dancing act, the humor diffuses a tense situation.

Her relationship with her Vulcan friend is well-drawn, as she remembers a time when the two teamed up to win a Starfleet Academy survival simulation. Her attempt to override Spock's computer lockout is priceless, as is McCoy's glee telling Spock his countermeasures have been circumvented.

Kirk and Spock are taken prisoner quite easily, but taking them back to the Enterprise is a key mistake. The female commander's tricks appear to be for naught. The last page of the book is so simple, it's profound.

After the "cosmic scramble" between Klingons, Gorn, Romulans, Tholians and several other races, our hero must face Mr. Scott— after what she did to his engines. Carey doesn't specify what Scott says, leaving it to the imagination.

DREAMS OF THE RAVEN

Brain-sucking beings swallow consciousness so people wake up in the "Raven's" body in DREAMS OF THE RAVEN by Carmen Carter. This is a nightmare for Starfleet personnel who become ensnared in the bodies of the monsters.

Dr. McCoy suffers emotional breakdown after four of his doctors are dispatched. After an emotional letter saying his wife was getting married, Bones got drunk before striking his head in a fall. He develops amnesia and returns to carefree days of a young cowboy in Waco, Texas— a young doctor yet to face the horrors that build year by year.

THE ROMULAN WAY

THE ROMULAN WAY by Diane Duane and Peter Morwood could be titled Romulan History 101. Duane and Morwood craft a novel of Romulan History.

Chapters switch back and forth from the time Romulans left Vulcan to the time McCoy was captured on a raid and returned to Romulus to stand trial for crimes in the Classic Trek episode "The Enterprise Incident." McCoy is sent to find out if a Federation spy has "gone native." She has learned to think and act like a Romulan.

McCoy is alone on Romulus with Lt. Nhrat, the Horta, who appears in several Trek novels including TIME FOR YESTERDAY, THE WOUNDED SKY, DOCTOR'S ORDERS, and MY ENEMY, MY ALLY. Ael shows up to save the mission, while the Federation mole is forced into a position that allows history to unfold.

Chapters flash back from the story of Bones, the rock and the mole, to in-depth reports on how the rift in the Vulcan-Romulan union altered galactic history in this sector. The ill-fated first contact with the Federation is brought out as the Romulans form an empire after one ship is spotted.

The two peaceful worlds explode into xenophobia leading to millions of deaths on both sides. Romulans love their planet so much there is a death penalty for pollution. In fact, Romulans were underestimated because all of their factories and heavy industry were underground.

THE IDIC EPIDEMIC

THE IDIC EPIDEMIC by Jean Lorrah is the sequel to her THE VULCAN ACADEMY MURDERS. Everyone not a murderer or victim in the first novel returns.

The Enterprise is transferring exiles along with Dr. Corrigan, his Vulcan wife, her father, the healer Sorel, Sarek and Amanda when reports of a deadly plague divert the ship. The disease is spread by interaction between aliens.

On this planet, Klingons wed Orions and Vulcans wed Rigellians. The disease causes madness, including homicidal delusions. It effects both copper- and iron-based blood and is most contagious among half-alien children.

The IDIC principle is symmetrical as diversity proves vital to the cure. Xenophobia and fear of disease are given a full airing with madness causing racial outbursts. The Vulcan exiles are green supremacists delighting in the misery, until it boomerangs into Engineering.

Sarek and Amanda show signs of madness and Spock becomes the focal point in ending the epidemic.

IDIC stands for "Infinite Diversity in Infinite Combinations", and Spock notes that humans have boiled down a concept Vulcans have debated for centuries into a four letter acronym.

The relationship between one of the Vulcan girls and the leader of the Vulcan expatriates resonates as does Scotty's reaction to the takeover in his beloved engine room. The Klingon who has a Vulcan wife and Orion ex-wife is a key player.

The book stands on its own and is an outstanding sequel. Sarek and Amanda get great parts, especially when Amanda goes to the bridge to slap Spock in the face.

TIME FOR YESTERDAY

TIME FOR YESTERDAY by A.C. Crispin evokes strong emotions. Spock's son Zar returns from YESTERDAY'S SON.

The Enterprise crew is diverted to fix the Guardian of Forever. Spock returns to Sarpeidon (Classic Trek episode "All Our Yesterdays") to find his son, dead 5,000 years, and attempts to get Zar to fix the time-space continuum.

Zar's relationship with his soul-mate, Wynn is priceless. He is the leader of the trade city of New Arean in the Lakreo Valley. Twenty years have passed since he last saw his father and the other Enterprise crew members.

Fourteen and a half years have passed for Kirk, Spock and McCoy.

Zar's relationships with his Second-In-Command, Cletus, his valet, Voba, and his warrior-priestess of a wife, Wynn are too rich for words. Add thousands of soldiers meeting in battle, planetary systems (named after Superman characters) being destroyed in stellar expansion, starships caught in the event horizon of black holes and dissolved by temporal speedups in space-time.

Zar's first encounter with the landing party in the dungeon is tremendous, as is Zar's first talk with Wynn. Wynn is a great character. When she and Zar meld, it creates a great moment. Zar restores the Guardian, fights the originators, restores Deheberan, fences with Sulu and melds with Uhura. There is no weak link in this book.

TIMETRAP

After an incident involving a Klingon attack, Kirk finds himself on board a strange ship where Klingons don't act like Klingons in TIMETRAP by David Dvorkin. They act more like NeoVulcans.

This story is hurt because fans of THE NEXT GENERATION know Klingons don't change that much. It is an elaborate ruse to force Kirk to reveal information, much as Riker believed the Romulans were doing in the TNG episode "Future Imperfect."

Kirk's relationship with the Klingon female is intriguing. Klingon honor and loyalty are stressed, despite the bizarre turn of events. Dvorkin and his brother are co-authors of the TNG novel THE CAPTAIN'S HONOR.

THE THREE-MINUTE UNIVERSE

Stephen Hawking would not approve of the physics of THE THREE-MINUTE UNIVERSE by

Barbara Paul. However, the author did go to a lot of trouble to look up terminology.

Still, the novel is better if the whole idea of mini-big-bangs is left out. The soul of the story involves Kirk, Uhura, Scott and Chekov with a starship run by murderous children. Chekov, Uhura and Scotty strive to establish a working relationship with their alien counterparts, while Kirk naturally charms the female captain.

It is cruel to compare the alien navigator with the mythical Sulu. When Sulu finally does appear, that chapter excels because Sulu doesn't understand why the aliens know him, much less worship him.

The way the beings affect the crew is interesting. This story is best when it deals with the personal interaction between the two crews of space travelers.

MEMORY PRIME

Artificial intelligence has advanced to the point where they have become sentient. A Vulcanoid assassin penetrates the Memory Prime complex, successor to Memory Alpha from the Classic Trek episode "The Lights of Zetar".

Scotty's relationship with the eccentric physicist is classic, as is Kirk's reaction to being relieved of command in MEMORY PRIME by Garfield and Judith Reeves-Stevens. Spock is suspected as the assassin, and his escape leads to the battle to stop the real assassin. The alien minds realize the entire galaxy is one living being yet fail to report it since no asks.

The sabotage of the Enterprise is well done, as are the various attacks on Memory Prime's Andorian security force. Scotty's lost love Mira Romain (Classic Trek episode "The Lights of Zetar") returns to play a key part in the plot.

A Federation official tries to dissuade her from Kirk, before he realizes it is Scott she has a relationship with. Kirk and Spock use an ingenious code system to communicate.

The final chapters are confusing, with Spock and the assassin traveling through the neural nets. The opening chapter is interesting, when a Vulcan shows emotions, nearly marries the Klingon bartender and detects a Klingon android; all having little or nothing to do with the plot.

The relationship between the computer minds shows how intelligence can get out of hand, especially when combined with isolation. The highlight is when Kirk finds his ship taken from him and Spock's reaction to learning Kirk is his counsel.

VULCAN'S GLORY

Dorothy Fontana excels in all her Trek work and VULCAN'S GLORY is no exception. D.C. has written for Classic Trek ("This Side of Paradise," "Journey To Babel," "Tomorrow Is Yesterday"), TNG ("Encounter At Farpoint," "Lonely Among Us"), DS9 ("Dax") and one of the Classic Trek animated shows ("Yesteryear"). She also serves as an advisor.

This story is set in the years before Kirk and company took over the Enterprise, when Christopher Pike was captain and Number One was first officer. Their lives are examined in detail, revealing why Number One is called Number One, not because she is first officer, but because she was ranked No. 1 by her species that is genetically perfect (a la TNG episode "The Masterpiece Society").

The only two regulars on board are the Vulcan science officer, Spock, who joins his crewmates after a "discussion" with Sarek through Amanda, and a young Jr. Engineer named Scott, who brews radioactive moonshine in his first still on the ship. Spock must deal with T'Pring and Stonn before heading out, and falls in love with a Vulcan widow.

Her death is the reason Spock stopped smiling and started trying to suppress his emotions. The "Vulcan's Glory" of the title is a rare stone which has been missing for centuries. When Spock leads a Vulcan landing party to find the stone, rivalries flare. The stone is stolen, a crewman is killed and Vulcans fall under suspicion of murder.

Fontana does a fine job wrapping up loose ends and filling in the blanks about Scott and Spock's first voyage on the Enterprise.

THE CRY OF THE ONLIES

The Enterprise crew's encounter with a primitive life form is more interesting than the elements from two Classic Trek episodes tainted by their reintroduction. The first mistake inTHE CRY OF THE ONLIES by Judith Klass involves the death of Miri, the title character from "Miri". If her death had meaning, it might have made sense. Instead she is mentioned as having died, adding nothing to the story. Authors should refrain from changes unless they are vital to their story.

The Onlies' act nonsensical, even if one proves to be a hero. The author drags back the character Flint back from the Classic Trek episode "Requiem For Methuselah", again, for no good reason.

Kirk realizes Spock removed the painful memory of the alien android he fell in love with. This puts Spock in an uncomfortable position, and harms Kirk and Spock's characterization for no good reason.

The story of how the Enterprise relates to the primitive culture could be intriguing, but the errors kill the story. This novel libels too many Classic Trek characters.

THE KOBAYASHI MARU

In THE KOBAYASHI MARU by Julia Ecklar, a shuttlecraft commanded by Kirk is struck by a gravitic mine. That's right, just like in the no-win Kobayashi Maru test seen STAR TREK II. As they wait for Spock to lead the Enterprise to find them, Kirk, Sulu, Chekov and Scotty entertain McCoy with tales of how each found a unique solution to the puzzle. Spock never took the test. Each crewmember reacted differently to the no-win scenario and each solution explores how they reason.

RULES OF ENGAGEMENT

Kirk's tribbles come home to roost in RULES OF ENGAGEMENT by Peter Morwood. A Klingon captain who saw his career derailed by the events of "The Trouble With Tribbles" is sent to test an experimental ship similar to the prototype warbird in STAR TREK VI: THE UNDISCOVERED COUNTRY. The ship is controlled by another master ship.

Claymare, the Organian peacemaker from "Errand of Mercy," reappears and plays a key role. Kirk deals with a Federation fleet and inhabitants of a planet who are descended from Klingons.

Kirk uses psychology to win one Klingon's trust, but a mutiny forces Kirk to fight his new Klingon friend. His bluff works and his relations with other Federation officers is outstanding.

DOCTOR'S ORDERS

Kirk places McCoy in command of the Enterprise in DOCTOR'S ORDERS by Diane Duane, after he gets tired of hearing how easy the captain's job is. Then Kirk vanishes during an away mission.

Klingons and Orion pirates show up, putting McCoy to the test. The planet has three intelligent life forms and medical terminology in this book is daunting. McCoy must convince Starfleet Command he is competent as a nutty admiral takes over the mission and orders McCoy to make foolish moves.

McCoy uses his brass tacks personality to keep Starfleet at bay, learning what life is like for Kirk, with hundreds of lives dependent on his every move. At red alert, he bolts toward sickbay, then remembers his place is on the bridge.

An excellent chapter involves McCoy with the first Klingon captain. He gains his respect through bluster and name-calling. When Kirk returns to find McCoy leading the ship in battle with the Orions, he asks the doctor how he got the Klingons to fight alongside the Enterprise.

HOME IS THE HUNTER

Ensign Garrovick, the son of Kirk's captain on the Farragut, returns and is killed early in HOME IS THE HUNTER by Dana Kramer-Rolls. He dies by throwing himself on an explosive to save a child.

Garrovick was seen in the Classic Trek "Obsession." Kirk and crew are placed on probation by a Q-like entity with the power to alter time. The being sends three Enterprise crewmen back in time to test their actions.

Sulu is sent to medieval Japan during the rise of the Shogun Empire. He must prove himself in a variety of tasks without killing too many key people and altering history. He must find out what should happen before he can correct the timeline.

Chekov finds himself in a World War II Nazi prison camp. He must join an ancestor of Kirk's who also has a Roman Emperor's middle name, to help Krushev escape the Nazis. Pavel finds himself honored by Stalin and must find a way to save Kirk's ancestor without changing history.

When he returns to the future, he learns it really did happen. He was a hero of the Soviet Union.

Pavel realizes he can't help too much and is stunned to see his homeland as a Communist totalitarian state. He is prepared to kill himself to keep the KGB from getting his Federation knowledge. He and the 20th century Kirk must attempt to sacrifice themselves to save the other.

Scotty doesn't have to worry about the Prime Directive. He loses his memory and finds he can help the Scotts win key battles they lost historically. He does all he can, and meets his Scottish heroes, but cannot change the disad-

vantages the disorganized Scotts faced against organized English forces. He later decides he purposely lost his memory so he could help his people, even though history refuses to be mocked.

The entity is convinced humanity is worth studying after each completes their mission. The novel is a well-written time travelogue.

GHOST WALKER

Kirk's body is appropriated by an alien who is upset at the prospect of Federation interference in his homeworld in GHOST WALKER by Barbara Hambly. Kirk's mind must survive without his body until he can find a way to force out the being that has taken over his ship.

Kirk survives because of his love for his ship and ability to remain awake in mental limbo. He gets Spock to realize what happened.

A FLAG FULL OF STARS

A FLAG FULL OF STARS by Brad Ferguson is the second novel in THE LOST YEARS saga. It features more adventures of desk-bound Admiral Kirk.

Kirk and Lt. Cmdr. Kevin Riley help a reporter help a Klingon work with the Federation. Kirk is assigned to press relations and sent to describe the upcoming celebration in commemoration of the anniversary of humanity's first visit to Luna in 1969.

The story is notable for the character of the Klingon school teacher and physicist. A non-warrior with a pet kitten and heart of gold, this teacher does more to improve relations between the two cultures than thousands of other encounters.

When the Klingon makes a dramatic discovery, he attracts the interest of the Empire, who set out to recover his technological breakthrough. The Klingon risks his life to protect others.

Riley makes a mistake putting lives at risk and runs off to correct it by risking his own life. Captain Decker is set to take out his redesigned Enterprise and does a fine job commanding.

In an inspired case of truth melding with fiction, Kirk takes command of the Space Shuttle Enterprise and is forced to take on the Klingons in the historical relic. It is equipped with 23rd century technology.

RENEGADE

Lt. Commander Ben Finney returns in RENEGADE by Gene deWeese. Finney tried to gain revenge on Kirk by faking his own death in the Classic Trek episode "Court-Martial". He returns in another attempt to make Kirk pay for sabotaging his career on the Republic, when Kirk reported him for negligence.

He has a chance to realize the error. The Enterprise is called on to help two societies negotiate a truce. One combatant is a colony of the other, so the conflict is painted in bold strokes of colonial domination and individual independence. Kirk cares little about the political situation after two of his best friends, notably Spock and McCoy, are presumed dead in a terrorist attack.

The author soon shows how Spock and McCoy overcome a Klingon plot to subvert both worlds and destroy the Enterprise, while Kirk still doesn't know they survive. The Enterprise is again sabotaged as Kirk must learn what is going on before the entire Federation is disabled by Finney's ploy. Spock and McCoy assist Kirk to overcome the threat before it spreads.

LEGACY

In LEGACY by Michael Jan Friedman Captain Christopher Pike and Vina reappear from the Classic Trek episode "The Menagerie". They are living out the dream life when Pike suddenly has a vision of Spock.

Pike also features in the novels VULCAN'S GLORY, ENTERPRISE: THE FIRST ADVENTURE, and THE RIFT. This is the only Pike appearance after the accident on the Class J starship which led to his injuries, and his subsequent return to Talos IV.

Pike asks the Talosian magistrate to find out about Spock. What apparently caused the insight was Spock's encounter with an alien pirate both Pike and Spock dealt with in the first years of the starship.

In a separate story, Spock is injured, and Kirk and a landing party vanish. Then the Enterprise is called away to deal with the pirate, who is attacking a Federation colony.

Kirk and the landing party struggle to survive and understand the complex sexual relationship the planet has with itself. The injury to Spock interferes with attempts to negotiate an end to the hostage situation at the Federation colony.

The pirate is stunned to find Spock has fallen into the trap. Spock is the one who shamed the pirate, who has finally recovered from the humiliation.

In the end, Friedman invokes sympathy for the brutal character despite what he has done to Spock and his captives. McCoy and Spock battle over his health, and return to find the presumed dead Kirk and company playing a key role in saving Spock, who has unwittingly joined the (planetary) sex act.

THE RIFT

THE RIFT by Peter David is an outstanding novel combining the two eras of Classic Trek to tell a story which brings together several characters from the STAR TREK universe. Captain Pike and the Enterprise are still on their way home from the attack on Rigel VII and initial encounter with the Talosians. The ship encounters a rift in space with the same properties as the Bajoran wormhole on DEEP SPACE 9.

It is stable, yet only appears at intervals of three decades. Pike, for a brief instant, sees the bleak future he will face as he travels through the wormhole.

When the Enterprise responds to a greeting from an isolationist alien culture, they travel through to meet them. Navigator Jose Tyler meets a woman on the other side who will change his life. Pike is barely able to retrieve Tyler before the rift collapses and the ship returns to Federation space.

This novel reveals why the ship's computers have Majel Barrett's voice. Number One and Spock install the voice command functions and she uses her voice, a voice that commands respect. Number One's relationship with Pike is also explored.

The story resumes at the next opening of the rift. Admiral Kirk is assigned to escort a Federation party to meet with aliens on the other side. The party reunites characters from disparate Classic Trek episodes. Ambassador Robert Fox from "A Taste of Armageddon" is dispatched by Starfleet, along with Doctor Richard Daystrum, from "The Ultimate Computer," and the previously mentioned Jose Tyler, who is now a Starfleet Commodore.

An Andorian and a Tellarite are thrown in for comic relief. Kirk must bring them together to work out a solution to problems that could leave Spock and the landing party trapped on the other side of the rift.

Spock and Kirk must deal with the unimind of the alien world with Daystrum's help. The holodeck technology featured in TNG begins with Daystrum's discovery on the distant world.

FACES OF FIRE

Kirk is forced to deal with an angry ambassador after he delays a mission to provide medical check-ups for a Federation colony in FACES OF FIRE by Michael Jan Friedman. The mission becomes personal when Kirk finds his former lover, Carol Marcus assigned to the station.

Kirk does not know about his son, David, but McCoy finds out and is compelled by medical ethics not to tell. Spock figures it out when he is left behind to do research and finds himself hiding from a Klingon attack force that seizes the colony.

Young David Marcus leads a band of children, who hide from the Klingons, then join with Spock to confound the Klingon plot. David and Spock's actions help elevate the Klingon second officer to command. That officer, Kruge, will later order the death of a hostage in STAR TREK III: THE SEARCH FOR SPOCK and David will lose his life to protect a young Spock and Saavik.

Spock is impressed by David's actions. The implications of David growing up without a father are explored.

The civil war the Enterprise is sent to end is interesting. A plant Carol gave Kirk to distract him from finding out about David plays a key role in working out a compromise that saves the day.

THE DISINHERITED

In THE DISINHERITED by Peter David, Michael Jan Friedman and Robert Greenberger, Uhura is sent on a mission to assist the Yorktown in making contact with an unusual species that uses sign language to intensify the meaning of words. Her new captain is known for raiding other ships for personnel, so Kirk is afraid he might lose her.

A highlight of the novel occurs when she tells Kirk she wants to stay to complete her duties. Kirk thinks he has lost the best communications officer in the fleet.

Her relationship with a fellow Bantu African who serves as the Yorktown's communications officer is complex. Her heritage allows him to open up to her. After a stormy beginning she is able to help him find a way through his psychological difficulties, much as McCoy helps Lt. Bailey in "The Corbomite Maneuver."

Lt. Chekov is a key player. One of the funniest scenes shows McCoy working on a report on the young navigator which Sulu notices. Bones decides that as helmsman, Sulu has a relationship with Chekov and decides to tell him that the young officer is jumpy.

Scotty and another officer overhear and Sulu brings it up with them. An upset McCoy makes a few smart remarks that confuse the situation, just before Spock and Kirk enter for the briefing.

McCoy's sarcasm is misconstrued as fact, leading to outstanding comic dialogue between McCoy, Kirk, Spock, Scott and Sulu.

On a more serious note, Chekov panics and accidentally destroys evidence, and even worse, Kirk sees him do it. Then he jumps up on the bridge and suggests an alternate plan while Kirk is giving orders during a battle. He is banished from the bridge, but works with Scotty to find a way around the aliens' defense measures.

ICETRAP

In ICETRAP, L.A. Graf gives a gut-wrenching roller-coaster ride that never lets up for a second. This is one of the most intense Trek novels.

Each member of the two away teams has more lives than a cat, with each chapter ending with a main crew member seconds from death. Chekov and Uhura are lost in a snow covered region, forced to fight off hostile aliens, friends who turn out to be enemies, and near-death at every turn. The chapter ends with Sulu falling off a cliff.

Meanwhile, McCoy and Kirk travel in an underwater vehicle beneath icecaps. When a disease causes the submarine's crew to begin to go insane, McCoy is attacked by the crazed surgeon and forced to overcome his fear of water when the ship is ruptured.

An unusual underwater alien plays a key part in the story. This novel is so constantly intense that by the end, the shock value is lowered.

SANCTUARY

Kirk, Spock and McCoy chase a pirate ship down to a planet and watch the ship crash in SANCTUARY by John Vornholt. When they travel by foot to look for survivors, they find their shuttlecraft gone when they return.

The three are trapped on a planet called Sanctuary, which criminals flee to, but can never leave. They find themselves ostracized when the aliens learn they are pursuers, rather than pursued.

They travel to a city where riff-raff congregate, after dealing with Klingons, Gorn and other outlaws in the mountains. They are all aware of who Kirk is, so the landing party tells of their escape from the dreaded Kirk.

They eventually find a boat and travel to a more idyllic island and meet two women who unknowingly help them figure out what is going on. One double crosses them and they find themselves back in the first city, where they face a fate worse than death. The Solarians create new members of their sexless race by castrating and lobotomizing some of the prisoners who flee to this world.

The first girl who helped them disguises herself as an alien to rescue Kirk, Spock and Bones before they can be mutilated. They escape with the aid of a friend, and find a hiding place where technical escapees hide from the aliens. They watch a failed attempt to penetrate the planet's shield, and decide on a way to get up where the Enterprise can rescue them.

Vornholt crafts an outstanding novel in his first attempt at a Classic Trek tome, equaling his work in the TNG novels MASKS, CONTAMINATION, and WAR DRUMS. Subtle character shadings outshine the dialogue to advance the story to a full and satisfying conclusion.

DEATH COUNT

Sulu, Uhura and Chekov enjoy shore leave at a Starbase, until Orion storm troopers move in and start thrashing people and their property in DEATH COUNT by L.A. Graf. The trio stand up for a shopkeeper and Chekov, now Security Chief on the Enterprise, engages one of the Romulans. He is promptly tossed in the brig, forcing Kirk to delay departure until his wayward officer can be retrieved.

The shopkeeper is so grateful he gives Sulu a small pool and some invisible lizards. This small gift plays a key role in a tale of treachery, murder and sabotage aboard the Enterprise.

The green-skinned storm troopers return to brighten Chekov's day. Meanwhile he deals with deaths and enough other problems to make an average security officer resign in disgust. The fearless Russian avenger risks life and limb, sacrificing himself for his shipmates on more than one occasion, only to cheat fate again, a la Kirk and Spock.

Sulu, Chekov and Uhura all get more to do than usual and the chemistry between them makes the more outlandish schemes seem commonplace. Their behavior on shore leave echoes the Classic Trek episodes "Man Trap," "The Trouble With Tribbles" and "Naked Time".

This book, at times, is just as nerve-wracking as ICE TRAP. Chapters end with regulars facing death, feared dead, or cheating death at the last second. The style overwhelms, but the characters carry the story.

SHELL GAME

SHELL GAME by Melissa Crandell is remarkably similar to the TNG novel, THE ROMULAN PRIZE, both released at about the same time. A Romulan derelict is more dangerous than it first appears.

Chekov seems out of character, yet shows his usual heroism. The Romulan doctor is a well drawn character who avoids the stereo-typical motives often given the most misunderstood race in the TREK universe. Their behavior is otherwise predictable. The alien is given license to severely wound our favorite characters, with some attempt to justify.

A good novel. Characterization is strong, if constrained.

THE STARSHIP TRAP

THE STARSHIP TRAP by Mel Gilden offers the kind of politician you want to jettison out the nearest airlock. The kind that screws up the mission, endangers the ship and crew and annoys the hell out of Kirk and Bones. He does see reason and accept that his position against Starfleet was a stupid one to take. Doing it on Kirk's ship, playing word games with Klingon captains, was simply political suicide.

WINDOWS ON A LOST WORLD

Kirk, Chekov and a security team find themselves instantly transformed into crab-like bodies when they step through the title windows on the lost world in WINDOWS ON A LOST WORLD by V.E. Mitchell. The signs are clear. Someone went to a lot of trouble to keep anybody from stumbling into these gruesome Nazi crabs who kill whole planets in mass genocide.

Each being has two brains. One set has the genetic information the being needs to survive; the other carries the trapped consciousness of each member of the ill-fated group. Kirk is the only one able to keep his self-awareness since brain-transference is old hat to him.

Chekov thinks he's one of the creatures, causing the gruesome death of a crewman. He considers Kirk an elder crab.

As an independent male, Kirk is given the personality of a treasonous crab about to face execution. A woman from a female-supremacist planet becomes a queen crab. When Kirk's crab mind impels him to mate with her, he barely survives. She sends him off a cliff to his death, only to have a Transporter save his shell at the last second.

The evil crab culture wiped out all life in their region of the galaxy and another ancient race. They tried to bury everything to keep anyone from finding it. They were almost successful, but Chekov and his female nemesis found one clue they overlooked.

These Classic Trek novels issued by Pocket demonstrate a willingness to explore the boundaries of STAR TREK far beyond the limited scope found in the Bantam novels.

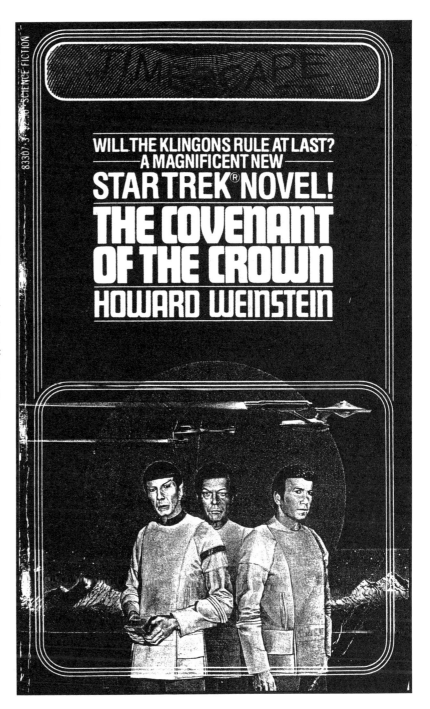

Howard Weinstein's THE COVENANT OF THE CROWN.

Profile:
LAURELL K. HAMILTON

Laurell K. Hamilton was a published novelist when she wrote NIGHTSHADE (NEXT GENERA-TION #24—Pocket Books), which was published in 1992. She'd never written fan fiction but wrote the novel because she was a fan of the series. She'd previously written an original fanta-sy novel, NIGHTFEAR, published early in 1992 while her NEXT GEN novel, NIGHTSHADE, appeared in late 1992.

Laurell describes NIGHTFEAR as "J.R.R. Tolkein meets Robert E. Howard." She is under contract for a 3-book series with Ace Books. Her initial decision to write a STAR TREK novel actually came from her association with Keith Birdsong, who is the cover artist for the majority of the NEXT GENERATION novels.

"I had talked to him and he said that after he'd done STAR TREK that his career had really taken off, and he encouraged me to see if I could do a STAR TREK book," she said.

Laurell contacted her agent and told her that, should the opportunity arise, she'd be interested in writing one of the series novels. Shortly thereafter the editor at Pocket Books contacted her agent, looking for someone who could deliver a NEXT GENERATION book quickly in order to fill a slot which another writer had canceled out on. The author recalled, "My agent promised him faithfully that I could deliver.

"I came up with one idea and Paramount rejected it because it was too inter-related with the show."

That idea had picked up the abandoned plot thread from the end of the first season episode "Conspiracy" regarding the intelligent worms which could take over human bodies. The episode had ended with a beacon having been detected which had been broadcast, presumably to the home planet. Laurell's idea was that the beacon said: "Come and get it," and she wanted to write about what happened when the parasitic worms returned.

"I had a week to come up with another idea," she said, "which I did. I read it to the edi-tor over the phone; he had a few suggestions. Shortly thereafter it went to Paramount and was approved. Then suddenly I was writing a STAR TREK book."

A NEXT GEN FAN

Laurell came to STAR TREK later than many others because, as a child, she was never allowed to watch the original series. She remembered, "My grandmother didn't like it so I didn't

BY JAMES VAN HISE

get to watch it. I didn't see any STAR TREK shows until I stayed over at my cousin's and saw the shows in reruns. My husband is a STAR TREK fan, and it wasn't until after I got married that he got me watching the classic reruns. That's where I became a fan."

She became such a big fan that when they moved from St. Louis to California in the fall of 1987, when THE NEXT GENERATION was going to premiere, they found that their new apartment couldn't be equipped with cable TV right away. So they went out and rented a hotel room the night THE NEXT GENERATION began to insure that they wouldn't miss the first episode.

"I actually prefer the NEXT GEN to the old," she stated, "and I think that's mainly because there's more women's roles. I also really like a large variety of the cast. I especially like Worf, Captain Picard and Data. On DEEP SPACE NINE, I've watched it, and some of the characters I'm starting to get a feel for; some of the characters are still very nebulous, like the Captain. He hasn't quite gelled as a character yet. I would have trouble writing him. So NEXT GEN is my favorite, but I'd say that DEEP SPACE NINE has a lot of potential."

WHEN SUCCESS IS A MIXED BLESSING

While STAR TREK books have a large following of readers at large, in the community of professional science fiction and fantasy writers, the series is often looked down on as being little more than "creative typing." That expression is borrowed from another writer who has written STAR TREK fiction but who doesn't take it all that seriously compared to his original work.

"I've had people say disparaging things to me because I did a STAR TREK book," Laurell explained. "I've had people say, I didn't think you'd do a STAR TREK book! Most people have been very nice about it, but when you do a STAR TREK book you open yourself up to stuff like that. I was told by one person who had done a STAR TREK book back in the '80s that I would never be rid of that fact. That I would always be known as somebody who did a STAR TREK book. But for me it's been a positive experience, as far as working on NIGHT-SHADE. I know other people have had problems but I didn't have any."

It took her about 4 months to write the novel and she explained that it was one of the hardest assignments she's ever had. She said, "It wasn't just because of the time pressure but because it had to be a certain length. If I got really into an idea and wanted to expand, I couldn't do that. Around 300 pages was the ideal length. So I had the length preset, and these weren't my characters, and there are all sorts of things you're not allowed to do with the characters.

"In the end you have to make everything all right so that no matter what you do with the characters they don't change. But it was interesting to have characters that were in somebody else's world; somebody else's playground. They set the rules and I knew that going in, so that didn't bother me. But it was harder than writing my own stuff."

Her deadline was so tight that she got a copy of the printed cover from the publisher while she was still writing the novel. "That was kind of a shock," she said. "It was like, well, I'd better finish it now because the cover's done! It was thrilling to see the cover, but at the same time, because I hadn't yet finished the book, it was a little bit of extra pressure. It was unsettling."

YOU MEAN I CAN TORTURE CAPT. PICARD?

When Laurell wrote NIGHTSHADE, she'd never read any of the numerous STAR TREK novels. She noted, "I knew from browsing the books just what I wanted to do, but it's almost impossible with the number of books out to really know what's been done, especially in the Classic Trek novels. I think it would be hard to come up with a brand new idea for them."

While she was able to write NIGHTSHADE the way she wanted to, there was one slightly different approach which was changed early on. She recalled, "In the original idea I had an ambassador as what Captain Picard is in the book. I was originally going to kill the ambassador off, but the editor thought it would be better if Captain Picard played the ambassador. But I said, 'I'm not allowed to kill him off, right?' And he said 'No,' but we came up with an alternative. Captain Picard wasn't originally going to be on the planet because I felt like Picard would be pushy. But it worked very well."

She continued, "One thing that I wanted to do, and didn't do in the original book that I turned in, was to torture Picard towards the end. I sent it in without having tortured him and the editor came back and said, 'You know, I think this part would work better if we tortured Picard.' And I said, 'I'm allowed to torture Picard?' This was before we saw him tortured on the show. 'What do you mean by torture? Messy medieval torture or clean science fiction torture?' And he said, 'Clean science fiction torture.' So I got to torture Picard. I was very careful and very discreet on the sexual innuendo and the violence. I kept it toned down because we had such a short time that if Paramount had any major problems with it then it would have been a real problem meeting the deadline.

"So there's nothing I would change in NIGHTSHADE, but if I ever got a chance to do another STAR TREK book, I'd probably be a little more daring and see if I could push the envelope a little bit."

THE FUTURE FOR A ONE-TIME TREK AUTHOR

It is sometimes debated as to just how wide the age level of the audience is for the STAR TREK novels, particularly since Pocket Books is going to start releasing a special Young Adult line. She said, "I personally talk to a lot of people at book signings, and a lot of what I would consider 'young adults' read the books. The age range is very broad for STAR TREK. They range from pre-teen up to what seems to be no limit on age."

The 3 book series she has sold to Ace will begin seeing print in October 1993, with the first one in the series titled GUILTY PLEASURES. "It's set in modern day St. Louis," she said "with a few minor changes like legalizing vampirism, and a character who raises the dead for a living, and legalized execution of vampires. What I've done with that is something science fiction does very well, which is to take an idea and go all the way with it; explore it as far as they can, and I've done that with horror. Everything is real. It's fun to use fantasy or science fiction like STAR TREK, and then to go in and work it into the modern world where you have Oreos and Nikes and you don't have to reinvent the wheel all the time."

Although Laurell hasn't named the series, the publisher has put a small banner across the corner of the first book labeling it "Anita Blake—Vampire Hunter."

Laurell has been a published writer for 5 years and she broke into professional writing through the sale of short stories. "My first short stories were purchased by Marion Zimmer Bradley for an anthology," she recalled. "I've been in two SWORD & SORCERESS anthologies, DRAGON magazine, and MARION ZIMMER BRADLEY'S FANTASY MAGAZINE. I've sold to various anthologies," including a superhero anthology co-edited by John Varley which will be published in 1994.

Chapter 4
POCKET SPECIALS

Publishing a new STAR TREK novel almost every month isn't enough for Pocket. Sometimes a book cries out for a special release to make it stand out from the pack.

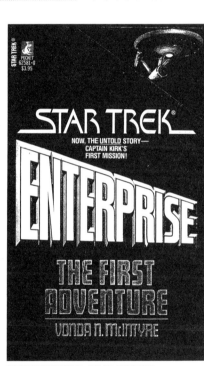

ENTERPRISE: THE FIRST ADVENTURE by Vonda N. McIntyre.

The following Trek Classic novels were issued as special books not numbered in series like other STAR TREK novels. They are special publishing events even though they are written by authors who have previously contributed to the Pocket Books STAR TREK novel series.

SPOCK'S WORLD

SPOCK'S WORLD by Diane Duane made Trek novel history in an impressive run on the bestseller list. The entire STAR TREK catalogue was catapulted from "kiddy sci-fi" into a legitimate school of drama.

The book opens the mind and heart, exposing readers to history, science and literature. It is absorbed subconsciously before the casual reader realizes he is learning.

Duane has shed light on medicine (DOCTOR'S ORDER'S), sociological chaos and war (THE ROMULAN WAY), quantum astrophysics (THE WOUNDED SKY) and how prejudice, honor and betrayal are all different sides of the same coin (MY ENEMY, MY ALLY). This book may have done more to revive STAR TREK than any event since the first film's premiere.

BY ALEX BURLESON

Kirk is on vacation in Ireland when he is called back to the ship on an emergency. Vulcan is threatening to pull out of the United Federation of Planets and recall all of its citizens, shutting out the universe, disowning those who stay with their new lives such as Spock, Sarek and most importantly, Spock's mother, Amanda, whose name we learn is translated as "beloved." Amanda does not appear before the council but makes the strongest impact.

This novel is written in the same style as Diane and Peter Norwood's THE ROMULAN WAY. One chapter returns to the first days of Vulcan, the next to the current crisis.

One of the most beautiful chapters presents the creation of the Vulcan stellar system; how the gasses logically congeal and form the logical planet. Vulcan was an Eden until a stellar event caused the climate to change forcing life to adapt.

Intelligent beings who live underground appear to speak to key Vulcans in history, such as Surak and "the Wanderer," the first Vulcan to become curious. He was the last one out of Eden as the stellar radiation turned Vulcan into Hades.

McCoy ruminates on the name of the god of the forge being used for Vulcan. Vulcan's own mythology is similar.

Surak is pictured differently than expected. Instead of walking around in a robe carrying a sign, he was a regular person who found he could not sit still after finding out anti-matter weapons were being created which could destroy the entire planet. Surak's struggles are given full shadings and his relationship with his disciple who joins the Romulan offshoot migration is detailed.

The past unfolds quickly, at first, then slows chapter by chapter as the author shows how the past affects the present and the future.

The delightful glass spider from THE WOUNDED SKY returns, with Scotty's initial added to her name. She gives a wonderful defense of academic freedom before biting some-one who postulates that she doesn't exist on the leg.

Kirk scolds the precursor to an android. Still, she did play a key role. Scott is given a good turn as he makes his engineers take apart the engines and directs various drills to prepare them for power loss, gravity loss and so on. Kirk is amused, yet proud of his engineer's devotion.

Sarek uses his position as ambassador from the house of Surak to urge a Vulcan with-drawal when T'Pau insists. Kirk again faces the woman who saw him die in T'Pring's last foolish stunt. The Vulcan Matriarch makes her death elegant by first making it look like T'Pring's treachery killed her. And by choosing a Terran, Amanda Grayson, to replace her as Eldest Mother in the House of Surak. That puts Vulcan's fundamentalists in a bind.

Sarek's early years are explored in detail, as was the way he and Amanda met and fell in love. They had Spock and dealt with the press and bigotry.

Amanda tells a dirty joke Sarek is unaware of. Sarek likes 23rd century baseball and sends T'Pau a video of the World Series (refuting NEXT GENERATION's claim that baseball will be extinct).

It is revealed how Vulcans developed the inner eyelid, from the Classic Trek episode "Operation Annihilate," the mental powers used throughout, and what McCoy would call that "damnable logic". It finally comes through in the end.

Terran voters should be ashamed to look at election returns. Everyone on Vulcan votes. They would sooner force a mind-mild than miss an election. Spock seems amazed that not every-one is civic minded. Vulcans could teach how to control negative emotions, use logic, pay more attention to what is important and less to how we look and what we own, and why we kill for no good reason.

Diane Duane gives delivers a Vulcan that learned its lessons.

ENTERPRISE: THE FIRST ADVENTURE

In ENTERPRISE: THE FIRST ADVENTURE by Vonda N. McIntyre, a friend of Commander James Tiberius Kirk gets him drunk just before he is scheduled to become the youngest starship captain. Winona Kirk is there, along with Sam, to see the dashing young hero of the Faragut disaster assume command as Captain Pike is kicked upstairs to commodore.

Kirk visits with Gary Mitchell, who is still recovering from the mission, and Carol Marcus, that blond technician Gary set Kirk up with. He does not know she will soon bear him a son.

Kirk is outraged with Admiral Nogura when he decides to give him an easy mission, escorting a vaudeville troupe on a 23rd century USO tour of starbases. He couldn't get off to a worse start.

The woman who runs the circus is reduced to tears, while Winona and Sam are convinced Jim is becoming a bully and a boor. Nogura is about ready to take back the command when Kirk straightens up.

Nothing initially goes right for the crew. Bones is kayaking and rafting in the Grand Canyon and nearly misses the flight. Kirk calls his ex-wife, looking for him. At the last minute he checks in and sprints to the bridge, injured and covered with dirt.

That is Spock's first vision of the doctor. Spock and McCoy's initial encounter is hardly cordial. Spock accuses him of wanting to use his unique anatomy as a Guinea pig.

Sulu wanted to be assigned to the border patrol, near his adopted home of Ganjitsu, protecting the border worlds from pirates. He is upset Kirk picked him. He nearly gets his wish when he almost wrecks the ship as it first leaves space-dock. Kirk angrily orders Spock to take over and Sulu is forced to redeem himself. Little hint Sulu would one day be a famous captain.

Kirk and Spock get off on the wrong foot when Spock overhears Jim's request for Gary Mitchell as First Officer. The Vulcan is ready to bolt.

Kirk and Scott almost come to blows. Kirk can't get the engineer to realize it is his ship and not the Scottsman's.

The cast molds together to solve the mystery and enjoy one of the few peaceful meetings the Federation had with the Klingon Empire. Kirk becomes the first Federation Captain honored by the Klingons.

The carnival troupe acts as comic relief, with flying horses and Sulu being recruited for a stage role. Spock uses his logic to disrupt a magic show, with Kirk ready to strangle the impolitic officer. When the Klingons see the magic, they believe it's sorcery, until the magician who runs the troupe is forced to explain her tricks.

The Klingons are insulted. The disastrous show could lead to war until the idiot thespian, who insists on mangling Shakespeare in his own image, takes the stage. The Klingons are overcome by the Bard's words and the mission is salvaged. A female Klingon wins a top-of-the-line state-of-the-art battleship in a game with the son of the Klingon KGB.

A very satisfying novel about the first trip of the ship under the new command.

STAR TREK IV— THE VOYAGE HOME

Ecological and environmental points are stressed in Vonda N. McIntyre's STAR TREK IV— THE VOYAGE HOME. All of the time stream continuum errors from the film are corrected.

In the movie, an elderly antique dealer buys Kirk's glasses. In the novel, it's an old hippie.

Kirk and Spock have trouble getting "exact change" for the bus, and the garbage man talking about his problems turns out to be a writer quoting one of his stories to a friend. Gillian is a well drawn character.

The opening scenes on Vulcan are well done as Kirk deals with Starfleet brass ready to hang him out to dry. McCoy objects to the time-travel scheme and Kirk suggests he stay behind in an escape pod.

McIntyre's novelization is based on the screenplay by Steve Meerson, Peter Krikes, Harve Bennett and Nicholas Meyer, taken from a story by Leonard Nimoy and Harve Bennett.

STAR TREK V— THE FINAL FRONTIER

The film viewer gets a brief glimpse of Jonn as he is cured of his pain by Sybok. The reader of STAR TREK V—THE FINAL FRONTIER by J.M. Dillard gets a complete look at how his life drifted downhill until the Vulcan touched him and took away his pain.

It is remarkable how effective Dillard is at explaining how he was able to win over the most loyal bridge crew in Starfleet. This novel is an enjoyable look at an underated tale.

Sybok's character is given dimension. The mission placed on his shoulders by his mother is shown to be far more than insane ramblings.

Dillard's novel is adapted from the screenplay by David Loughery which was based on a story by William Shatner, Harve Bennett and David Loughery.

STAR TREK VI— THE UNDISCOVERED COUNTRY

Carol Marcus is seriously injured when Klingons attack the scientific research station she is working at in STAR TREK VI: THE UNDIS-COVERED COUNTRY by J.M. Dillard. Kirk waits to see if she will live or die but is called away to Starfleet Command.

This addition explains why Kirk is enraged at the Klingons at the time of the meeting. The "Let them die!" speech is more effective in this context.

The Klingons are given more background as they are examined and their motivations chal-lenged. The Deltan president shines as he is forced to decide between Kirk and McCoy and the chance for peace.

Captain Hikaru Sulu contemplates his role as captain when the shock wave pulls him from his complacency. Sulu is outraged by the trial and decides to risk his career to help his former crewmates. Commander Rand's role as communications officer on his ship is explained and other characters on the Excelsior are detailed.

The reasons Valeris did what she did are finally revealed. She was not a "normal" Vulcan. Her parents lived far away from their homeworld when her mother was killed and her father was shocked into manic-depressive behavior, causing him to refuse to allow Valeris to undergo the mental disciplines. When she finally does receive training, she has been poisoned by years of hearing her father seek revenge.

She is reluctant and tries to let both Kirk and Spock know how she feels, but neither listens. She is ashamed Spock calls her his suc-cessor as she is betraying him.

Dillard shows how Valeris agreed to give Spock the information willingly. She is prepared for a vicious attack and brain damage until Spock politely asks her permission, stunning her into consent.

Admiral Cartwright's motivations are detailed, as are those of Colonel West. The feel-ings are given in-depth analysis and Kirk's hatred is purged by the sorrow he feels for Gorkon, one of the few Klingons he likes.

More on Captain Sulu and Col. Worf should have been added, but Dillard would be hard pressed to improve this novelization of the screenplay by Nicholas Meyer and Danny Martin Flynn, based on the story by Leonard Nimoy, Nicholas Meyer and Danny Martin Flynn.

THE LOST YEARS

THE LOST YEARS by J.M. Dillard tells the tale of what happens to the Classic Trek crew when the Enterprise finally returns from the historic five-year mission. The novel reveals the feelings of the bridge crew as they bring the ship in for a massive refitting.

Kirk is not planning to get stuck at a desk. He requests assignment to the USS Victorious as captain. Spock gets upset with Kirk when his captain recommends Spock become captain of the Science Ship Grissom.

Chekov, Sulu, Uhura and the others deal with the dissolution of the crew. McCoy returns to the woman he fell in love with in the Classic Trek episode "For The World Is Hollow And I Have Touched The Sky," only to find she has fallen for someone else. He returns to Vulcan and falls in love with a fortune-telling, cigarette-smoking wildwoman who wanders into his life.

Spock agrees to get McCoy permission to tour the sacred area at Gol. Spock has become engaged to marry T'Sara and settle down and leave Starfleet.

McCoy is uncomfortable in the Vulcan heat and goes to sleep in the space vessel where it is cooler. He is on hand to see the vessel stolen and finds himself in the middle of a 10,000 year old Vulcan death match, with the planets' future hanging in the balance.

McCoy is furious when Kirk accepts promotion to admiral at Starfleet Command after Admiral Nogura waves beautiful Vice-Admiral Lori Ciana in Kirk's face and they fall in love. Kirk signs on as a trouble-shooter and realizes he is going to be stuck to a desk.

Lori helps Kirk when his ship has been sabotaged. In fact, her actions save the day.

Lt. Comdr. Kevin Riley, from the Classic Trek episodes "The Naked Time" and "The Conscience of the King," and the novels A FLAG FULL OF STARS and PROBE, serves as Kirk's Chief of Staff. Lori changes his attitude. Kirk is impressed with Lori and they marry.

They will eventually let that contract expire. Lori ultimately dies in the transporter incident in Gene Roddenberry's novel STAR TREK: THE MOTION PICTURE. Her relationship with Kirk

is explained and expanded on in Brad Fergeson's sequel to this novel, A FLAG FULL OF STARS.

The Vulcan plot involves the katra of two Vulcan legends restored to human form. The Vulcans are forced to commandeer bodies to continue a battle begun before Vulcan reformation.

Spock, with the aid of an ancient Vulcan woman, uncovers what is going on and leads the team to oversee the outcome of the battle. The evil Vulcan has strong mental powers and uses a rare error by Spock to hurt their chances.

The woman McCoy has fallen in love with, Drew, is forced to give her life to save Kirk, McCoy, Spock and the Vulcan Matriarch.

McCoy is livid when Spock calmly flies the shuttle away leaving Drew to die. He wishes Jim would fire a phaser at the Vulcan, never realizing she is happy to play such a significant part in Vulcan history. His anger towards Spock eases as he realizes how much it affected him.

Spock breaks off his engagement and prepares to leave for Gol to learn the Kolinar discipline. Kirk finds he is going to be more constrained than he imagined. McCoy drowns his problems in drink, then decides to devote his time to the causes Drew was passionate about. This sad ending helps explain their reactions when the crew is reunited in STAR TREK: THE MOTION PICTURE.

FINAL FRONTIER

FINAL FRONTIER by Diane Carey is set in two separate time periods. It begins when Captain James T. Kirk visits his mother in Iowa. The captain struggles to come to grips with the death of the woman of his dreams, Edith Keeler. The woman he allowed to die to save the Federation has been haunting him since his recent visit to the Terran 1930s in the Classic Trek episode "City On The Edge of Forever."

Kirk is in the barn reading old letters his dad sent him before he vanished on a Federation mission. As Kirk reads the letters, we are introduced to the father, George Kirk, who helped set James on the road which led to his destiny.

George was working a quiet security job when he and his assistant were kidnapped and taken from the Starbase. After they awakened they found they were on a special mission, under orders from George's old friend, Robert April.

April explained that he wanted George to serve as First Officer on the top-secret mission to test the brand new Federation invention—the starship. George was awed by the beautiful vessel and learned to interact with the crew.

Robert's easy-going command style was not well suited for saboteurs on his ship. George began an investigation and the clues fell together.

The sabotage sent the Enterprise past the neutral zone near Romulus. Damaged in Romulan space, the crew found a way to effect repairs, defeat the saboteur and deal with the xenophobic Romulans.

Kirk is joined by McCoy and Spock at the barn as he begins to understand his father.

BEST DESTINY

BEST DESTINY by Diane Carey is a sequel to Carey's FINAL FRONTIER. The novel shows two sides of the career of James Kirk. The story begins with the events following the novel STAR TREK VI: THE UNDISCOVERED COUNTRY.

Kirk and the crew are bringing the ship home after their tour to the "second star on the right." The Enterprise receives evidence of an anti-matter explosion, forcing them to believe the USS Bill Of Rights, commanded by a former member of Kirk's crew, was destroyed.

As Kirk approaches, he looks back on his first trip aboard the Enterprise. The early memories play a key part in resolving the tale.

A 16 year old James Kirk led a bunch of kids to run away from home and sign on as merchant sailors. His father, George reacted to both Kirk and the people who hired him.

George promised to take Jim into space, but after the tragedy on Tarsus IV, Jimmy soured on space travel. The elder Kirk took Jim on a surprise visit to a starship.

Kirk met Captain April and acted like a spoiled brat, convinced not to do anything he thinks his father wants. The teen's heart stopped as he stared at the starship which would change his life. he was dumbfounded to learn his dad named it.

His first words on the bridge were, "What stinks up here?" and later Kirk said he always wondered if the ship forgave him. Most of the crew were ready to send the little brat out of a torpedo tube, but an exasperated April insisted on bringing Jim on a landing party in a shuttle-type craft. The grandmotherly first officer took the Enterprise on a diplomatic venture while the Kirks joined April and two others on the mission.

A pirate vessel with unusual technology severely damaged the craft. At one point, George insisted on sending Jimmy to get help to save his son.

This wasn't the same Jimmy. After Kirk made a few mistakes injuring a female crewman who became his friend, he started learning proverbs that eventually led to his command style. Kirk couldn't stand to see his crew die and aimed his escape vessel into a kamakazi suicide craft as his father watched helplessly.

April explained to George how Jimmy had matured enough to give his life to save them all. They were about to attack an enemy ship when its gravity fails and the ship is crippled. April realized young Jimmy survived and put a monkey-wrench in the pirate's plan.

Young Kirk faced off against a young rebel, the pirate's son who built the shield. The two met in a battle of wills and Kirk maneuvered the son into killing his own father. Kirk's father is overtaken with pride as he slipped aboard the pirate ship at the last second and heard his son talk about how much his crewmates now mean to him.

Situation under control, father and son were closer than ever. Jim Kirk decided on a career in Starfleet, just like dad. Throughout the story, flash backs are shown of the last mission. It all makes sense when it turns out the young pirate is the one holding the Federation ship.

The rivals face off over an ancient world with advanced technology. Kirk's rival destroys all the invaluable technology when he tampers with the defense systems. The entire intergalactic transporter system is destroyed, so he becomes a laughingstock instead of a legend.

The unique Enterprise-class design (which Carey calls Constitution class) outperforms the new Excelsior class Bill Of Rights. Starfleet decides not to decommission her after all.

Scott is as happy as Kirk when the Deltan Federation President honors them, in sharp contrast to the way they were treated with by Starfleet at the end of STAR TREK VI— THE UNDISCOVERED COUNTRY. The stories provide bookends for Kirk's storied career.

STRANGERS FROM THE SKY

Margaret Wander Bonannoas crafts a masterwork in STRANGERS FROM THE SKY. The crew of the Enterprise is examined at different points in time. The present is right after STAR TREK: THE MOTION PICTURE and before THE WRATH OF KHAN.

Doctor McCoy enjoys a novel that suggests Vulcans visited Terra earlier but the facts were suppressed. The book causes mental trauma in Kirk to such a degree that he is declared clinically insane.

His distress affects Spock, aboard the Enterprise, serving as captain on a training mission. One key scene shows Spock meditating when he thinks of the word "alone." A Vulcan speaking aloud during meditation is akin to a human arriving nude at his wedding.

Kirk is fixated on something a blond woman once told Spock and him. The novel offers excerpts from the book which caused such distress in Kirk.

Two kelp-farmers lives are altered, as well as that of the captain and first-mate on his ship, not to mention the two Vulcans who stand history on its head. As Spock and Kirk are released into McCoy's care to try a Vulcan mind-meld after Spock has gone insane as well, the female doctor mentions an old name that stirs a memory.

When she is diagnosing Kirk for her students, one suggests his fantasies compensate for a dull life. The doctor points out Kirk has had the most exciting life ever.

McCoy believes Kirk's other mental manipulations, such as the exchange with Sargon in the Classic Trek episode "Return To Tomorrow," could be behind his problem. Then Kirk remembers who the blond woman is.

The novel moves back in time to one of Kirk and Spock's first encounters. Kirk delights in browbeating Spock when a planet disappears from sensors. He offends the Vulcan who stays up all night and finds the planet again. Kirk leads a landing party consisting of Spock and the three crewmembers who will meet their death in the Classic Trek episode "Where No Man Has Gone Before."

The five are transported back in time by a time-traveling Egyptian for whom time runs backwards. Kirk, Mitchell, Kelso and Dehner show up, but Spock is missing. The Egyptian is afraid his interference kept Terra and Vulcan apart, so Spock couldn't exist.

His fears prove unfounded. Spock rematerializes in the United States, and goes to Boston to contact his ancestor, Professor Grayson, a peace negotiator.

The landing party in Egypt hears about aliens and tries to find out if Spock could be involved. They split up across the planet to solve the mystery.

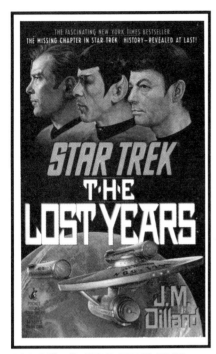

J. M. Dillard's STAR TREK: THE LOST YEARS.

The two Vulcans' reactions to their human hosts are priceless, and the submarine captain turns out to be quite Kirk-like. The kelp-farmers adopt the Vulcans and vow to protect them. Kirk and Dehner join the investigation. Gary Mitchell arrives in a snowmobile and Spock arrives to tie the story together.

The Dehner message and "alone" referred to the fact that neither Kirk nor Spock could solve the mystery alone. Kirk could not convince the formidable female Vulcan captain, yet Spock was condemning her to years of isolation by revealing his presence. When she reads Spock's thoughts, she understands how the two worlds will grow together, just as the captain and first officer, who are just getting to know each other.

Bonanno does an excellent job melding the story from many separate fragments, and drops in familiar faces, including the Vulcan and Terran woman from the novel DWELLERS IN THE CRUCIBLE. The author also adds humor, such as Spock's host calling him Benjamin—as in Dr. Spock, the noted peace activist and baby doctor.

This tale is as much fun as a barrel of Vulcans. The stories reinforce each other.

PROBE

PROBE by Gene Deweese and Margaret Wander Bonanno is overshadowed by the controversy that went into its release. An article in PEOPLE magazine detailed how Bonanno disowned and disavowed the novel after Pocket Books objected to the story and brought in novelist Gene Deweese (RENEGADE, and THE PEACEKEEPERS) to rewrite the planned sequel to STAR TREK IV: THE VOYAGE HOME. Margaret said one page she wrote was retained, with the rest changed beyond recognition.

Her Trek novels have always featured strong characters in addition to the regular Trek cast. In DWELLERS IN THE CRUCIBLE, the Enterprise crew plays a secondary role, until they debrief the captives at the end of the book. The Terran and Vulcan females, Deltan hostages and Klingon and Romulan abductors make up most of the story.

In STRANGERS FROM THE SKY, Bonanno revived the landing party from the Classic Trek episode "Where No Man Has Gone Before," adding two kelp-farmers, two Navy officers, two Vulcan survivors, an Egyptian time-traveler and a long-lost relative of Spock. In addition, she introduced an Aboriginal Australian Dreamtalker, an Island boy Kirk befriends and a psychologist who treats Kirk.

Despite the introduction of new characters, the stories are successful. The problems arose over Lt. Comdr. Kevin Riley, who is promoted to Federation Ambassador in PROBE. In the published novel, he is barely heard from, suffers an injury and spends the mission in a coma in sickbay.

Deweese brings back the title Probe from STAR TREK IV, yet doesn't capture the humor of that novel. The Probe is preparing to return in a decade to check on George and Gracie when it finds itself in Romulan space. Romulans suspect it is a Federation weapon.

An unusual peace conference takes place as the Enterprise and a Romulan ship are dispatched by the Deltan President of the Federation and the Romulan Praetor. An archaeologist, who is a musical conductor in New York, finds herself summoned by Uhura to assist the Federation. Both her skills come in handy. Music and archeology intermix in the confusing plot.

Efforts to talk with the Probe prove intriguing, yet the tale turns tragic when the ship learns that the intelligent superwhales that built the Wanderer have faded into extinction. Perhaps those proud superminds relocated before their planet lost its ability to support them. And perhaps humanity will as well.

PRIME DIRECTIVE

The opening chapter of PRIME DIRECTIVE by Judith and Garfield Reeves-Stevens sets the tone as this adventurous novel leads us to the true final frontier. Disgraced heroes restore their reputations. Debates concering the Prime Directive are some of the most tortured philosophical queries in STAR TREK history.

An anonymous manual laborer attracts his female Tellarite supervisor. The laborer saves a Tellarite pup by risking his life following a breach in the asteroid's skin.

At first he is cheered as a hero. Then when his identity is known, he is spat at and reviled. He is the man who destroyed a planet and lost his command.

His name is Jim. Jim Kirk. How did this happen to the most illustrious captain in Starfleet history?

The dream of stars grew dim. A Starfleet admiral's report lists Kirk alongside Ron Tracey (Classic Trek episode—"The Omega Glory") as a captain who went bad. Scotty cries over what's left of the Enterprise, destroyed when a nuclear war claimed Kirk's career and Scotty's bairns. Scott must deal with people who don't show the ship the respect he insists upon. Worst of all, Lt. Styles is in command.

Scott reads in his mail that Ensign Spock has resigned from the fleet, the last of the infamous "Enterprise Five" to do so. Dr. Leonard McCoy punched a Starfleet admiral; Ensign Uhura is being court-martialed on Luna, Earth's moon. Sulu and Chekov are off to the Rigel system to find work as pirates on an Orion slave ship.

Kirk is a man without a future. He meets a former Starfleet officer familiar with his record who offers to help him travel back toward the planet he allegedly killed. As Kirk travels with the female captain, he tells her the story of what went wrong.

This novel uses rich characterization and first rate plotting to involve the reader!

A LOOK BACK

These novels explore the STAR TREK universe in unique and exciting ways. Fans often complain that some of these should have been made into motion pictures instead of those which were presented for our viewing enjoyment. Unlike the Bantam STAR TREK novels which often seemed cranked out for a paycheck, the authors of the Pocket STAR TREK novels, and especially these specials, clearly love what they are doing and put their heart and soul into their books.

Chapter 5
NEXT GEN & DEEP SPACE

In the '70s, Bantam relinquished the contract to publish STAR TREK novels because they felt the field had been mined out. In fact the richest veins had yet to be uncovered as the '80s and '90s have proven.

In 1987 when STAR TREK: THE NEXT GENERATION premiered, the first TNG novel was an adaptation of "Encounter At Farpoint." This was followed with occasional original NEXT GENERATION novels until now there are more than two dozen and they are published regularly, as are those devoted to the new addition to the line, DEEP SPACE NINE.

Both numbered and unnumbered NEXT GENERATION novels have appeared. While ENCOUNTER AT FARPOINT is the first release, it was issued without a number. The official numbering began with the first original NEXT GENERATION novel.

GHOST SHIP

This first original TNG novel, GHOST SHIP by Diane Duane, is well-written, but fails to stand out like Duane's Classic Trek novels. Deanna has a psychic experience with a Soviet naval vessel from 1994.

At the time, Duane couldn't know the Soviet Union would soon dissolve. The naval officers are absorbed to live in an energy form that allows them to survive for centuries in a disembodied state. When they contact the Enterprise crew, they cry out for an end to this form of existence.

Picard is uncertain. He immerses himself in a deprivation tank to gauge the impact of such an existence. That convinces him to do as Troi says.

BY ALEX BURLESON

THE PEACEKEEPERS

While investigating a derelict vessel in THE PEACEKEEPERS by Gene Deweese, Data and Geordi are transported several parsecs by a device long abandoned by an ancient culture. Rather than be perceived as trespassers, they pretend to be inventors of the transporter technology.

Geordi makes the call as Data plays along. On the Enterprise, they figure out what happened. Riker and Tasha plan to reproduce the effect, find Data and Geordi and send back a message via subspace radio.

It was a good plan. Unfortunately, the radios didn't survive the transport. Will and Tasha are stranded along with the original duo.

Deanna feels her Imzadi's thoughts in subspace and gets Picard's attention just in time. Geordi, Data, Will and Tasha are stranded in deep space, orbiting a planet as they fall toward the atmosphere.

The Enterprise arrives in time to save the day. Lt. Worf gets a great turn, as he terrifies the people of the planet into accepting each other, if only to fight him off.

There is a tragic death, but that death is not in vain. The relationship between the battling brothers is intriguing, although Deweese never fully explains the reasons.

THE CHILDREN OF HAMLIN

In THE CHILDREN OF HAMLIN by Carmen Carter, as the Enterprise transports farm settlers to New Oregon, they are diverted to respond to a distress signal and find a starship under attack. They rescue the survivors and drive off the alien 'ship'. Picard is stunned to learn that Starfleet has placed him under the command of the ambassador who commanded the mission that led to the destruction of the first vessel.

NIGHTSHADE by Laurell K. Hamilton.

Picard is put off by the ambassador and his young assistant. Ruthe's presence plays a key part in the novel, even if it does take the bridge crew forever to figure out the obvious.

Wesley's relationship with the farmer boy is well-scripted, as is the conflict of the farmers' old fashioned ways against 24th century values. The farmers have a brother-sister based social structure and the boy lacked the vital uncle role model stressed by custom. Wes helps open his mind up to the wonders of the Enterprise and he helps Wes learn to interact with the cultural subset.

One of the best chapters involves the crew's reaction to a yellow alert. Picard notices the ship change speed and asks Riker for a report before Riker can contact him. The next time, Riker contacts him instantaneously.

When Tasha hears the alert, she sprints to the bridge and harangues Worf for not calling her earlier. He replies, "I was busy."

Deanna is startled awake and put off when Riker tells her she's not needed, but realizes she was more upset at being awakened from a sound sleep. Geordi chides Data after the android gives a definition of yellow alert, instead of just saying, "I don't know."

The funniest reaction is that of Acting Ensign Crusher who has snuck his farmer friend into engineering. Wes calls the bridge to report and is ordered back to bed by Picard.

The actual Children of Hamlin play a key part in the tale. Communications with the aliens is handled very well as Carmen conveys the difficulty in dealing with the complicated form of musical being.

The story of the little girl is heart wrenching with the rescue a very rewarding tale. Tasha enjoys giving Beverly some of her own medicine when the doctor is forced to breathe a liquid atmosphere.

Author Carter brings loose ends together. At one point, it seems the story has ended. Then it begins again with a vengeance as Picard and the ambassador form an uneasy alliance to save a child. Carmen infuses the story with rich character shadings.

SURVIVORS

SURVIVORS by Jean Lorrah is the tragic story of Tasha Yar. The hardships of her childhood, her rescue by Starfleet, her last key mission before her death, and the crew's forced acceptance of the security chief's demise are all presented.

Tasha and Data are sent on an away mission in a shuttle craft to evaluate a request for aid from the Federation. While on the long voyage, Data and Tasha confront their feelings about each other.

She tells him of her life and the novel flashes back to earlier events. Her struggle with withdrawal as a child born addicted to "joy dust" and battles with the rape gangs are shown as tragic glimpses into her psyche.

This novel serves as a fine epitaph to a TNG character whose shadow continues to fall in TNG episodes and novels.

STRIKE ZONE

Captain Picard is forced to place the Enterprise in the middle of the centuries-long dispute between the Klingon and the Kreel in STRIKE ZONE by Peter David. Meanwhile, a dwarf casts a spell over Wesley, driving the acting ensign to distraction in an attempt to find a cure for the disease that is killing him.

Two savage cultures get hold of ancient technology capable of wiping out most of the life in the galaxy. Geordi LeForge finds himself stuck over a disintegration chamber and Worf and Wesley face down phasers set to kill. The bridge is taken by an armed commando team.

Despite all that, this is one of the funniest books ever written. Laugh out loud funny when Riker walks in on the elf seducing Troi . . . or interrupts Worf, who is. . . er. . . preoccupied with the 1/4 Klingon daughter of the 1/2 Klingon ambassador.

The novel weaves back and forth from funny to sad. Betrayal followed by acts of bravery. Peter David crafts a masterwork in his first TNG novel.

POWER HUNGRY

Howard Weinstein has written other STAR TREK novels including DEEP DOMAIN, and wrote the script for the STAR TREK animated episode "The Pirates of Orion." Weinstein brings a sense of environmental awareness to his novels, which feature ecosystems out of control and politicians unwilling to give up control, against people who love and respect the land.

In POWER HUNGRY by Howard Weinstein, Riker is sent down to accompany an idiot ambassador and is immediately attacked. Riker is taken by the people who live in caves and protest the destruction of the planet.

Picard and the others dine on sumptuous fare, as the rulers live like kings while the peasants starve.

Picard must beam down, then beam over to save Riker under attack. Riker is shocked to see Picard beam into a battle zone.

Weinstein shows how one voice can gain power, if only a mediator can reach common ground with both sides. To paraphrase Worf, Klingons don't fight in burning houses. This novel carries that proverb to a planetary scale.

MASKS

John Vornholt's first TNG novel, MASKS shows two away teams forced to adapt to a hostile planet. They struggle to reach a common goal, independently.

The ambassador is painted as a hero, a descendent of Meriwether Lewis, of Lewis and Clark fame. He quickly turns against the away team of Picard, Worf and Troi.

They encounter a band and move forward as guests of the female leader, in hopes of finding a way to continue their mission after they lose contact with the Enterprise. Riker, Data and Polaski accompany a second away team that runs into a little old peddler, who escorts them to the fair.

Each away team runs into perils. These include the aforementioned ambassador, bands of red-masked bandits and attacks from the planet, which is geologically unstable.

When Riker and his band are attacked, he asks Wesley to provide a diversion. He does. His photon torpedo nearly destroys them all.

Geordi, who is in command, is about to fry Wes on the stake, when Riker notes that he had asked for the diversion. It was just a bit of overkill.

Picard and his group become intermingled with their band in more ways than one. Picard falls in love with the beautiful leader.

When John Vornholt appeared at the Starbase Houston Trekfest in 1992, he bragged that he was the first writer to let Picard have

sex. He made the act of taking off their masks very erotic.

Everyone on the planet wears masks, not just for protection, but as social custom. Showing their naked face is the ultimate compliment. That is why the old peddler is shocked at the bare faces of the second away team. The masks the first team wears down are very funny. Worf's is hysterical.

Vornholt said he wanted masks as a metaphor for what we hide in our professional and private lives. He succeeds in making people believable and reactions very understandable.

THE CAPTAIN'S HONOR

The Magna Romans who appeared in the Classic Trek episode "Bread and Circuses" are reexamined in THE CAPTAIN'S HONOR by David and Daniel Dvorkin. They are now in the Federation, yet democracy has been an uneasy fit on a planet where the Roman Empire never fell. The captains and officers are patricians, with a few proletarians among the bridge crew.

Riker falls in love with the leader's daughter. She turns out to be a formidable leader in her own right even if a trip to a "magical holodeck" makes her unsure of what is real.

Subversion through education in an attempt to teach a pacifist society how to defend itself is brought home as the students react to Worf's classes. Worf and the Romans are amazed to find that the colonists would rather die than suffer the dishonor of killing. They exile their war heroes.

An Enterprise security guard falls in love with a Roman officer and plans to transfer aboard when tragedy strikes. She single-handedly saves the ship.

The battle of wits between Picard and his counterpart is well-drawn. Each pushes the other past the point of no return. Giant cats who eat humans, and each other, shows hunger can drive an entire species mad. The interaction between the space-voyaging, human-eating kitty-cats is interesting, but the female security officer is the star.

A CALL TO DARKNESS

An away team is investigating a crippled starship that was carrying the daughter of a friend of Captain Picard's in A CALL TO DARKNESS by Michael Jan Friedman. Picard, Polaski, Worf and Geordi are whisked away to the planet's surface and processed as slaves.

Each loses their memory and has no idea where they are or why they are there. Picard and Geordi are thrown together when one risks his life to save the other, then vice-versa.

Worf has no idea who he is, but feels there is no honor in combat for no reason. He feels his reluctance to kill makes him a coward, until Polaski regains her memory and takes the Klingon into her confidence.

A group of freedom fighters on the brutal planet joins to help the away team find a way to reverse the mental process and save crewmates from destruction. Picard figures a way to end the mental coercion without violating the Prime Directive and transports the slaves back to their homeworlds.

The debriefing in Ten-Forward is very illuminating. Various aliens explain their plight over the years of fighting for another being's enjoyment for no reason.

A ROCK AND A HARD PLACE

In A ROCK AND A HARD PLACE by Peter David, Commander Riker is sent to an Arctic planet named Paradise to contact an old school friend and investigate a mysterious animal. Meanwhile, a new first officer is assigned to the Enterprise.

Commander Stone is considered crazy by most—a genius by a few. He and Picard butt heads over ship operations and Stone's conduct

on a bizarre away team mission. Stone tells lies about his scars to everyone who asks, until he finally breaks down and admits the crime he has never been able to forgive himself for.

It is an example of how a moral person with a Prime Directive dilemma is forced to stand by and watch atrocities committed, unable to act and forced to live with the guilt. It transforms Stone from an ice-hearted monster into a misunderstood victim.

His early attacks on Wesley and Data anger Picard, until Picard realizes Stone must be trying to make him angry. A standoff with a phaser and a meeting with Stone's former captain are also standout chapters. David does a great job of filling in the backstory of Riker as his friend, his wife and daughter are each fleshed out.

GULLIVER'S FUGITIVES

Fundamentalists leave Earth and form a government where all fiction is outlawed and the Bible is law. People suspected of "thought crimes" are brainwashed and given new identities.

A group of rebels hoard books and memorize them. When Troi has a mental flashback, the crew investigates the planet and finds evidence of a missing Federation ship. When the Enterprise makes contact, the leaders visit the ship, then kidnap Picard and leave robot devices to attack the ship.

Riker, Troi and Data head to the surface to look for Picard and are immediately taken prisoner, except for Deanna who escapes and meets up with the underground. Picard has his memories edited, but a member of the underground who does not take to the brainwashing watches his memories on a viewscreen and joins with Riker (who is about to be blanked) and Data (who is about to be disassembled) to restore his memory. They help find Troi and the power center on the planet.

Meanwhile, on the Enterprise, the robots are attacking. Geordi is in command and Worf, Wesley, Wes's zen-warrior girlfriend, and Geordi's blind musician assistant save the ship. Wes's use of Shiva to tie into quantum mechanics is interesting, as is Wes' relationship with the security officer.

Worf shines as he hunts down the armed robots for hand-to-hand combat, since they have trouble reading Klingon minds. They are forced to believe there are no aliens, which keeps them from accepting him as a being.

The appearance of an alien species on the planet plays a key role in resolving the story. The escape by the dissenters and the true identity of the alien leader are high points.

Worf's friendship with the alien visitors is well done, as is Troi's realization that they had unknowingly started the crew on the mission when they used their technology on Troi. Worf's designs on being a writer shows a new side of the Klingon, who finally realizes the pen can be deadlier than the sword.

Picard's knowledge of Shakespeare allows both Geordi and Riker to figure out what the aliens did to the Captain. The alien dissenter Amoret saved the mission and the away team, as Geordi's assistant helped save the Enterprise.

In a nice touch, Picard thanks them for saving his ship as they sleep. The musicians' attack on food taboos is hilarious.

DOOMSDAY WORLD

Geordi, Data and Worf go on an away mission to assist an archaeologist who was a mentor to Geordi in DOOMSDAY WORLD by Peter David, Carmen Carter, Michael Jan Friedman and Robert Greenberger. They discover an ancient civilization and deal with the conflict between the Federation and the K'vin (named after the book's editor Kevin).

Picard makes an unpopular decision to leave a colony unprotected. Tension on the bridge and in the ready room is drawn out, with even Wesley questioning Picard's decision.

Meanwhile, attacks are occurring on the planet, as relationships deteriorate. When Geordi's friend is killed, he takes it personally, which helps lead the away team in the right direction.

The planet itself is a giant suicide weapon and a misguided patriot on the planet sets it in place. The Enterprise is nearly caught in the wormhole created by the planet, but Worf has a delightful solution to the problem.

Riker and Troi react to the devastated colony, and are both at odds with the captain. When a woman tries to seduce Data, Worf steps in and the interaction between the Klingon and Orion are outstanding.

The alien invasion plot is predictable, but the way the Enterprise maneuvers the survivors rescues the story. Interaction between the Federation ambassador and her K'vin counterpart are well done, as is her intimidation of Picard.

The novel is structured so well the reader never realizes four authors are at work. They share the same voice, thanks to the crisp editing of the real K'vin, Kevin Ryan.

THE EYES OF THE BEHOLDERS

In THE EYES OF THE BEHOLDERS by A.C. Crispin, the Enterprise is ordered to investigate the disappearance of a Federation cargo ship and Klingon warship. The Enterprise is captured and the crew learns what did in the other two crews.

They are in an alien art museum. The species posseses an appearance so out of the human frame of reference that it makes those who look upon it ill. The beings make telegraphic sculptures which produce violent emotions in those exposed.

Picard drops shields to transport an away team to the cargo ship. As a result, mental illness is introduced to the Enterprise.

Crispin effectively describes an away team encounter in which Data, Geordi, Worf, Riker and a Tellarite doctor are overcome by the lethal artwork.

EXILES

An alien culture deals with their opposition by banishing each culture to colony planets in EXILES by Howard Weinstein. One of the cultures formed after expulsion specializes in preserving ecosystems and saving extinct species and even restoring species that have vanished.

The colony requests the Enterprise help it negotiate with the original planet; which is itself destroying itself with pollution. The second planet is being torn up by geological stress, so they request use of an uninhabited planet controlled by the original planet.

An unusual pair of alien sacred animals is featured. Beverly is outraged at the idea of pets in sickbay but learns to love the sacred little creatures.

Their keeper, a young man who loves animals, has a crush on Troi. It is hilarious when the young man misinterprets Deanna's attempt to calm him as an attempt at seduction. Later, when he is attacked, he awakens in Deanna's arms, making him believe his dreams have been fulfilled.

Riker and Data begin negotiations and are abducted in a shuttlecraft. They face perils in the giant ship and the alien ambassador and ruler have good senses of humor, making them far more palatable than the usual Trek ambassador.

The two alien command units are given proper background, much as in Weinstein's earlier POWER HUNGRY. The alien computer with a sense of humor is the best depiction of artificial intelligence since Diane Duane's "Miora", the recreation computer in SPOCK'S WORLD.

The third alien who brings the ship of vengeance is a tragic character ill-suited for the role history has for him. At one point, Picard informs the populace of the Enterprise he has decided to sacrifice the ship and all the lives aboard to protect a planet. That is one of the truly tense moments in TNG history with Riker contacting the ship at the last second to inform them of the true situation.

Howard does a great job scoring his points on how fragile an ecosystem really is. That ties this book in the same green ribbon as POWER HUNGRY and PERCHANCE TO DREAM.

FORTUNE'S LIGHT

Riker must travel alone to a planet to investigate a crime a friend has been accused of in FORTUNE'S LIGHT by Michael Jan Friedman. Riker and his friend both were assigned to the planet and the other stayed behind. His friend meets an end similar to that of Jackson Carter in Peter David's A ROCK AND A HARD PLACE.

Riker's friends all seem to have hard luck. On the planet, Riker must deal with a difficult female co-investigator. They finally overcome mutual distrust and work together to solve the puzzle.

Back on the ship, Data gets lost in a 21st century baseball game that Will had programmed into the holodeck. Data plays the part of a phenom brought up in the playoffs to make a key hit in Alaska's only major baseball game.

Picard watches and is upset that Data is loyal to the team's manager who smashes water coolers with bats. His concerns are muted when Data explains he "feels sorry" for the beleaguered manager and does not emulate his style or actions.

Both stories work, but no element ties other crew members into the mix.

An exception occurs when the Klingon security chief walks out on the field during Data's routine and is attacked by the baseball security staff. They do not impress Worf in the least.

CONTAMINATION

John Vornholt combines a traditional murder mystery with a detailed look at super-clean recycling procedures in CONTAMINATION. He does a good job describing the lifestyle of the hundreds of scientists working on every deck. They have little to do with the missions the bridge crew undertakes in every story.

One leading Federation scientist dies in an accident in ae cleanroom. Her despondent attitude and marital difficulties lead Deanna to suspect foul play.

When Worf finds evidence of equipment sabotage the investigation begins. Deanna works closely with the Klingon for the first time since the birth and death of her son, Ian. John does a first-rate job getting inside Worf and Deanna's heads to reveal exactly what they are thinking at each step of the investigation.

Another crewman dies in a brutal phaser attack. Wesley's interaction with Chief O'Brien is priceless. His friendship with one of the suspects plays a key part in the investigation.

The attack on the shuttlecraft carrying Picard, Riker, Data and the Kreel delegates is well done. Vornholt effectively uses the Kreel as comic relief, with Riker forced to fend off advances from the Kreel who keeps flirting with him.

BOOGEYMEN

In BOOGEYMEN by Mel Gilden, Picard and Data accompany Wesley to a holodeck. The ensign is going to attempt to complete the Kobayashi Maru, the no-win scenario. With Data and Geordi, he developed a program which gets harder and more unpredictable each time.

While on the holodeck with the "Boogeyman" program running, Picard, Data and Wes experience a malfunction. They find them-

selves trapped in a version of the Enterprise controlled by the Boogeyman.

Picard must deal with a bizarro Dixon Hill mystery and Data must find a way to interface with the computer. Picard overwrites the program and succeeds, at some cost. That cost is that the program spreads throughout the real ship.

Q-IN-LAW

Place your bets, the main event: Lwaxana Troi vs. Q, for the heavyweight title of the space-time continuum.

Mrs. Troi arrives to attend a wedding on the Enterprise in Q-IN-LAW by Peter David. Q appears at the wedding and both parties insist he remain.

Q develops a romance with Lwaxana, much to Picard's chagrin. Q uses his influence on the bride and groom to drive both families apart. The young Romeo and Juliet destroy their love and then themselves.

Then Lwaxana receives the power of the Q. The two Q engage in the wildest fight imaginable inside, outside and throughout the Enterprise.

At one point, Riker asks Picard what they should do. Worf suggests they sell popcorn. The humor pours from page to page. The Genesis Planet serves as the site of the ceremony and Q gives a tribble to Worf, with predictable results.

This is the funniest of the TNG novels, and the basis for an outstanding audio-book with Majel Barrett and John de Lancie as narrators. Q-IN-LAW is impossible to read without laughing out loud.

PERCHANCE TO DREAM

A shuttlecraft carrying Data, Troi, Wesley, Gina (from EXILES) and Kenny is captured in the tractor beam of a ship full of refugees. The shuttle disappears and Picard and the female captain spar over the fate of the craft. PERCHANCE TO DREAM by Howard Weinstein offers an interesting tale.

When Picard and the female argue they are transported to the planet. Picard prepares a fish dinner, French-style, and tries to bridge the cultural gap. His counterpart returns the favor by saving his life during a planetquake. They return to her ship, where Picard realizes her peoples' dire straits.

Riker is suspicious when Picard appears on the other ship, but agrees to send Geordi over to keep the ship from blowing up. The mysterious transportations are accomplished by unusual aliens evaluating the crews to see if they are alive.

They mold the planet when not sleeping for centuries, and were awakened by the seismic tests performed by Data's away team. The away team is stashed in a cave, where Troi and Data keep an eye on Wes, Gina and Kenny who interact as real teenagers probably would.

Data contacts the aliens. Picard is transported to join the away team to work out the plan.

One notable character is the daughter of the alien captain. Her relationships with the alien first officer, her mother and Picard are well developed, particularly that is more adult than the 'adults'.

Picard takes the alien captain on a tour of his hometown of Labare, then tells Wes and Kenny to program a recreation of the aliens' home planet. They were victims of an unthinkable genocide; only a few thousand survivors remain from a population of several million.

They were persecuted out of experience. They weren't paranoid; everybody really was out to get them. Data shows subtlety in not mentioning the genocide of American Indians in his Thanksgiving analogy, and Weinstein shows the aliens would not fight the way settlers and natives did in the tragic days in which millions died on both sides.

SPARTACUS

The first chapter of SPARTACUS by T.L. Mancour is a treat. The rest of the book does not slow down as the storm which starts the story pitches the Enterprise out of the Federation.

Picard must face two genocidal groups and work out a compromise. The Enterprise is trapped in a massive space storm which causes problems with all systems.

Reports of destroyed nacelles and antimatter explosions are common. The ship spends days at red alert and everyone is wound up tight as a spring.

When the storm breaks, the Enterprise offers to assist a vessel damaged in the storm. An away team visits the ship and is shocked to learn that the humans are really androids.

The androids were keeping their true identity unknown since they did not want to be considered property. Machines had few rights on the world they fled.

Data, naturally, strikes up a relationship with the group. The philosophy they share helps him to realize the android emotions he neglects.

CHAINS OF COMMAND

The Enterprise's appearance shocks the human overseer of a world where all humans are treated as slaves in CHAINS OF COMMAND by Bill McKay and Eloise Flood. The slaves see the "free" humans and begin a revolt.

The overseers work for a race of avians who believe humans to be lower animals. The humans migrated from Terra in the early days of space colonization and passed through a wormhole. The birdlike aliens found them very uncivilized and put them to work doing menial labor on what amounted to prison planets.

Riker leads an away team to the surface where they come under fire from the overseers' weapons. A group of freed slaves saves the away team.

The Enterprise loses communication with the away team when the head bird signals for reinforcements. Picard goes to the planet to meet with the slaves.

The slaves cause discomfort for Troi, since many have not seen a woman in years. Beverly is upset that Picard takes measures to protect female crew members, but realizes it is a prudent precaution.

The crew sets up a base camp on the planet. Picard and Troi are taken prisoner by a group of slaves afraid the Enterprise will not join a war of genocide against their avian oppressors.

A child who befriends Beverly carries the knockout toxin and suffers severe brain damage. The child reminds Beverly of Wes, so she takes him under her wing.

Doctor Selar insists that Beverly leave the child in her care, since Crusher was affected by the toxin. An armed away team is unable to follow the trail and heavy metals in a crevice prevent a search by scanners.

Picard, Troi and their abductors are attacked by an alien species that lives in the hot caves where they are being led. Data learns to speak the "chicken's" language and operates the computer. Picard realizes the cave-dwelling aliens are a branch of the avian race, survivors of a war millennia ago.

Picard tricks the aliens by offering to fix their faulty equipment. He makes his way to the wrecked shuttlecraft their captors used to take them from the slave settlement.

The novel shows how things are not always how they seem and helps prove that the theory of IDIC is applicable to races far different from humanity. The use of humans as "lesser animals" is reminiscent of the novel THE PROMETHEUS DESIGN. This book shows how it is possible for rationalization to overcome logic.

IMBALANCE

In IMBALANCE by V.E. Mitchell, the Enterprise is dispatched to negotiate with the Jarada, the insect race referred to in the TNG episode "The Big Goodbye." An away team beams down to open negotiations. They soon find that the Jarada are going through a chemical imbalance that has led the violent race to the edge of anarchy.

Each member of the away team faces problems on the planet as they flee for their lives through a giant anthill. Attacks on their lives are frequent.

Keiko Ishikawa O'Brien faces an unusual dilemma. She must deal not only with the Jarada, but with a jealous Miles O'Brien, who believes she is being entirely too friendly with a co-worker.

The crew discovers the antidote to the Jarada sickness and saves the race, despite the hostility manifested against the away team. The Jaradan system contains a complex system of planetoids, many in eclectic orbits, causing trouble for navigation and leading to imbalance.

The intense novel forces the away team to fight to survive, but no greater meaning is apparent. The aliens are too private to ask for help, putting the crew in the middle of the problem.

WAR DRUMS

John Vornholt couches his warning on Terran prejudice in this parable entitled WAR DRUMS that marks Ensign Ro's first starring role in a TNG novel. A group of wild Klingons, who survived a starship crash, are attacking a human colony. Both sides try to eliminate the other.

Picard sends a non-human away team to deal with the problem. When the human director complains, Picard notes he did not even realize he had done it, yet refuses to change it.

Worf is outraged to find a young Klingon held in squalor by the humans. Betazoid Troi and android Data help Worf make contact with the Klingons, while Bajoran Ro Laren is left to communicate with the colonists.

Worf uses the holodeck to good advantage to gain the trust of the Klingon child. He is then forced to get by without help from the ship after the Enterprise is called away on a diplomatic mission.

Ro develops a relationship with a little girl and her father, the security chief at the station, after she is nearly killed by a deadly insect. Worf forms a relationship with the boy he rescued from the squalor and a girl, who kills the leader of the Klingons who refuses to work with the Federation team. Ro conducts oceanographic research and realizes a giant tidal wave is about to destroy both humans and Klingons.

The colonists wait until the away team convinces the Klingons to turn themselves in, then traps them. Worf and Troi are taken hostage while Data escapes. Ro has already escaped with the girl and her father.

Data assists Ro in freeing the others. They eventually contact the Enterprise, which is too far away to assist.

Vornholt is big on metaphors, using the title MASKS to show how we hide our feelings. In CONTAMINATION he showed how insanity can make people mistrust each other. In WAR DRUMS prejudice is shown for how silly it is, when skin tone and custom keep people from joining together.

NIGHTSHADE

Picard, Worf and Deanna travel to a dark, depressing planet in NIGHTSHADE by Laurell Hamilton. Picard is accused of treason and faces execution by torture. Deanna finds the people are able to broadcast emotion, which drains her. Worf attempts to free Picard. The Enterprise is sent to assist a disabled ship, which turns out to be a trap, designed to lure them from their away team.

The subject of the novel makes it very hard to read. Sympathy and empathy persist despite the despicable acts of the aliens.

A light moment comes when Worf and Troi rush the prison to free Picard. Picard is upset at the attempt, but the aliens then admit they plan to torture him.

Picard is willing to face torture to improve relations, but even he is unwilling to die for the cause. Past the depressing part, the rest is enlightening.

GROUNDED

A dramatic opening chapter in GROUNDED by David Bishoff propels the story into overdrive. Picard and his bridge crew must stand by and listen as a bureaucrat informs them that the Enterprise has been declared a total loss and is about to be destroyed.

The story flashes back to the events leading up to the mission which could cost the crew its home. Picard is ordered to proceed to a scientific outpost where an old flame of Jean-Luc's is stationed. She and her son are the sole survivors of an attack on the settlement. Riker, Worf, Beverly and the away team face an intense rescue operation.

The crewmen and the shuttle bring back mud from the planet that has achieved sentience due to unique planetary magnetic fields. Picard's intuition tells him something is amiss, so he calls for a Priority One inspection. A faulty reading sends the Chief Engineer and his repair crew out the airlock to inspect the hull manually.

Bishoff effectively builds tension as the ship comes alive, kills a crewman and hurls the rest into space. The relationship between a young autistic girl and her android tutor is a special treat.

Deanna and Beverly both feel for the girl, who apparently has empathic abilities that cause her to retreat into a catatonic state. When the scientist's son's secret is revealed, it is gripping. The girl finds a way to reach him, much as other similar mental rescues appeared in the novels TIME FOR YESTERDAY and YESTERDAY'S SON.

THE ROMULAN PRIZE

In THE ROMULAN PRIZE by Simon Hawke, Picard and company are stunned to find a giant version of a Romulan warbird with a dead crew in Federation space. When the sensors confirm the deaths, and that there is no air or life support, the crew lets down its guard.

That nearly proves fatal. The Romulan Commander allowed his crew to be given a death-simulating drug and bet on Geordi restoring life support before they were revived.

When they revive, away teams are beamed to key spots on the Enterprise. Picard is on the away team to the Romulan bridge, while Riker is forced to surrender the ship. Worf kills several Romulans before being subdued.

The Romulan commander is an expert on human psychology. An early meeting with the Romulan Praetor is well scripted as Hawke gets inside the Romulan mindset. This is proved when he shows the chess game going on aboard the two ships.

Riker goads his Romulan counterpart into a holodeck fight and holds his own despite the other's greater strength. He shames the green-supremacist in front of his men.

DEEP SPACE NINE NOVELS

EMISSARY by J.M. Dillard remains true to the Rick Berman/Michael Piller script. The author adds background to the characters with an emotional look into what they are feeling.

Sisko has not gotten over the death of his wife, Jennifer. His inability to grieve puts him at risk of losing his health and career. By pro-

tecting the Bajoran wormhole prophets, he saves himself, as well as the Bajorans.

Kira's antagonism is abated when Sisko is called to Kai Opaka. Kira's belief in the Kai's wisdom is brought out as the story shows why the Bajoran first officer is the way she is. Likewise, the story of Dax is spelled out in considerable detail.

Some sections of the book differ from the scenes in the televised episode, some fall close and others correspond.

J.M. Dillard makes the premiere on paper as satisfying as the film canvas director David Carson used to create the televised two-hour episode. O'Brien's accent as he fusses with the computers brings back fond memories of another miracle worker.

THE SIEGE by Peter David is an astonishing novel by a writer with a sense of purpose. Humor rises to the top and makes the reader laugh out loud, but is immediately submerged by dark forces.

Odo makes a hilarious comment. Quark does outrageous things. Dax tells a wicked joke. Bashir screams, "Kiss me you fool!" Then a gut punch of print hits like hand grenades.

There are at least five very graphic deaths. They are not gratuitous but an integral part of the story.

THE WRAP-UP

An exhausting overview of so many books that all you can do is pick and choose—unless you really want to try to read them all. Peter David clearly emerged as the fan favorite in the NEXT GENERATION novels just as Diane Duane did in the Trek Classic books. They are by no means the only fine writers. Many excellent books have been crafted from the varied elements which comprise the increasingly complex STAR TREK universe.

Chapter 6
NEXT GEN SPECIALS

ENCOUNTER AT FARPOINT

David Gerrold is best known for his screenplay for the Classic Trek episode "The Trouble With Tribbles", co-writing "The Cloud Minders" and the Classic Trek animated stories, "More Troubles, More Tribbles" and "Bem". He is able to build around the screenplay written by Gene Roddenberry and Dorothy Fontana, to flesh out the initial portrait of the crew of the Enterprise D in ENCOUNTER AT FARPOINT.

There is tension as Riker chaffs at working with a machine for a second officer and is stunned to find his "Imzadi," Deanna Troi, assigned to the same ship. Beverly must confront the ghost of Jack Crusher, who comes to the surface as she and Picard are reunited. Gerrold does a great job of giving details of the doctor's career and a version of Jack's death.

This novel's treatment of death is far different from that in the TNG novel REUNION (not to be confused with the TNG episode "The Reunion"). Q's motivations are explained in detail as the new Trek legends are given a proper sendoff.

METAMORPHOSIS

Fans of the android second officer will be thrilled to read METAMORPHOSIS by Jean Lorrah, a tale of an away team mission to a planet where the aliens spin time-strings to perform magic. Data saves the life of a woman who has journeyed through a dangerous swamp to meet her destiny and allow her people to unite with their neighbors.

Data and the leader help each other through a torture chamber of tests. Then Data gains his fondest wish. He finds himself transformed into a human body, cloned from his android DNA. The bridge crew is suspicious, but the human convinces them he has Data's memories and personality.

In an ironic note, Data's nemesis, Katherine Polaski, first recognizes him in his new human form. Lorrah's novel delights as the reader follows Data as he learns what he has been missing, as well as what he has been spared. Every sip of liquid and bite of food is played for full effect.

BY ALEX BURLESON

Lorrah is a master of dialog, best seen when Picard calls the human Data on the carpet for sending Wes to work with the pirates-with-hearts-of-gold. Data shows Picard that his fears are unfounded and Picard asks him how he got to be so wise in just one day. Data replies his android persona would have done the same thing.

His uniqueness as an individual is emphasized, much as it was in the TNG episode "Measure of a Man" and "The Offspring". Jean does an outstanding job of letting Pinocchio come out and play.

VENDETTA

VENDETTA by Peter David is one of the most intense novels ever put to paper. It is so good it's scary.

The Borg return in force. The successor to the planet-eater from the Classic Trek episode "The Doomsday Machine" arrives to do battle with the Borg monolith, powered by none other than Guinan's sister, Delcara.

The Borg had destroyed her homeworld and killed her family and children. She escaped and fled to Guinan's homeworld where she and Guinan wed into a sisterhood relationship. She again started a family and, for a second time, watched them die at the hands of the Borg. She is an empath and once appeared to Picard in a vision.

Peter David does a great job with the details behind the encounter showing how Cadet Picard responded to his stern taskmaster of a teacher. This novel is as good as it gets, with enough tension for a dozen books, yet with skillful writing which ties the story together into one tale.

REUNION

The bridge crew from Picard's former vessel, the Stargazer, gathers on the Enterprise to escort an ensign they served with, who eventually became captain, back to his homeland to be sworn in as king. Worf has an uneasy relationship with the regent to be, as his race has warred unceasingly with Klingons.

In REUNION by Michael Jan Friedman, the two are involved in a combat exercise in the holodeck that would have killed them both, had O'Brien not become curious. The two bond and eventually work together to help solve the crime.

A second assassination attempt leaves Picard's former first officer near death, and Picard is forced to take action against the former officer. A romance between Riker and the older comm officer is well crafted, as is Beverly's relationship with the Amerind doctor she worked with at Starfleet medical.

One item of note is Friedman's description of Jack Crusher's death, which occurs under different circumstances than those outlined in David Gerrold's ENCOUNTER AT FARPOINT. In this book, Jack dies while trying to detach a damaged nacelle, and Picard rescues the security chief, leaving Jack to die. Had Picard gone after Jack, all three would have died.

The chief has become an alcoholic and Guinan forces him to face that fact. She sends him to Beverly to confess his sins.

The identity of the murderer is unexpected. The ghost of Jack Crusher plays a key part in finding a way to tie the various clues together.

The battle in the Transporter room is well done, with Picard and the accused killer joining to end the assassin's reign. The regent even asks Worf to join his honor guard.

UNIFICATION

Executive Producer Jeri Taylor uses her inside information to craft UNIFICATION, based on the script she co-wrote with Michael Piller. Ambassador Spock is missing, perhaps having defected. Picard is called in and must meet with Perrin and Sarek to investigate his son's behavior.

Sarek, just before he dies, gives Picard a key piece of information. The book reveals how Sarek processes the information.

Several characters not shown in the episode are fleshed out. Highlights include the multi-armed piano player who falls for Riker and Worf and the ship's barber, Mr. Mott, advising Picard on strategy.

RELICS

The 23rd century's favorite miracle worker appears in the 24th century. Following the crash of a shuttle taking him to a retirement colony, Scott reports to the bridge and agrees to stay and risk his life with the bridge crew in RELICS by Michael Jan Friedman.

In an ironic twist, air is lost in the passenger compartment and most of the bridge crew is killed in the crash. The young protegé of Scott fails to survive three generations in the transporter beam. Scott's reaction to Worf is priceless.

The ensign who shows him to his quarters has a key role in an away mission inside the Dyson sphere. He puts the team at risk, then risks his life to save Riker.

The absolute highlight is Scott's trip to the holodeck. In the novel, he calls up holographic doubles of his old friends. When Picard enters, Scott introduces him to Kirk and realizes Picard knows the real Spock.

That makes him realize most of his friends are dead, which pushes him into depression. His relationship with Geordi is explained, and many references are made to Classic Trek episodes, including "The Naked Time," "Elaan of Troyius" and several other events.

IMZADI

IMZADI by Peter David begins with Captain Kirk and a landing party about to leave Gateway (here called Forever World) after his ill-fated journey through the Guardian of Forever that led to the death of Edith Keeler. As Kirk tells the team, "Let's get the hell out of here," he is being watched by Commodore Data.

Data, captain of the Enterprise-F, is on assignment. He and his chambeloid science officer discuss the time-streams with the scientists. Data then encounters a bitter, broken Admiral Riker.

Riker has never gotten over the death of his Imzadi, Deanna Troi.

Data tries to cheer him up by telling him he saw Deanna alive in another time-line. Data is horrified to find Riker planning to disrupt the time-stream to save Deanna.

Captain Wesley Crusher of the USS Hood has delivered Riker to Betazed for the funeral of Lwaxana Troi. Data is to return him to a Starbase. An autopsy proves Deanna died from a poison unknown at the time of her death. Data tells Wesley Deanna died from unexplained circumstances.

This is one of the finest novels in any genre.

THE DEVIL'S HEART

Carmen Carter fashions a classic in THE DEVIL'S HEART as Picard is encircled by a stone which comes from the Guardian of Forever. The Enterprise is diverted from a poker game on a Starbase to investigate an illness on a Vulcan archeology mission.

Picard's nose for mystery leads him to find the rare stone which has played a vital role in galactic history. Picard dreams of the plight of previous holders of the stone as several disparate groups try to win back the treasure. Worf is impressed by Picard being the new owner, pitting him against Troi, Riker and Beverly who are worried about his preoccupation with it.

The flashbacks are effective, as is a nightmare where Picard must watch the Borg kill the women he cares most about, Beverly and Guinan. The commander of the Starbase is well drawn out and her character's relationship with Guinan's fellow listener is well done. Plots and twists bounce back and forth as intrigue is the name of the game.

Besides writing novels for the Pocket Book Specials devoted to STAR TREK: THE NEXT GENERATION, Michael Jan Friedman also writes the comic book series for DC Comics.

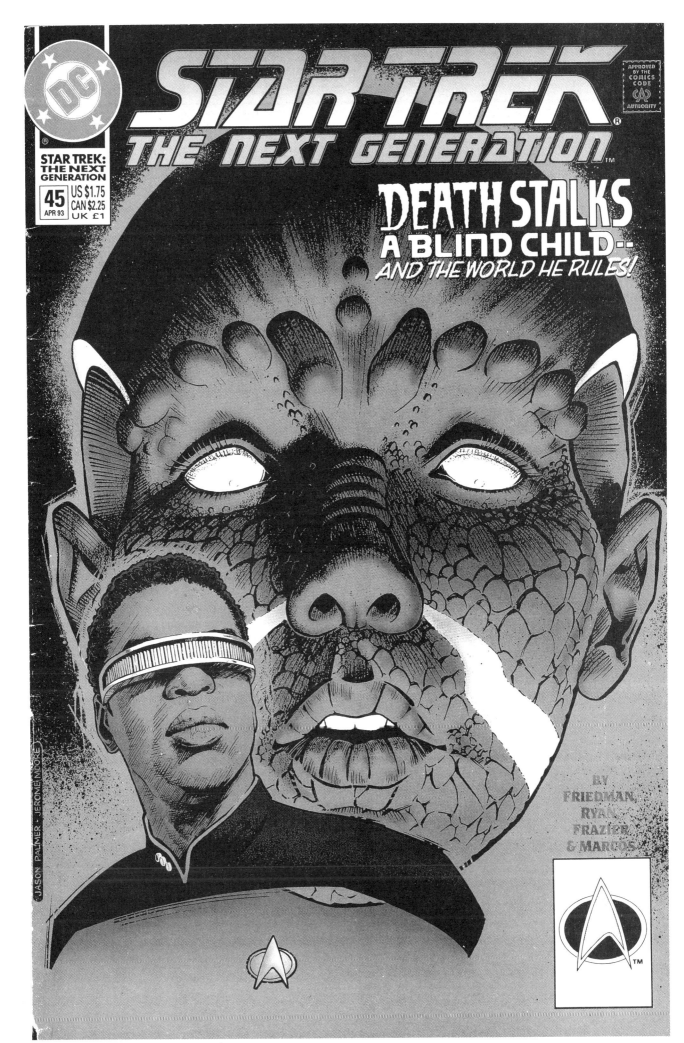

Profile:

Ann CRISPIN

Ann Crispin's first novel was YESTERDAY'S SON. Since its sale she has gone on to write a couple novels in the short-lived "V" series as well as original novels in her own STAR BRIDGE series. She has just completed her fourth STAR TREK novel, which is slated to be published in hard cover in June of 1994.

When she wrote YESTERDAY'S SON she submitted it to Pocket Books through author Jacqueline Lichtenberg to editor David Hartwell in 1979. It then sat at Pocket Books without any action for three years. "I never have really understood what the delay was because it took a year to ship it to Paramount and get it back. But then after that it sat for two more years before they decided they wanted to buy it even after Paramount had approved it," she recalled.

Unlike other STAR TREK novel writers who had practiced their craft in fandom writing fan fiction, Ann Crispin wasn't even aware of the fan fiction arena until after she'd written YESTERDAY'S SON. She recalled, "I live in the country. I had been to a couple conventions in Washington, D.C. just to hear Gene Roddenberry speak, but that was, I think, before they had a lot of fanzines for sale or else I just hadn't gone to the dealer's room with money to buy. So I wasn't aware that there was fan fiction until YESTERDAY'S SON was finished. It's not that I turned up my nose at it. It's just that I didn't even know that it existed.

"I remember that it was a big surprise to me when I turned over the manuscript to Jacqueline at a convention in New York in 1979. I remember that it was George Washington's Birthday and we all got snowed in all weekend with Jimmy Doohan. I had another copy of the manuscript with me, and I was amazed when I went into the dealer's room and found all these people selling books! I just had no idea that all that existed. I met Jean Lorrah for the first time; she was doing STAR TREK fan fiction. I met Leslye Lilker, who was doing SAHAJ, and

BY JAMES VAN HISE

she snubbed me," Ann said, laughing. "I told her very shyly that I had written a story about Spock's son, too, and she was very scornful."

THE MANY FACES OF FANDOM

"I felt very intimidated," she continued. "Everybody had these fanzines and they looked pretty good to me. I had the manuscript with me and basically I told somebody that I'd written a STAR TREK story, and she said, 'Oh, we'd be interested in looking at it.' You know the way fan fiction editors are always interested. Her name was Ann Elizabeth Zeeke; a very nice woman. She did a lot of STAR TREK fanzines and for all I know she may still do them. I've gotten a little bit out of touch.

"She sat there in the dealer's room glancing at it while trying to run her table. Then she had someone who was helping her take over the table and she ran into the back with my story and she didn't come out for quite awhile.

"I went to lunch and when I came back she said, 'I read your whole book and I really love it and I want to publish it.' But I said that it's just been submitted to Pocket Books. She said, 'No, don't do that! That's a really dumb thing to do! They'll wreck it! They'll make all these changes.' I said, well, let me think about it.

"I was just beginning to realize what a dumb thing it was to write a STAR TREK story as a first effort because I was beginning to dimly realize that if Pocket wouldn't buy it there was no place else for it to go and I'd never see any money for it. But at least here was someone who was willing to publish it if Pocket didn't. So I said I'll wait and see what Pocket has to say. Well Pocket didn't say anything, and until I heard from them I felt that I couldn't let it come out in a fanzine. I guess that was about the only smart thing I did because that would have probably scratched my chances. If I had run into the fan fiction people first I probably would have done that."

WRITING MORE STAR TREK

Once YESTERDAY'S SON was published and was well received, Pocket Books indicated that they would be interested in a sequel, which turned into TIME FOR YESTERDAY a few years later. When she wrote YESTERDAY'S SON, she decided that it was unlikely that Paramount would allow Spock to have a son running around permanently in his own timeline, so she didn't even try to work that out. Instead she let the story tell itself and felt that it worked better artistically to have Zar return to his own time at the end of the first book.

She said, "I didn't plan it, but it made more artistic sense for him to go back because I think the ending was more poignant to have him go back. It's hard to talk about your own work and put labels like that on it. You know what you tried for and you hope you succeeded."

The NEXT GENERATION novel she wrote, THE EYES OF THE BEHOLDERS, was written when Pocket Books approached some of their senior STAR TREK novelists about contributing books to the new series. "They were getting flooded with a lot of NEXT GENERATION proposals from people," she recalled, "but Peter David can't write all of them by himself. So they were asking me and a bunch of other people."

Pocket told Ann that they wouldn't be interested in getting another Trek Classic novel from her until she wrote a NEXT GENERATION novel for them. She said, "I think that was probably caused by the fact that they had a pretty solid listing of books lined up for the original Trek, but they needed NEXT GENERATION books at that time."

THE SECRETS OF SAREK

Ann had been working on a Trek Classic hard cover for Pocket Books for the past year, which she has just finished. The book is called SAREK. She said, "This is a Classic Trek book so it takes place right after the sixth movie. It is kind of the bridge book between situations that we saw at the end of STAR TREK IV, where Spock and his father were on pretty good terms. But then something happened to the point where Spock wasn't there at his father's deathbed and they were obviously at odds. I don't believe it was just the Cardassians.

"I think there were interpersonal factors going, too. So that's what I had to put in, that would drive them apart again in a rift that would not be healed. And the reason I take that it was never healed was that Perrin (Sarek's last wife) came along later on and did things; that she obviously hated Spock. From everything she said, she couldn't stand him. I didn't deal with Perrin in my book, though. I think that Perrin came along anywhere from the year 2310 on. I put her somewhere in the year 2330 range. Just from her apparent age I'd say she was in her mid-fifties, but he couldn't have met her much before 2310."

The novel covers 80 years out of Sarek's life and has many plot threads as well as some controversial elements. "It's very emotionally wrenching because of things that happen with Amanda in the book, and it's been a very difficult book to write," Crispin revealed.

Because she raised the subject of Amanda in that context, this led to the obvious question—Does the book deal with Amanda's death? Since THE NEXT GENERATION introduced Sarek's subsequent wife, Perrin, many have wondered what happened to Amanda in those 75 years during Classic Trek and THE NEXT GENERATION. Being human, she must have died somewhere along the way. Crispin reluctantly revealed that she did indeed tackle this subject head on.

She insisted, "If people don't like what happens to Amanda in my book, it was not my idea to do it. It was Pocket's. They figured that was the right place to deal with a heavy subject like that, and after all, Amanda is in her

90s at the time of STAR TREK VI, so we know she went at some point. But that was not my idea. I want to absolve myself of the responsibility. My editor made me do it. But it's not easy. It was like, 'Me? Do that to Amanda?! Oh I can't! I just can't!' But I thought about it and I thought that if they don't get me to do it in this book called SAREK, which is probably the best place for it, they'll get somebody else to do it someplace else. I guess it was professional pride because I thought, well, I know that I could do it as well as anybody; maybe better. So I'll do it."

FROM FAN TO PRO

Ann has been a STAR TREK fan since the series originally began airing in 1966. She said, "I came into the third or fourth episode aired, called 'What Are Little Girls Made Of?' I watched every episode from that point on until third season when I was in college. But third season was so bad that I didn't watch a lot of those episodes until it got into reruns. So I was a fan from the very beginning. At the time I wrote YESTERDAY'S SON I'd read every one of the pro novels, and that was one of the things that made me keep going because I thought, 'I can do better than this. I know I can.'

"I remember VULCAN! by Kathleen Sky. I'm sure she's a very lovely person, but that was a silly book and everyone was out of character. I thought somebody should write a book and have these people act like the way they are on the TV show. They don't have to twist the characters and bend them to make them interesting. That was my philosophy and it seems to have worked okay.

"I try not to extrapolate too much beyond what we've seen. With everything I do I have at least one precedent. With all the shows and all the movies and all the books, you can justify almost anything in Trek at this point. You can have Spock act all wonky and basically just point to something in the movies and go, well, in the movie he did this under these circumstances and make it sound justified. But in the old days it was pretty cut and dry."

Addressing the age and interests of the average reader, she said, "I don't think that it would hurt to get a little more real science fiction into the STAR TREK novels, especially into the NEXT GENERATION novels where they've always had a little bit more emphasis on that anyway. Plus, they don't have as arresting characters as the original to fall back on."

Ann continued, "I'm sorry, but they don't. The [TNG] characters were set up from the very beginning to . . . not have a lot of personality; not like Kirk, Spock, McCoy, Uhura, Sulu and the rest. They really don't. The two most human characters are the Klingon and the android. I think this could work in some ways if the people who are writing it are also fans. But I'm pretty sure that a number of them who are doing this are not really fans and they never thought about writing a STAR TREK novel. So I would be interested to see if they can get any kind of simpatico going."

THE STAR BRIDGE SERIES

"I'm the only person I know of who has managed to really draw in any tiny proportion of the STAR TREK reading audience into her non-Trek books. That's because I wrote a series that was deliberately aimed at attracting the attention of the STAR TREK reader as well as the SF reader. The fifth book of that just got turned in. I get a fair amount of mail from people writing to me about STAR TREK books and saying at the bottom, 'Oh, by the way, I picked up your STAR BRIDGE novels and I really like them, too.' Plus at the STAR TREK conventions I find a fair amount of STAR BRIDGE books at this point," she noted.

Ann continued, "I made a very conscious effort to write about adventures out in space, with the emphasis on character rather than hardware. Lots and lots of interesting alien cultures. People having adventures with alien cultures pretty well describes a lot of STAR TREK. That's how I set my series up and it appears to be working. I also get people who say, 'Oh, no, I never read anything but STAR TREK books,' but I also get a fair number of people who have picked up the first book [in the STAR BRIDGE series]. If they pick up the first book they usually read all of them, which is nice.

"The funny thing is that the converse isn't true. I get a fair amount of science fiction fans who read the STAR BRIDGE books and they say, 'Well, I never read Trek novels but maybe I'll read yours.' But it doesn't seem to go very equally the other way. It's surprising when I go to a science fiction convention. People are somewhat aware that I did 'V' and STAR TREK, but most of it focuses on my own SF and fantasy. The people who read my STAR BRIDGE, and my fantasy that I've written with Andre Norton, seem to be those who read some science fiction anyway. But the people who are dyed in the wool, 'I never pick up anything unless it's Trek,' they don't read my other stuff. That's okay. I can live with that. The books do pretty well by themselves. I would never have to write another STAR TREK book at this point, and probably won't after SAREK. That just about killed me."

Opposite page: Ann Crispin's YESTERDAY'S SON, featuring the story in which Spock finds his own son living five thousand years in the past.

47315-8 · $2.95 · SCIENCE FICTION

TIMESCAPE

SPOCK DISCOVERS HIS
OWN SON—LIVING 5,000 YEARS IN THE PAST!

—THE NEW—

STAR TREK® NOVEL

YESTERDAY'S SON

A. C. CRISPIN

BORIS ©

FANZINES
THE FAN'S WORLD

Chapter 7
A BRIEF HISTORY

STAR TREK fandom was born one night in 1966 when that venerable TV show premiered. During most of the '70s fandom is all that kept the memory of STAR TREK burning brightly rather than fading into rerun obscurity, but it has many sides and facets.

Beyond the rim of the star-light
My love is wand'ring in star-flight.
I know he'll find in star-clustered reaches
Love, strange love a star-woman teaches.
I know his journey ends never,
His star trek will go on forever.
But tell him while he wanders his starry sea
Remember, remember me.

—Gene Roddenberry

Part One:
"Be Careful What You Wish For"

In the beginning, the concept of STAR TREK glimmered in one man's mind as an incredible dream, a dream for a future all mankind could look forward to. It's not unlike the dream of many great men of

BY WENDY RATHBONE

history: a society where all races, men and women, are equal. Where unlimited opportunities await every individual. Where knowledge and exploration of the unknown, both outer and inner space, is valued above all else because it is our way to ensure our civilization's survival.

The dream grew and changed, endured make-overs and rewrites, quivered from the tortures of censors and critics, and finally, on September 8, 1966, went out over the airwaves in scrambled pieces which coalesced into images on television sets all over the United States of America. Those images, created by Gene Roddenberry, became the first episode of a story called STAR TREK, a legend which was to span decades and contribute animated stories, feature films, a spin-off series, and thousands of books and fanzines containing novels, short stories, artwork, poetry, articles, interviews and analyses.

And why?

Of course it would be easy to answer that the excellence of the show, its commercial success, and the unique (for its time) background of space with the optimistic foundation of a United Federation of Planets contributed to STAR TREK's survival through the years. That easy answer is not the entire truth.

The real reason behind STAR TREK's much deserved longevity is, quite simply, the fans.

STAR TREK LIVES!

STAR TREK fandom is a legend unto itself. No other group of television series admirers has

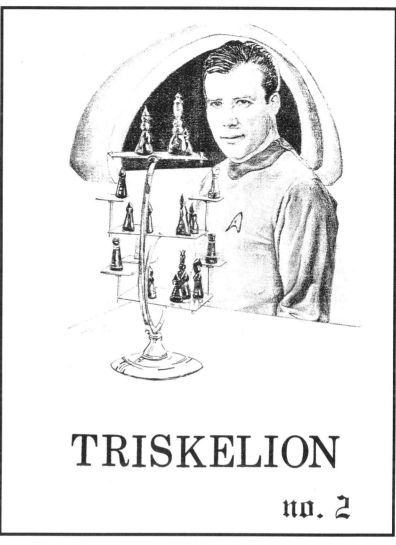

TRISKELION is one of the earliest STAR TREK fanzines. Issue #2 from 1968 even includes a non-fiction piece about STAR TREK technology by science fiction author Hal Clement.

ever been quite so vocal, avid or creatively constructive in expressing their love, obsession and respect for a phenomenon that, as the classic it is, speaks to the soul. The first indication that such a legion of fans for STAR TREK existed, aside from the enormous amounts of mail received by the actors and producers of the show, was after the second season when the network announced the impending cancellation of the series. A letter-writing campaign, headed by a multi-talented, energetic fan named Bjo Trimble, virtually changed the destiny of the doomed show.

She had access to many fans through her association with science fiction fandom, and access to Gene Roddenberry after she became fan liaison for STAR TREK, and therefore was the perfect person to inform fans that they could, quite possibly, influence the future by making themselves heard. Bjo started a domino effect by sending out flyers on how to write letters to the 800 or so people she knew, and telling them to pass on flyers to others.

Because STAR TREK fans are people of all ages and job descriptions, word got out quickly and easily to a large variety of establishments, including hospitals, universities (the entire Princeton graduating class wrote in), newspapers, and even such places as NASA and Polaroid (which at the time was one of the holding companies which owned NBC). So NBC received letters from their own stockholders as well as high school kids, scientists, doctors, lawyers, housewives, babysitters, dog-walkers, couch potatoes. . . you get the picture. According to Bjo, quoted from David Gerrold's 1973 book THE WORLD OF STAR TREK, "the mail to NBC had topped one million pieces." This prompted NBC to come on the air "with a precedent making announcement one night, right after STAR TREK, that the show had been renewed and would everybody please stop writing in."

The fans did not stop there. Writing letters to get their favorite TV show back on the air was only the first of their many ambitious projects.

THE BIRTH OF FANZINE FANDOM

Though with their first mass effort they managed to get their one episode a week for approximately 26 weeks, after the season ended in 1969, the show was finally, irrevocably canned. The hunger for more inspired the formation of clubs, conventions and a famous little item known as the fanzine.

A fanzine is an amateur press publication done for a fan's own pleasure and is usually non-profit with a print run anywhere from 10 to 1000 copies. Fans publish them in order to make their stories and opinions available to other fans in a uniform, organized package.

Actually, STAR TREK fanzines have existed since the early days of the show. One of the first, entitled SPOCKANALIA, came out in September of 1967 and featured articles and stories about Vulcan culture, Vulcan psychology, even Vulcan anatomy complete with a diagram of the supposed six-chambered Vulcan heart. Other famous 'first' fanzines had such creative titles as T-NEGATIVE, GRUP, STARBORNE, ERIDANI TRIAD, KRAITH and GUARDIAN OF FOREVER.

It wasn't long before thousands of other fanzine titles abounded. Fanzine mania swept through Trek fandom with a contagious enthusiasm to share, express and create.

FROM ONE FAN TO ANOTHER

Many pro writers including Ruth Berman, Jean Lorrah, Jacqueline Lichtenberg, Juanita Coulson and Della Van Hise (to name a few) got their start in STAR TREK fanzines. Fanzines publish (to this day) fiction and poetry and articles about all aspects of STAR TREK imaginable. Subjects range from intricate mathematical analysis of the warp drive to that shocking, age-old speculation as to whether or not Kirk and Spock could be lovers.

Fanzines are one of the major forces which have kept STAR TREK alive from the '60s until now. They serve to keep fans in touch with each other, as well as with the 'feeling' for the show they love. Excitement is maintained by reading and rereading stories about their favorite characters, interviews with the actors and articles about future STAR TREK projects. This, in itself, may be what set TREK fans apart from the usual TV aficionado.

Through fanzines, a Trek fan can walk new roads into their obsession and, as a result, find new energy to keep the obsession charged. Thus, for Paramount, fanzines are a form of free advertising. They keep STAR TREK fandom growing during 'dry' times, and with fandom alive and well, the movies and new TV series result in commercial successes far beyond ordinary predictions.

THE ENTERPRISE INSTITUTIONALIZED

Without the 'activities' of fans, and their specific contributions, STAR TREK would not be where it is today. What specific contributions have the fans made, you may ask?

Do not forget two very major, very important things that happened because of STAR TREK and its fans. First, the Air and Space Museum in Washington D.C.'s Smithsonian Institution.

The museum opened in 1976. It houses models of the Kitty Hawk, earlier forms of flight machines, The Spirit of St. Louis, a satellite, moon rocks, astronaut props and an exhibit entitled "Life in the Universe?" where-in hangs none other than a glistening 11 foot model of the U.S.S. Enterprise given to the Smithsonian by Paramount Television. The model is the actual one used in the filming of the original '60s STAR TREK series. Blueprints of the starship are also displayed.

In an article by Carol McGreggor in the magazine ALL ABOUT STAR TREK FAN CLUBS (published April, 1977), she writes, "It is fitting that the Smithsonian's National Air and Space Museum selected the 'Life in the Universe' exhibit to display the Enterprise. STAR TREK not only serves as an example of the quest for other life forms in the universe, but also reinforces the concept of peaceful coexistence, equality and respect for other living things."

The authors of STAR TREK LIVES, Jacqueline Lichtenberg, Sondra Marshak and Joan Winston wrote in their 1975 book concerning the Smithsonian exhibit: "No higher tribute could be paid to the spirit of STAR TREK except that tribute which has been paid and is being paid by millions and tens of millions of people:

the supreme tribute of letting the spirit and meaning of STAR TREK's bright vision of Man's future touch their own lives."

They go on to write, "It is already apparent that STAR TREK is much more than just a television show which came and went. The efforts of millions have been directed toward its rebirth. Millions have been moved profoundly."

THE FIRST FLIGHT OF THE ENTERPRISE

Could it be that STAR TREK has actually changed lives, even the direction of the future? Would the Smithsonian exhibit be there if not for the act of Bjo and her letter-writing campaign back in '67? Do the fans really have that much power? Well, take a look at the second major event that occurred in the '70s, in our own NASA Space program.

On September 17, 1976, The New York Times reported a historical moment; the unveiling of the first space shuttle. Its name? USS Enterprise. Present at the unveiling were Gene Roddenberry and most of the STAR TREK actors.

Originally the shuttle was to be named Constitution. That was changed when NASA was deluged with letters begging them to name their first true space craft after the imaginary vessel in STAR TREK, the Enterprise.

Once again, Trek fans united. Once again, their power to be heard, to make an impact out of love for and commitment to the vision of an optimistic future generated by a television show, persevered.

The impact is astounding. Fans actually contributed to making history because of a belief, and because of an obsession to make that belief come true. If anyone tells a STAR TREK fan they're wasting their time, that it's just a dumb old TV show, that they should "get a life," that person has obviously forgotten the major contribution that STAR TREK fans have made.

Destined for obscurity in 1967, STAR TREK came back. Though it was then canceled again after its dubious third season, the spark of its impact had only just begun.

Now the names Kirk, Spock, Klingon, phaser and tribble are household words. References to STAR TREK are everywhere in fiction, movies, TV, articles and plays. STAR TREK has become a historical event integrated into cultural behavior as if it were real. Or will be. And all because of the fans!

Art by Ken Mitchroney, done in the '70s. Ken is now a professional artist working in the animation industry.

PART TWO:
"From the '70s to the '90s — A Retrospective"

Being a fan twenty years ago, or even ten years ago, was a very different sort of phenomenon than it is now. In the '70s, when the first STAR TREK conventions sprouted up, there was no hope of revival. There was no series of original novels, no feature films, not even the concept of a NEXT GENERATION TV series.

Gold Key put out a children's STAR TREK comic book. Some coloring books were printed up. There were some spaceship models, a few toys, and the James Blish books. Fans starved for new information, new material, more fuel for their fiery obsession. For their almost-religion of a more than promising future.

Fans sewed their own costumes. Fans constructed their own props. They wrote stories. They formed clubs. They created characters for themselves to playact in those clubs and at the very popular STAR TREK conventions. If the show was dead, they could keep it alive by attempting to 'live' it.

Out of the virtually unlimited power of the fans, two massive groups popped up. STAR, an organization whose name stands for Star Trek Association for Revival, had chapters all over the United States with over 15,000 (a conservative figure) members. Their primary goal was to get STAR TREK back on the air by writing letters, holding meetings and conventions, and proving that there was a commercial market out there for such an ambitious new project.

MEETING THE FANS

The second organization to spring up was the Star Trek Welcommittee. Volunteers helped to answer mail from new or out-of-touch fans wanting answers to all kinds of questions. The Welcommittee, which still exists today, helped people find information on conventions, clubs, fanzines, penpals, etc. They were instrumental in bringing together people who were otherwise isolated, or thought they were the only crazy person in love with a man with pointed ears.

And there were the conventions. Surprisingly successful conventions. Conventions with thousands in attendance. That phenomenon, probably more than any other, got the attention of the Hollywood producers and executives. Conventions came to the attention of such magazines as VARIETY and TV GUIDE, and communicated to the world, both fans and non-fans, that this phenomenon was real, a growing force and something that could not be ignored.

It was not enough attention (yet) to bring back the show. The fans did get two seasons of an animated STAR TREK series, though, with most of the actors reprising their roles as the voices of the cartoon characters.

So the fans kept doing what they knew how to do best by sending letters, attending large conventions, writing, sewing costumes, building props and making their enthusiasm known to as many people as they could all over the world. Because of the lack of material to placate a mind hungry for STAR TREK, fans were forced to be creative. This made fandom in the '70s seem new and exciting. This was untrod territory, a place for ground-breaking revelations about the characters, about relationships and about science and the future.

THE BIRTH OF A GROUNDSWELL

I don't think young fans of the '80s and '90s can even imagine what the Trek 'dark ages' of the '70s was like, and how it contributed to the energy and power of our fantasies. How it created what kids now take for granted. It seemed as if everyone who was a fan of STAR TREK was 'family,' a distant friend we had not yet met.

Conventions were like stepping through an enchanted doorway into another world. The force of fandom was palpable. We longed for rebirth. We believed we could make it a reality. We wrote letters and scripts and reviews and novels. We wished. We dreamt. We burned with inspiration.

In the early '70s, with only the Gold Key comics and Blish books to keep us warm (and, yes, David Gerrold's books, too), we'd gather in front of the TV during reruns, audio tape the episodes with clunky, gritty sounding recorders and memorize the lines. But it was fun.

The suffering only made the longed for even all the sweeter when it arrived. This suffer-

ing contributed to the phenomenon of STAR TREK as we know it today.

FANDOM: A UNION OF OUTSIDERS

Another difference in being a STAR TREK fan in the '70s, as opposed to the '90s, is that in the '70s it was literally not 'cool' to be a Trekkie. Many people who did not understand the show had no tolerance for those who did.

Also, many of the people drawn to the show were, in some cases, loners, outcasts, introverts, misunderstood geniuses and many labeled as 'freaks'. The show spoke loudly to those people who were/are 'unsettled,' and who may have had less hope for the future than the average individual. STAR TREK brought hope into those homes. It said that anything was possible and imparted that feeling to its viewers. It awakened people. It opened minds. It distracted people from their sadness, their sickness and their personal pain.

Still, even now, disapproval toward fans from people not at all interested in STAR TREK exists. It is usually a form of intolerance and prejudice. Why? Probably because Trek somehow threatens their perfect little microcosm of existence.

Fans must themselves admit they can become obnoxious with their enthusiasm. The obsession that many people have for Trek probably takes away time from family or friends; or perhaps the love of the TV show dominates dinner table conversations until family members want to shove their fanson/daughter/husband/wife down the garbage disposal unit.

It is more 'cool' to be a STAR TREK fan now than it was when there was nothing new regularly in print or on the air. There is more to share these days, more access to STAR TREK items and to fellow fans, and more to watch, read and discover that's already out there.

Because of this access today, and the even larger number of fans who now exist, there is less of a need to bug loved ones and afflict friends with neverending thoughts and impressions of "Amok Time". Having more access also means more people can share the experience together and not feel as isolated.

SCIENCE FICTION IN THE MAINSTREAM

The cultural acceptance of STAR TREK into daily life, whether in jokes or speech-patterns or computer design, means that there is an understanding of the concept of Trek today that was not there in the '70s for the average non-fan. Acceptance and tolerance of fans is better than it used to be. But we are still a pretty shallow society, obsessed with things like appearance and financial gain, apathetic about things like voting and trying to change the world. We still have far to go even now, and STAR TREK now has a whole new world of problems and controversies to address in its continuing futuristic allegories.

Things have changed, but STAR TREK and its fans still have the powerful magic to make an impact on society, even to manipulate the future. In the '70s, in those turbulent pre-revival times, so starved were most of us for "space, the final frontier," that a wonderful thing happened. In 1977 a bizarre little movie with low hopes of becoming a hit opened in theaters nationwide. Its run lasted over one year.

The name of the movie was STAR WARS. And fans, having desired that kind of adventure kick-in-the-brain since 1969 when the last episode of STAR TREK was shown, saw the movie again and again and again.

STAR WARS, and its fans, was a major contributor in helping revive the dormant STAR TREK. Until STAR WARS, virtually nobody in Hollywood believed there was enough interest in science fiction adventure to warrant spending the money to make it. George Lucas proved all those 'nobodies' wrong.

Paramount saw all the money STAR WARS was making and wanted to do a STAR WARS themselves. Then somebody at Paramount said, 'Hey, we already have one of those ideas sitting on a shelf somewhere gathering dust. It's called STAR TREK. Let's go take a look and see if there's any possibility we could get rich off it like Mr. Lucas did off his sci-fi flick.'

THE REBIRTH OF STAR TREK

Fans went wild at the rumors. They lined up for hours outside theaters when the movie came out. STAR TREK: THE MOTION PICTURE today is not the most popular of movies to rent and watch. In fact, some fans hate it and don't understand how anyone could even take it seriously.

Ah, but they don't remember. When it was released in 1979, it broke box office records, got decent reviews, cost the most of any film of its time to make and brought in new fans. It stirred the blood of Trek lovers everywhere.

In no other of the STAR TREK movies do you see a scene of a huge recreation deck on the Enterprise where hundreds of people crowd to listen to Kirk give a morale-boosting speech,. Most of those 'extras' are fans responsible for giving us STAR TREK as it is today.

As much as some people hate to watch the movie, there is magic in it. It can be felt. If you remember, if you know what it was like to be 'without,' you can watch that movie and love every moment of it; every long uncut scene, every echo in it of episodes past, and value what it stands for. What it gave us. What the fans were able to do with a power that surprised even them.

THE SEQUELS ROLL ON

Some people are offended by enthusiasm and obsession, and the general cockiness of those who know what they love and adamantly oppose any change. Being close-minded is a personal choice. Trek fans knew what they liked, realized they wielded a lot of power and wanted more control over what would happen next.

They wanted their characters unchanged, young and brash. They opposed designs of the new uniforms, a new ship, the art of exploring powerful feelings such as 'death' if said death involved any main character.

Then along came a man named Nicholas Meyer, whose earlier science fiction film success, TIME AFTER TIME, won him the approval of Paramount and the job as director/writer of the next Trek project. He ignored the fans. He wanted to make a major impact with his film, not unlike that of a person picking up a shotgun to kill a fly. He wanted attention. And he got it.

In THE WRATH OF KHAN, still the most popular of all the Trek movies, Spock died. Nick Meyer made a lot of people mad, sad, amused, depressed, intrigued, insane, inspired, lost.

He also did one more thing. He gave fans back their power. After THE WRATH OF KHAN broke box-office records and played to great reviews, the fans used their power to demand THE SEARCH FOR SPOCK.

THE STAR TREK EXPLOSION

Now, It stands to reason that if fans can revive a very dead character, a character who's portrayer (no matter what he says now, it's on record that he, too, wanted the irritable, haunting character that wouldn't leave him alone—Spock—killed off) was reluctant to return (and ended up directing the goddamn thing!), there is no limit to what fans, when motivated, can achieve. Today, thanks to the fans of the '70s and early '80s, the enigma has become a monster.

Pocket Books publishes one STAR TREK novel a month, the quality far improved over the James Blish books of the '70s and the rather irritable Bantam novels of the late '70s and early '80s. STAR TREK: THE NEXT GENERATION is, as of this writing, going into its seventh very successful season. It receives Emmy nominations now. Critics have decided they like it. Syndicated reruns of both Trek and TNG often show back to back. Sponsors stand in line to buy commercial time during these shows.

THE UNGLIMPSED HORIZONS

Moving into the '90s, and beyond the recently celebrated 25th anniversary, STAR TREK fans have everything they could possibly want. Wide-eyed and weaned on a culture that makes references daily to the old show on TV and on the streets, can they possibly feel the same enthusiasm, the burning longing, the isolation, the excitement, the power of wishing for something so much that you'll go out of your way to actively engineer events to make that wish come true? Possibly, but the drive may be different. The '90s fans are not starved. They have it all.

STAR TREK fandom was and still is a unique force. If it was all taken away today, the new fans would get it back. They'd make the events of the '70s—such as the naming of the Space Shuttle Enterprise, and getting the Smithsonian to include a model of the Enterprise in its Air and Space museum—happen all over again.

STAR TREK fans are legion. They are a unique phenomenon, an entity unto themselves. Their historical accomplishments support that claim as fact. As Roddenberry's theme-song poem says, STAR TREK will go on forever, with its enduring life owed to its fans.

Chapter 8

STAR TREK FANFICT

While many STAR TREK fans find plenty to satisfy them in the endless stream of novels being published by Pocket Books, some want something more; something different. Fan fiction offers that alternative. The following chapter examines some of the types of fan fiction available and how it differs from the STAR TREK stories found in professional novels.

General STAR TREK stories can be found in abundance in fanzines. They offer readers expansions of ideas laid down in the series. These general stories usually follow the Trek universe of the series fairly closely, putting the STAR TREK characters and the Enterprise through a new set of action/adventure yarns or psychological character studies.

Since the possibilities of such adventures are endless, so are the Trek stories available in fan fiction. For example, many of these stories are sequels, or even prequels, to such aired episodes as "Mirror, Mirror," "City On The Edge Of Forever," "The Menagerie" and others.

There are many kinds of fan fiction, though. The following sections define some of the more specific categories.

GET - 'EM—THEY'RE STILL ALIVE!

"Get'-'em" stories never have a happy ending— well, almost never. In this type of story, one, if not all, of the main characters will no longer be alive when the end comes. Some of the best stories in fan fiction are to be found in this category. Most Get-'em's have a purpose other than the death of the

BY ALEXIS FAGAN BLACK, WENDY RATHBONE, DENNIS FISCHER, JAMES VAN HISE AND KAY DOTY

character(s). These stories often offer insights into characters which were previously undiscovered.

Perhaps the best known story of this type is "The Rack," published in the '70s in CONTACT #4. Written by J. Emily Vance, it deals with a very controversial subject: Kirk and Spock are accused of being homosexual lovers by Starfleet and must face charges.

Though these charges are not true, Kirk and Spock must attempt to convince Starfleet of their innocence, or become separated. Spock bwill be transferred to another ship and given a command of his own.

The tortures they go through are enormous. Though there is some dissent as to whether Starfleet would drum up such charges, or even if they would care if Kirk and Spock were lovers, the idea works within the framework given.

CONTACT was one of the most influential STAR TREK fanzines of the 1970s. Issue #4 (September 1977) ran 174 pages and included impressive fold out artwork by the late Pat Stall.

STAR TREK often uses its 23rd century setting to make commentaries on life in the 20th century. On a scale of 1 to 10, "The Rack" would have to rate somewhere in the range of 15 simply due to the emotional and psychological studies given of Kirk, Spock and McCoy. This is one of the best written, best illustrated, stories ever published.

The sequel to "The Rack," entitled "All The King's Horses, All The King's Men," was published in a fanzine titled FARTHEST STAR. It dealt with the continuing tragedy as seen from McCoy's point of view. "All The King's Horses" deals more with what too much power in the hands of the wrong people can lead to. It also illustrates "victory in the face of tragedy" when it is already too late for many of the people involved.

Get-'em stories are worth reading since, as Bev Volker pointed out in the editorial of CONTACT 4, "We all have that masochistic streak that loves to see our heroes suffer in our fantasies." While it is true no one likes a sad ending, it is also true everyone's lives are filled with some form of tragedy, both large and small. Get-'em stories deal realistically with the inevitable deaths of Kirk, Spock and McCoy by giving us insights into their lives. Did their lives have a purpose?

Another fine 'zine which presents emotional grabbers is GALACTIC DISCOURSE, published by Laurie Huff. Issue #1 of this 'zine features a beautifully written story entitled "My Life Closed Twice," which traces Spock's life many years after Kirk's death. It is marvelously touching and should be read by any newcomer to fan fiction.

Other stories worth mentioning are Bev Volker's "When The Time Comes" and "Not Yet Time," both of which appeared in CONTACT #3. These stories offer a view of how Spock might react to Kirk's impending death, and how he would face the reality that there is no hope. These two stories show the reader that not all endings are happy ones.

"MARY SUE, MARY SUE"

You can always recognize a "Mary Sue" character by the miles of flowing hair combined with long eyelashes and a heart that flutters when in the presence of her long-lost love. Mary Sue-type characters usually fall into specific categories and display some, if not all, of these characteristics:

1) She's the prettiest thing ever to be granted breath by God but, of course, sees herself as simply "average" and "not worthy of his love."

2) She's the smartest little thing ever to have entered Starfleet at the ripe old age of 13 due to her "superior abilities."

3) She's the loneliest creature ever to have been born. She was raised in a sprawling country home by an aging aunt after the untimely death of her parents while on safari in downtown New York. Her life has been one of "self-imposed solitude" laced with the "pursuits of intellectual development."

At least half of the Mary Sues are from the 20th century, and somehow, "through some inevitable twist of galactic fate," they come to be on the good ship Enterprise. Mary Sue characters are often from the 20th century because this makes it easier for the writer/reader to identify, and therefore far simpler to write. You could take any Gothic Romance, change the names and places, and have a Mary Sue story. Many believe Mary Sues are a direct projection of the writer's fantasy self into the STAR TREK universe.

This type of story is usually well written and enjoyed by many fans. They have a place in fan fiction, even if that place is only as a launching pad for new writers.

ALTERNATE UNIVERSE

Alternate universe STAR TREK stories are not to be confused with sequels or prequels to "Mirror, Mirror." This type of fan fiction is meant to offer alternative views of what could happen with the STAR TREK characters given a different set of circumstances or surroundings.

Alternate universe fan fiction is usually not intended to take place on the same time/space level as the STAR TREK of the actual aired episodes. It is often geared to appeal to certain interests of specific groups of fans.

For example, SAHAJ COLLECTED is a marvelous collection of stories, mostly by Leslie Lilker, which deal with Spock's son, Sahaj. The stories postulate that Spock had a brief encounter, brought on by pon farr, with a female Vulcan ambassador. He fathered a child, but had no knowledge of his son's existence until the boy was ten years old.

The stories are absolutely delightful and give a wonderful portrayal of a ten year old Vulcan boy and his father. The artwork throughout is absolutely beautiful. Most of the art in this 'zine is by Alice Jones, Signe Landon and Gee Moaven.

If you've always wondered what Spock would actually do with a ten year old "keg of dynamite," SAHAJ COLLECTED is definitely for you. Many of the Sahaj stories first appeared in Leslie's 'zine IDIC in the '70s. SAHAJ COLLECTED was recently brought back into print.

Another fine example of alternate universe Treklit is Dr. Jean Lorrah's treatment of Sarek and Amanda in her NIGHT OF THE TWIN MOONS series, which was also recently reprinted. KRAITH is one of the most well known alternate universe Trek fiction series. It involves a universe in which Spock becomes Kirk's liege and Kirk is bound to follow Spock's instructions and orders to the letter. The series is controversial and very highly detailed.

Also in the realm of alternate universe Treklit is DREADNOUGHT EXPLORATIONS, which takes place after the end of the five year mission. Kirk and company are placed in command of a dreadnought-class vessel and given a new assignment. The five issues of this 'zine feature excellent character development, good story lines and plots and many new and fresh ideas.

K/S or SLASH—
IT SPELLS CONTROVERSY

K/S or slash stories fall into the area of adult fiction offering tales in which Kirk and Spock are lovers. Although a small part of the fan fiction realm, it has an intense and loyal following. Most of the writers and readers of this fiction are women.

In the '70s when this sub-genre of fan fiction first appeared with such stories as "Shelter" and "Poses" by Leslie Fish and "Alternative" by Gerry Downes, it created shockwaves which have since subsided. Having gotten past years of variations on the "first time" story, current K/S tends to consist of regular STAR TREK stories and adventures in which the K/S relationship is just one facet of the mosaic, and sometimes a very minor facet.

Some stories include scenes of graphic love-making, branding them adults-only. Most publishers of such 'zines label them as either adult or "slash." Slash is the '90s designation for K/S, and is taken from the slash mark in the abbreviation, but it can also be applied to other characters explored in that manner, such as STARSKY & HUTCH "slash" stories and MAN FROM UNCLE "slash" stories, the latter having even been published as professional comic books in Japan. It's a whole wide world out there and there is something for everyone.

A few of the following 'zines are currently in print, but most are not. They are reviewed to examine the historical context of STAR TREK fan fiction. This section is followed by a review of currently available, new fan fiction.

THE OTHER SIDE
OF PARADISE

THE OTHER SIDE OF PARADISE #4 was published by Amy Falkowitz. This issue contains a complete STAR TREK novel titled THE ELDER BROTHER by Clare Bell. The story deals with Spock as he goes through strange and difficult changes during a several month period. After mentally communicating with a creature resembling in parts a fish, a whale, a bird and a dragon, Spock slowly loses his self-confidence and has a difficult time concentrating on his work.

McCoy and Kirk are the first to notice. Spock is aware something is wrong but wants to research the answer by himself. This doesn't work because he sees the world in a distorted way as a result of his illness. He can no longer play the Vulcan lyrette, makes mistakes, slips into the Vulcan tongue and seems to forget English.

Spock doesn't understand what is happening and becomes confused, frightened and ashamed. He is plagued by dreams that leave him visibly shaken. He feels his whole Vulcan heritage is in question and he is slowly going insane because of his human/Vulcan physiology.

Interesting characters are introduced in THE ELDER BROTHER. They are all Vulcans of a new starship in the fleet, the T'Pau Avreena. The Vulcans are at a loss to explain what Spock is experiencing, but they try to help. The T'Pau Avreena's doctor, T'Feyla, is the one Vulcan who attempts to understand Spock with more than logic. She and Christine Chapel begin to piece together the answer.

The novel is an excellent study of Spock. It shows the depths to which the others care for the Vulcan first officer and follows the set-up of aired Trek, concentrating on character. The story is too drawn out with tiresome details.

This 'zine is 119 pages of reduced type and contains over 30 pages of artwork. The outstanding pieces are drawn by Merle Decker and Nan Lewis. Several other artists contributed to the story. The result is a lovely zine.

STARBORNE

STARBORNE #1 was published by Michael Verina. The outstanding feature is the artwork. Surprisingly, some of these artists, including the best and the brightest, showed their brilliance in the pages of fanzines and then faded from sight.

The cover of STARBORNE #1 is a striking example of the artwork found within. It is a fold-out picture of the 'big three', Kirk, Spock and McCoy, by Mike Verina. The rest of the issue contains breath-taking illos by Verina, Gayle Feyrer, P.S. Nim, Wagner, Decker, Lewis and an absolutely fabulous fold-out of Kirk and Spock by Pat Stall especially rendered for the tear-jerking story "Forever Autumn" by Della Van Hise.

The stories, unfortunately, are not all of the same caliber as the artwork. "A Logical Choice" offers one version of "The Galileo Seven" asking what if Latimer and Gaetano had not been killed and Spock had to choose three of the seven crew members to stay behind on Taurus II? This action/adventure story deals mostly with Spock, Boma and Latimer.

"Trembles A Rarer Speech" has Spock visiting his mother on her death bed. It's a simple idea and not very exciting.

"En Quatre Parties" has Spock feeling guilty for not reaching Kirk in time to save Miramanee and her unborn child. It's a good story, but too short.

"Raftee" is confusing and lacks character depth. It is a disappointment.

The longest story in the 'zine, "Illusions," is also a disappointment. It has Spock's form being worshipped as a deity by a planet's primitive inhabitants.

The best two stories in the 'zine are "Forever Autumn" by Della Van Hise and "In Palaces of Sand," a less than two-page vignette by Toni Cardinal Price guaranteed to twist your heart.

A lot of work went into this zine and although the story content may be a let-down, STARBORNE's appearance is beautiful.

THE PERFECT OBJECT

THE PERFECT OBJECT, published by Mindy Glazer, deals with Captain Kirk. The crew is looking forward to a much needed, long overdue R&R which they take on the planet Manderlay. Manderlay is quite well-known for its shore leave conveniences, one of them being a special bordello by the name of Sunrise.

This is where most of the men take shore leave, including Captain Kirk and Dr. McCoy. Even Spock beams down for a look at the artifacts with which Sunrise decorates its spacious facilities.

The novel is original. The character, Dareet, a young woman Kirk takes a fascination to who happens to run the place, has a good time playing hard to get. Kirk likes a challenge.

The plot of THE PERFECT OBJECT is very basic. Kirk meets girl; Kirk becomes infatuated with girl; Kirk goes to bed with girl; Kirk loses girl.

For a Mary Sue story this is well written, but not a joy to read. It is a strange love story between Kirk and Dareet, two characters who lack appeal as written here. It isn't STAR TREK, and it isn't science fiction.

THE PERFECT OBJECT is 106 pages offset with 4 pages of illustrations, including three good ones by Nan Lewis, and a nice cover drawing of Kirk by Carol Walske.

CONTACT

CONTACT was one of the foremost STAR TREK 'zines of the '70s. Issue 5/6, published by Beverly Volker and Nancy Kippax, features 13 stories. Most deal with the characterization of Kirk and Spock and their friendship based on mutual respect.

The first story, "Woe To Him Who Is Alone" by Linda White, has an interesting premise. Kirk and Spock must find a way to locate an alien's friend before the alien becomes so overwrought with grief that he dies.

Spock is affected telepathically by the intensity of the alien's emotions and finds it increasingly difficult to control his. Kirk is there to help him through the turmoil, but several of the scenes are too saccharine.

"In Your Place" by Crystal Taylor is an excellent story about Kirk and an alien captain switching starships so each can learn from the other. The characterization is quite good with the varying reactions each crew exhibits toward their new commander.

One of the most infuriating stories in the 'zine is "Fire and Ice" by Sandra Gent and Virginia Green. Not only do Kirk and Spock suffer a major catastrophe, but the end leaves the reader hanging and angry with the writers for placing our favorite characters into such a traumatic situation.

"Shadowrider" by Susan K. James is a different sort of Kirk story as the poor guy loses his memory and through the aid of a mechanical device mentally becomes a native of a primitive planet. It's joining the crowd the hard way until Spock steps in to the rescue.

Many of the stories and poems are boring and several of the ideas have been tackled before. There's a whole scope of emotions and feelings to choose from and an entire galaxy to explore, yet fresh, original stories are rare.

HOME IS THE HUNTER is one of those rare finds. This lengthy novel comprises the second part of CONTACT 5/6.

The plot is mind-boggling, heart-wrenching, stomach-twisting, exciting, sad and violent. The characterization is excellent. Nancy Kippax and Bev Volker show writing talent with this novel.

HOME IS THE HUNTER is a portrait of Kirk. Kirk mends his wounds and come to grips with himself as being only human. Aside from the more gruesome scenes, which are minor turnoffs, this is one of the best fanfic STAR TREK stories. It is the STAR TREK version of THE DEER HUNTER, about imprisonment, torture and what it's like to come out the other side. It pulls no punches.

THE BEAST

THE BEAST, written and published by Teri White, is a STAR TREK novella dealing with Spock being accidentally thrown into the Earth of 1910. His memory is gone due to a transporter accident. He is captured, imprisoned and turned into "The Beast," a circus oddity for whom his "owner" charges admission to see.

The well-written story captures the emotional turmoil of a Kirk still searching a year later, and Spock, whose memories gradually begin to return until he realizes that somewhere there is someone named Jim who befriended him. This knowledge leads him to escape from his keeper.

The tale then follows Kirk's struggle to get Spock back to the Enterprise after finding him and traces the agonies they suffer trying to find a safe haven. Spock's memory is still not totally complete and he is portrayed very sympathetically from Kirk's point of view.

THE BEAST is a well written and nicely printed hurt/comfort and action/adventure story. It is a "psychological" story which gives new insights into the characters, rather than simply putting them through a series of actions like wooden puppets. In THE BEAST, Kirk and Spock live rather than just perform.

ANTARES RISING

ANTARES RISING features stories, poems and artwork. The lead story, "Ad Astra" by Lisa Smith is a tale of young pranksters aboard the Enterprise. The author shows she can handle dialogue with some humor.

Unfortunately, her story is weak in almost all other areas. Perhaps it would have fared better as a radio play, but it is enjoyable in its own way, albeit not necessarily believable. One of the touches I enjoyed was Ming, an apparently female Oriental Vulcan who sings "The Ballad of Lost C'Mell" and "The Green Hills of Earth" among other compositions.

A totally ridiculous but fun little piece is "Return of the Psi Syndrome" by Robert Byther. It refuses to take itself seriously and while the humor may not be everyone's cup of tea, it is fun.

Next is ". . . And a Star to Steer her by" by Don Osborne. Unfortunately this story is garbled. A quasar causes crew members to have dreams which they cannot distinguish from reality. There is absolutely no scientific explanation for this phenomenon, and the solution is to leave the vicinity of the quasar.

A quasar is an acronym for quasi-stellar radio sources. They generate more light and radio energy than 100 Milky Way galaxies and produce tremendous amounts of energy from the total gravitational collapse of their matter. The story did not make use of these facts. Instead it relied on scientific hokum and references to previous episodes. The result is poor science fiction.

Last is "The Disappearance of William B. Doran" by Marc Siegall, which may not be a scientific story but it is a delightful vignette. Like any other fanzine, this work has plenty of sweat, love and care poured into it. What makes it worthwhile is a good sense of humor and fun.

DREADNOUGHT EXPLORATIONS

DREADNOUGHT EXPLORATIONS #1-5 is a series of fanzines which chronicle the story of what happens to the crew of the Enterprise after the five year mission. The writing is some of the best since the "Federation and Empire" series which ran in that paragon of Trekzines, BABEL.

DE #1 starts off with the crew leaving the Enterprise and waiting to be reassigned. As the title indicates, they are assigned to one of the prototype Dreadnought ships; in fact the only one in existence, named the Federation.

The authors' pet character, Danior of the Trader Clan Abrasax and his pantha Altair are introduced. Danior is an Orion trader, space vagabond and general all-around good guy. Confronting the crew is an unknown enemy that has already succeeded in sabotaging the Federation.

Kirk must keep peace in a special alliance between the Federation, the Romulans and the Klingons, who joined to combat the threat of the unknown enemy. Kirk must test the new Dreadnought ship and keep himself from revealing military secrets while allied during the first crucial mission.

Luckily, most of the familiar crew have been asked to serve under Kirk. The ball starts rolling.

In DE #2, due to the alliance, Lexa, the Romulan female commander from "The Enterprise Incident," and Captain Koloth, appear among other characters. The plot concerns a mind-controlling alien presence that has been causing the sabotage.

DE #3 offers the exploration of the planet most likely the unknown alien's starting point. The planet is unstable and deserted, except for "sentinels" which cause problems for the landing party.

DE #4 pits the Federation against one, and later three, of the enemy's spaceships. Kirk undergoes a personal crisis when one of his friends is presumed captured and lost to the aliens.

DE #5 continues the story as the aliens invade Federation territory, the Enterprise is found after an alien attack, and Romulans plan to mutiny on their ship. These later issues contain other stories and poems and maintain a fairly high standard.

Except for a "Tell us about your many adventures" line or two, the dialogue is crisp and realistic. The characters are true to form and not over-emotional parodies of themselves while the plot is properly convoluted and interesting.

The description is weak, but is improving, and the authors are finally including that underlying philosophy that made STAR TREK a hit, but is missing from much of fan literature. In addition to entertainment and engaging characters, a story needs provide food for thought. DREADNOUGHT EXPLORATIONS is a good read. The 'zine has been collected and remains currently in print.

A TREK 'ZINE NAMED FANTASIA

FANTASIA #2 is an average in approach, if not in content. It has crisp layouts and reduced type so that its 38 page length is a bit deceptive. The 38 pages include as much material as other zines of 100 pages.

This issue offers several pieces of fiction. The one which stands out is "Yesteryear, Today & Tomorrow" by Leslie Fish. This story is a sequel to the animated STAR TREK episode "Yesteryear," but takes a unique approach, focusing on the Andorian, Thelin.

The tale begins with Thelin having strange dreams about an alternate life in which he is the first officer of the Enterprise. He slowly puts the pieces together until he arrives at a solution he finds difficult to believe. Subplots involve his relationship with other people on this Federation ship, the Yorktown.

The Yorktown is almost the opposite of the Enterprise. The Captain is a xenophobic jerk and the ship is poorly maintained. Thelin needs to secure an important position in Starfleet in order to help the people of his star system. Knowing that in an altered timeline he had this position is immensely frustrating to him. Thelin finally hatches a plan involving the Guardian which could bring him that coveted position.

What happens is unpredictable and imaginative, as well as suspenseful. Leslie Fish is one of the best writers to contribute STAR TREK fan fiction and this is one of her best stories.

Nice illos which she drew herself accompany the story. There is an underlying theme regarding Thelin's emotional involvement with the chief engineer which is very well handled. This story is a perfect example of excellent fan fiction. Characters, plot and science fiction elements are written in a very professional manner.

This 'zine also includes a nice little vignette in which Kirk mourns the death of Miramanee. There is also fine art by Gordon Carleton, Gayle Feyrer and Joni Wagner. Editor Jean Kluge secured a lot of talented people to produce a very good 'zine.

SAHAJ COLLECTED

These stories originally appeared in the fanzine IDIC. They are "alternate universe" which postulate that through some unusual circumstances, Spock wound up with a son named Sahaj. SAHAJ COLLECTED gathers the stories.

The first story in this series, "Loved I Not Honour More" by Trinette Kern explains how all this came about and returns to Spock's days with Christopher Pike. It's a good story.

"The Ambassador's Son," in which Spock first meets Sahaj when the boy is already ten years old, is even better. Some people are put off by concepts like this in fan fiction, but it is handled quite believably.

The writing on these stories is some of the best in fan fiction. Among the many illos are several by Alice Jones which are among the best ever published in any fan fiction 'zines.

Alice Jones was a legendary fan fiction artist in the '70s until she abruptly dropped out of fandom, never to be heard from again. Not seeing any new work from her in more than a decade is a great loss to fandom, as well as to the professional art world which she surely deserved to be a part of.

SAHAJ COLLECTED rates high.

THE WEIGHT

"The Weight" is a serialized story which appeared in the fanzine WARPED SPACE in the late '70s. It is the story of Kirk's struggle to regain not only his crew, but their respect as well. After a time displacement accident which left Spock and McCoy dead, the entire crew of the Enterprise is left stranded in an alternate time line, unable to get back to their own universe.

The crew deserts Kirk and sets up camp on the Earth of two hundred years from now. Kirk feels that if he could somehow get back his own time line, there would at least be a possibility of setting things straight once again.

Even though the crew and Kirk are in their own time, they are not in their own universe. The universe in which they are stranded is a society which has shunned science due to an error in judgment on Kirk's part. This is one of the few pieces of fiction where it is admitted that Kirk, Spock or any of the regulars could make a mistake.

Kirk discovers, quite by accident, a group of Anarchists who befriend him. They help him to see that there is still a chance of getting back to his own time. Yet, the Anarchists shun leadership, and Kirk knows they would be out of place in his universe. He must find a way of "balancing" things so that no one comes out on the bottom in the end.

In this parallel universe, all of Kirk's people have doubles. Kirk's double is a woman, Jenneth Roantree, "leader" of the Anarchists. Jenneth is Kirk born into the body of a woman. Kirk discovers she is his double in an astonishing and humorous way.

Leslie's story is highly detailed and often emotionally crushing. She makes her new characters move and breathe and live in a way which many professional writers simply cannot. Her portrayal of Kirk is both correct and stylistically beautiful.

In "The Weight" the reader comes to know other characters who soon become as important as Kirk, Spock, McCoy and the rest of the crew. Though there are many new characters introduced in other fan fiction serials, Leslie's portrayal of Jenneth Roantree, Quannechota, Sparks and the rest of the Anarchists is far superior.

"The Weight" was collected in a single volume in 1988 and, at the time, sold for $40.00 (for over five hundred 8 1/2 x 11 pages). For information on availability, contact T'Khutian Press, 200 E. Thomas Street, Lansing, MI 48906.

MODERN FAN FICTION FANDOM

Due to the small print runs of fan fiction 'zines, many are now out of print and have all but disappeared. A few, thankfully, remain in print due to the efforts of dealers who have made legitimate arrangements to reprint older, highly praised 'zines.

New 'zines continue to be published, though. The following section reviews some of the STAR TREK fan fiction 'zines of the '90s. All of the following 'zines are currently in print.

LIVING IN SPITE OF LOGIC

Moving from historic fan fiction stories to the modern realm we encounter the novel LIVING IN SPITE OF LOGIC by Ellen O'Neil. This story begins soon after the original STAR TREK series episode "Mirror, Mirror." Captain James T. Kirk is attempting to compose a report, with a notable lack of success. Starfleet Command is demanding details of the events that caused Kirk, Dr. McCoy, Scotty and Uhura to be transported into an alternate universe.

Simultaneously, events are occurring in that other universe which will plunge Kirk and his officers into a horror which will require all of their wits to escape. In the alternate universe, Spock has been arrested, interrogated repeatedly and thrown into the brig for his refusal to answer questions about a secret weapon called the Tantalus Device. The alternate Captain Kirk has disappeared, along with the device, and is assumed to be dead.

Spock is tried and found guilty of withholding evidence. He is sentenced to the prison planet Tau Ceti, where his telepathic powers will be surgically destroyed. Spock escapes to our universe, but is transported into the Empire universe.

The novel emphasizes the strong friendship between Kirk, McCoy and Spock in both universes as they all work to return things to normal. The author delves into the characters of both Spocks and gives the reader a fresh understanding of the Vulcan. She also gives the reader a glimpse into the differences, and the similarities, between the characters of the two universes.

O'Neil has written a fast-paced story, filled with danger, suspense and intrigue while remaining true to the characters. LIVING IN SPITE OF LOGIC is one of the best STAR TREK novels, professional or amateur, on the market. It is a must for Spock fans, and a collector's item for all fans whose hobby is STAR TREK literature. The 130 page, professionally bound book may be obtained by writing: Ellen O'Neil, 135 Hamilton Park, Lexington, Kentucky 40504. Send a self-addressed stamped envelope for price and availability.

STEADY AS SHE GOES

STEADY AS SHE GOES is a NEXT GENERATION anthology containing 5 stories. "The Gambler" is a drama. After Captain Picard is poisoned, Commander Riker must mediate a peace treaty between two warring worlds.

When it becomes apparent that the delegates are not sincere in their quest for peace, Riker calls upon his poker skills and introduces a very unusual "wildcard." He also finds a very unexpected "wildcard" of his own, in the form of a beautiful woman.

"Geordi's Adventure" is a comedy/drama wherein Geordi follows a mysterious trail in a search for answers about a missing probe. He finds much more than he bargained for in the form of a pretty young lady. He has been yearning for an adventure all his own, but soon learns the truth to the old adage: "Be careful what you wish for, you might get it," when a series of unhappy events leaves him wishing he'd never heard the word "adventure."

"Beverly Goes Shopping" is a comedy. Beverly returns from a visit to a planet which caters to human tastes, bringing with her a strange purchase. Her fellow Enterprise officers are intrigued, except for Captain Picard.

"O'Brien And The Lady" is a bittersweet love story that occurs long before his marriage to Keiko. The transporter chief "rescues" a frightened girl and unknowingly creates a serious problem for himself, and a possible breach of Prime Directive.

"A Matter Of Adjustment" is a drama wherein the Enterprise is ordered to Eridana V to evacuate the residents from their endangered world. A small group of rebels, who don't believe the scientists' reports, attempts to commandeer the Enterprise and return home.

Meanwhile the ship rescues a man from another time. Riker is assigned the task of helping him cope with his situation, and in so doing learns something about himself.

STEADY AS SHE GOES is 154 pages, spiral bound, and available from Peg Kennedy and Bill Hupe, Footrot Flats, 916 Lamb Road, Mason, MI 48854.

FREE FALL ONE

FREE FALL ONE is another STAR TREK anthology. It opens with "McCoy Finds A Refuge" by Kay Doty. This touching story concerns McCoy's bitter divorce and custody battle over his daughter, Joanna. There is also a bittersweet romance and the story of his first two years after the doctor's unplanned enlistment into Starfleet.

"On Call" by Charmaine Wood is an account of the demands, frustrations and achievements of one very hectic day in Dr. McCoy's life on the Enterprise. "The Poachers" by Jill Thomasson details how McCoy vanishes on a routine exploratory mission. The victim of a kidnapping, he will die if Kirk and Spock do not discover his whereabouts in time.

"Landing Party" by Magee Gilks is about an old man who reminisces about his first landing party with the illustrious Captain Kirk while serving aboard the Enterprise. "Any Day Now" by Jeane McGrew asks the question, what if STAR TREK were not entirely fiction?

In "Checkmate" by Charmaine Wood, the Enterprise is in port for repairs when two female inspectors come aboard to oversee the work. The story tells how Kirk fares in his relations with these two very different ladies. "Captain/Hero" by Zaquia Tarhuntassa is a Kirk fable.

This zine is a special treat for McCoy fans in particular. It is 120 pages long, available from Bill Hupe and Peg Kennedy, 916 Lamb Road, Mason, MI 48854-9445.

FREE FALL TWO

Published by SpartiWerks and edited by Zaquia Tarhuntassa, FREE FALL TWO is available from the same address as FREE FALL ONE. In the lead story, "Rain Daughter" by Magee Gilks, the plot brings together an ancient world of human sacrifice and the modern world of the Federation. Captain Kirk and a young Starfleet ensign are caught in the middle. It is a beautiful story of family love and tradition.

"The Admiral's Shore Leave" by Kay Doty deals with Captain Kirk deciding that he, Dr. McCoy and Spock will investigate a somewhat unfriendly planet before allowing crew members to take shore leave. The three get into a fistfight with locals, nearly kill themselves in a vehicular accident with Kirk at the controls and find an unwanted bride for McCoy, before being rescued by the Enterprise.

"Season's Greetings" by Charmaine Wood is a tender story of a meeting between McCoy and his daughter, who comes aboard the Enterprise to spend Christmas with her father. After their all-too-short visit, she takes a special gift from McCoy back to her duty station.

"Pendulum" by Magee Gilks is a story which begins soon after the end of STAR TREK IV: THE VOYAGE HOME. Thirty-nine people become suddenly ill with anemia, and doctors are unable to find a cause. Aboard the science ship Cartier, Dr. Gillian Taylor is experiencing similar symptoms. A well-written, thought-provoking tale of the effect time-travel could have on history.

"An Old Country Doctor Goes Home" by Charmaine Wood is a short-short story with Dr. Christine Chapel and Dr. Leonard McCoy. To say more would spoil the surprises.

"The Haunted Castle" by Kay Doty begins when a mysterious Starfleet commander is reported to be causing trouble on the planet Arvon, and Lieutenant Uhura and Lieutenant Leslie are sent to investigate. When they disappear, Kirk gets little cooperation from Arvon's Commandant Baiseek.

Leslie and Uhura have strange adventures that lead them to a horrible discovery. As they attempt to extricate themselves from captivity, they are drawn to each other.

"To Have And Have Not" by Kay Doty is a sequel to "McCoy Finds A Refuge." Leonard McCoy is in love, and after a rather startling disclosure, proposes marriage, but duty comes first. Before the nuptials can take place, a disastrous event in the far reaches of the galaxy must be attended to first.

THE DEFOREST KELLEY COMPENDIUM

Edited by Laura Guyer, THE DEFOREST KELLEY COMPENDIUM is a largely non-fiction volume, published in 1991. It contains 205 pages of material about the career of DeForest Kelley. Included are photos, illustrations, interviews, movie and television credits and convention appearances. This is a must for collectors of Kelley/McCoy memorabilia.

Half of this book is devoted to reviews of his STAR TREK episodes and movies. Also included are 40 pages of poems and fiction. The cover is a color photograph of Kelley in his red uniform worn in the last 5 movies. Computer graphics are by Scott Guyer, Barb Schwartz and Michael Schwartz.

For information about current availability contact Laura Guyer, 7959 W. Portland Ave., Littleton, Colorado 80123.

EXPLORATIONS

EXPLORATIONS is a compilation of NEXT GENERATION fiction written by Carol Davis. Much of this was originally published in SHIP'S LOG SUPPLEMENTAL, a fanzine founded by David. The book also contains two articles describing the six weeks that Carol spent working as an apprentice writer at Paramount Pictures with the STAR TREK: THE NEXT GENERATION writing staff.

For information about the availability of EXPLORATIONS, write to The Fandom Press, c/o Tim Perdue, 412 Second Avenue South, Humboldt, IA 50548.

A MATTER OF HONOR

Compiled by Bill Hupe and Peg Kennedy, A MATTER OF HONOR contains a collection of NEXT GENERATION fiction and poems written by a number of writers. Also featured is artwork by different artists. The cover of the spiral bound book is a color illustration of Captain Picard.

For information on A MATTER OF HONOR, contact Bill Hupe and Peg Kennedy, Footrot Flats, 916 Lamb Road, Mason, MI 48854.

WHERE DO I GO FROM HERE?

There are two immediate possibilities open for those who want to plug into the current fan fiction scene. There's the bi-monthly publication, THE ZINE CONNECTION (sample copy $3.00, from Jean Hinson, 7830 DePalma Street, Downey, California 90241). The other is the DIRECTORY OF STAR TREK ORGANIZATIONS, which also lists many 'zines ($3.00, available from the STAR TREK Welcommittee, c/o Judy Segal, P.O. Box 414, Pawling, New York 12564).

The information in this chapter is current as of mid-1993, so explore the furthest reaches of STAR TREK fandom!

Chapter 9

LEGENDARY FAN WRITER

In the Seventies and Eighties, getting Leslie Fish to write a story for you was a real coup. She was one of the half dozen or so most respected writers in fandom and it was no surprise that she eventually turned pro. That STAR TREK novel sale has still eluded her, but mostly because Paramount and Pocket impose more arbitrary restrictions than she's comfortable with. ("You mean I can't have McCoy and Spock drown in Chicago in a parallel universe?").

Leslie Fish is an artist/writer regarded by many as one of the finest talents STAR TREK fandom has produced. She has written all kinds of Trek fiction and all of it is marked with an important subtext of drama and humanity. Her lengthy serialized novel, THE WEIGHT, is probably the most ambitious and successful continued series. It shows what new ideas exist untried in STAR TREK fan fiction.

Her Thelin stories, "Yesteryear, Today and Tomorrow" in FANTASIA #2 and "Winterlight" in MATTER/ANTI-MATTER #2, continued the Andorian character who had been briefly introduced in D.C. Fontana's animated STAR TREK episode "Yesteryear." With Thelin, Leslie expands the STAR TREK universe in exciting ways.

In SEHLAT'S ROAR #5 she wrote a thirty-page article called "A Sociopolitical Survey of the Rim Worlds". It postulated various original societies on the worlds of the Rim.

BY JAMES VAN HISE   Artwork accompanying this interview is by Leslie Fish.

VIGIL

BY THERESA HOLMES

ART BY LESLIE FISH

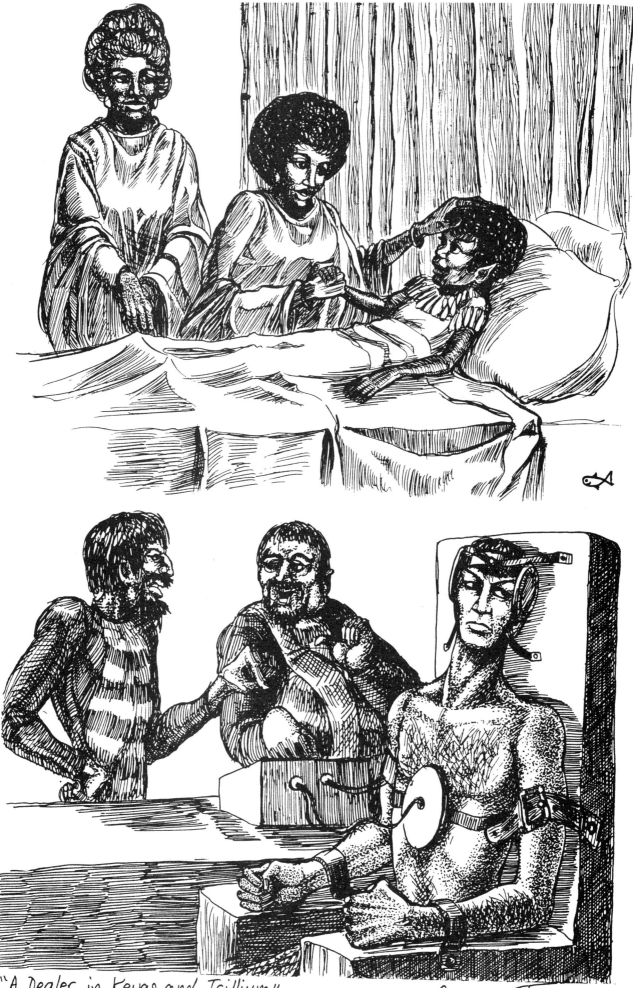

"A Dealer in Kevas and Trillium"

Leslie Fish

Leslie became involved in STAR TREK fandom in 1975 when she simultaneously acquired the address of the STAR TREK Welcommittee from the non-fiction book STAR TREK LIVES and learned about an upcoming STAR TREK convention in her home town of Chicago.

HER FIRST CONVENTION

"Before then I was a typical isolated fan, thinking that nobody but me still watched old reruns religiously," Leslie recalled. She managed to get into her first STAR TREK convention on the strength of her home made STAR TREK songs. She explained, "I had a lovely time. I subsequently wrote to the Welcommittee for their directory and began writing to and ordering 'zines. I decided that a cheap way to get 'zines would be to contribute. The rest is history."

Leslie only began to write STAR TREK fiction after discovering that fandom existed. She said, "I believe I had some minor poems and illos printed in some small 'zines. I tried writing a story which I subsequently abandoned for lack of interest, and wrote a few short vignettes for small zines, most of which weren't published until many moons after I'd sent them. A few never saw print at all. Surprisingly enough, the first piece of ST fiction of mine to actually get published was part one of 'The Weight'."

"The Weight" was originally written as a reply to a short story, "The Sixth Year" published in the fanzine, WARPED SPACE. "At the end of part one, all the elements necessary for Kirk to get back to his own universe are spelled out; where the crystals are, how to get them, and who's willing to help. However, the readers demanded a sequel. People wanted to see the whole adventure of setting time right and dealing with the consequences," she recalled. "Being an obliging sort of fool, I gave the readers what they wanted—three years worth! Once I got into the story; once the implications started showing up and demanding to be dealt with, the damned thing began to stretch like the Midgard Serpent. One cause of this was probably the effect of serialization. After each chapter the readers would write LOC's, point up problems, ask about details, and in the next chapter I'd work in answers to the questions raised. 'Twas one helluva writing experience. Educational, at least."

ANARCHISTS ON THE ENTERPRISE

At one point in "The Weight," a group of characters, called the Anarchists, on an alternate Earth timeline, are brought aboard the Enterprise. They adapt rather quickly to the ship in spite of a 300 year difference in technology.

"The Anarchists pick up on Starfleet technology quickly for several reasons, all of them based on historical examples. Remember that they're highly motivated, well-taught and exceedingly intelligent people. In the environment they come from, the unintelligent wouldn't live long. They already have a grasp of the basic theories involved and all they have to learn are the numerous details of applications. It's been done many times in real life. Note such cases as the first Israeli Army of Liberation, the skills of the Viet Cong, the various resistance armies of World War II, and the amazing battles of the Anarchists against Franco in the Spanish Civil War," she said.

She continued, "Also bear in mind that Roantree's people spend their time concentrating on learning the new technology to the exclusion of everything else. That lopsided learning is one reason Kirk is able to keep the truth from them for so long."

WHICH SOCIETY IS MOST EFFICIENT?

In "The Weight," Leslie portrays the Anarchist society as being, in its own way, preferable to the more efficiently ordered structure of the Federation. She insisted, "Well, natch, being an Anarchist myself, of course, I side with the Anarchists. What-the-hell, what prompted me to write 'The Weight' in the first place was the annoyingly inaccurate depiction of Anarchists in 'The Sixth Year.' Certainly I think the Federation could jolly-well benefit from Anarchist ideas. I think any society with government could benefit from them!

"As for the Anarchists benefiting from 'the efficiently ordered structure of the Federation,' heh! What makes you think that the Federation's structure is that efficient? Remember Spock's sour comment in 'The Mark of Gideon,' or the pretty picture of the ambassador in 'A Taste of Armageddon' or the fatheaded bureaucrat in 'The Deadly Years' or the legal bind Kirk gets stuck with in 'The Cloud Minders' or. . . shall I go on?"

She did, and continued by saying, "Fact is, as no less than Thomas Paine pointed out in the opening paragraph of COMMON SENSE, governments do not create social order; societies do that of themselves. Governments can only limit and control, from the top down, social orders that already exist. Remember, humans are social animals. Indeed, the social instinct may be the only provable 'instinct' that we possess. Living in orderly groups is one human behavior that is universal, throughout all history and all over the world, common to the entire species. Show me an isolated human and I'll show you a very sick and miserable human. We build societies as readily as spiders build webs, bees build honeycombs, or beavers build dams. We build societies around common proximity (you have to get along with your neighbors) or around common tasks and problems (look at the PTA or the AMA or any labor union) or around something as esoteric as common interests (such as TREK fandom!)."

THE NATURE OF SOCIETY

She explained, "Take a random group of people from backgrounds as wildly different as you can get. Say, a Borneo headhunter, a Mexican housewife, a Korean farmer, a Swedish painter, an American nurse, a French engineer. Put them together in a common situation (desert island, plane crash, Trek convention, hospital ward, kidnapped by a flying saucer, whatever) and within 24 hours they'll have a rudimentary society set up complete with manners, morals and division of labor."

THE ATTRACTION OF FANDOM

Asked what initially attracted her to participating in organized STAR TREK fandom, Leslie stated that there were many reasons. She noted, "For one thing I simply enjoyed being able to talk about dramatic, stylistic and thematic aspects of STAR TREK with people who knew and cared what I was talking about. For another, I liked the general grade of people I ran into in fandom. STAR TREK fans struck me as intelligent, creative, open-minded (if sometimes naive, mostly through lack of experience) and humanely oriented.

"Finally, I discovered that STAR TREK fandom, thanks to the sheer number of 'zines, readers, editors and detailed LOC [letter of comment] writing critics, just happened to be the best school for beginning science fiction writers that I'd ever run into. Do you know how many fan writers have gone on to become pros? I can think of half-a-dozen offhand, and I certainly don't know everybody in fandom. That's not counting artists, editors and costume designers and model-makers, either."

Like anything, fandom has both positive and negative aspects. "Aside from the positive aspects I just mentioned," she said, "I think STAR TREK fandom is also a fine example of the amazing amount of work people can do by themselves, voluntarily, organized by nothing more (or less) than an ideal. Being an anarchist myself, I'm always happy to find such examples.

"The negative aspects are no worse than one could expect to find in any organization: petty politics and personal ego-tripping (more common among clubs than 'zines). Failures of various projects due to lack of experience. Assorted touches of social, religious and political prejudices. Occasional faction fights, and so on. As an old SDS'er [Students for a Democratic Society], I've seen all that before and think that its effect on fandom is rather mild and nothing to worry about."

THE MANY SIDES OF FANDOM

As indicated by some of her comments, Leslie's interests extend far beyond the confines of STAR TREK fandom. In fact, as a member of the Students for a Democratic Society in the '60s, she participated in the notorious demonstrations at the 1968 Democratic National Convention.

She recalled, "Hell, yes! I was in the Chicago Follies of 1968 and in dozens of other anti-war protests, large and small, all during the '60s. I was also in various Northern civil rights demonstrations, all sorts of university reform activities, Vietnam Veterans' protests, drug law protests, police brutality protests—you name it."

In the '70s, besides writing a long, complex STAR TREK novel called THE WEIGHT, Leslie was also one of first fan writers to seriously tackle writing K/S stories, now called "slash" by modern fans, referring to the slash mark in the abbreviation. She explained, "When I got into fandom, K/S was already a much discussed premise around the fan grapevine (I believe Mary Manchester outlined her 'Continuity Theory' a year earlier), but it was still very hush-hush and underground. Having lived in various 'undergrounds' for a good part of my life, I thought this was an idea that deserved to surface. 'Alternative' [by Gerry Downes] hadn't been printed yet, but I did see a copy of Diane Marchant's 'A Fragment Out of Time' in GRUP #3. That convinced me that a K/S story could be printed in a fanzine, so I wrote one (a longish and fairly soft-core story called 'Descensus Averno') and sent it off to GRUP."

ROLLING BACK THE BOUNDARIES

She continued, "The story was accepted and I was told that it would be printed in GRUP #5 or #6, but it took a year for #5 to be published and another two years before #6 came out and my story wasn't in either of them for reasons known only to the gods and the publisher. Meanwhile I'd written 'Shelter' as a triple literary exercise, attempting to: 1) Write a convincing K/S story which could be printed somewhere besides GRUP, 2) Have the precipitating incident be something other than the 'underground' usual cause of pon farr, 3) Describe a love scene only, or at least primarily, in terms of one sense—sound.

"I sent the first version to Connie Faddis, for whose subsequent advice and criticisms I'll always be grateful, then sent the finished version to WARPED SPACE for their promised 'double X-rated' issue #20. WARPED SPACE accepted it and in-between acceptance and publication, (the other story) 'Alternative' was printed."

Since the K/S premise explores the concept of the Kirk/Spock friendship expanding into the realm of expressions of physical love, reactions to it tend to reflect an individual's own personal philosophies on the concept in general rather than to the stories in particular. Leslie explained that this hasn't always been the case.

"I've run across quite a few people who dislike K/S for legitimate reasons," she said. "Connie Faddis, for instance, makes a good case for the unlikelihood of the K/S relationship because sooner or later pon farr would show up, and there's an excellent chance that a human male couldn't survive that. I think she has a good point there.

"The only ceiling limit we know to the violence of pon farr is that Amanda has survived it (happily), and for all we know she could be a remarkably tough lady, physically as well as mentally. Spock would absolutely not involve his beloved Captain in an affair that had a high probability of killing him!"

DIFFERENT STROKES FOR DIFFERENT FOLKS

She continued, "Another legitimate objection is Paula Smith's. She complains that most K/S stories are dull, unconvincing and poorly written. Since Paula is one of the best writers in Trekdom [and one who went pro, with such science fiction stories published as "African Blues" in ISAAC ASIMOV'S SF MAGAZINE] and has written a couple of K/S stories herself, I'd say she has every right to insist on such high literary standards.

"No, it isn't honest objections like these that make me tear off scorching letters. What makes me get intemperate about anti-K/S proponents is all too often encountered blind prejudice about the whole concept. This prejudice usually disguises itself behind the phrase 'out of character,' but what it really means is that 'Our heroes could never do such a dirty-dirty thing because they're not fairyish.' This, of course, assumes that any form of same sex affair is automatically dirty-dirty and that nobody would ever indulge in it except for a true lavender 99% impure stereotype drag queen, complete with lisp, mince and limp wrist. ARRGGHH! Needless to add, this is totally contrary to the observed facts.

"Truth is, under the right circumstances (and feelings) anybody could do it. Kirk's observed skirt-chasing and Spock's observed reticence wouldn't prevent any such thing. Hell, I can tell you in 9 short words how to cause the most macho-masculine posturing skirt-chaser to go to bed with other men, absolutely guaranteed: Give him only male company for about 5 years. Prisons are notorious male/male rape palaces. The incidence of same-sex affairs is the Army's best kept secret, and never mind what happens in the Navy. Repeat: given the right circumstances and feeling, anybody could do it.

"Probably this is what the distinctly prejudiced anti-K/S faction is most afraid of because of the unspoken implication that it could even happen to them. Quel horreur! I weep great crocodile tears for their fears."

THE ANDORIAN CONNECTION

Other short stories Leslie has written in the STAR TREK universe involve the character Thelin, who was created by D.C. Fontana but only appeared briefly, and with no real background, in the animated episode "Yesteryear." These are among her best stories, though, and are titled "Yesteryear, Today and Tomorrow" and "Winterlight." They were written as sequels to tie up loose ends to previous stories, including D.C. Fontana's "Yesteryear."

She recalled she "originally invented my triple-sexed, carnivorous, aggressive versions of Andorians in a scholarly article for SEHLAT'S ROAR #2 as an exercise in alien anthropology. First officer Thelin, who might have had Spock's place on the Enterprise, seemed to be perfectly set up as a tragic hero, and also in a good position to exemplify Andorian society to us outsiders. I think hoc is too good a character to abandon. Besides, hoc's so useful for tying up loose ends of stories that leave me feeling unsatisfied, so I expect to write a lot more stories about huius adventures hereafter." The terms hoc and huius are interchangeable and are used instead of either "him" or "her" because Thelin is something of a hermaphrodite and a specific term of gender would not be applicable.

"As to whether or not Kirk and Spock will figure in Thelin's future," she said, "well, since I've usually written Thelin stories in reaction to other stories, and since most STAR TREK stories (fan and pro) revolve around Kirk and/or Spock, the odds are very good that Thelin will run into them again."

ARTISTIC INFLUENCES

Leslie is a double-threat, both a writer and an artist. She has usually illustrated her own fan fiction.

She said, "I've been drawing ever since I could remember, although I think my writing is better than my artwork, despite all the practice. I've seen and studied the work of so many artists that I don't know which ones to credit as influences. I can only try to list the ones I like, both in Fandom and out, in no particular order: Connie Faddis, Caravaggio, Gayle Feyrer, Norman Rockwell, Marty Seigrist, Winslow Homer, Renoir (Pere), Gilbert Stuart, S. Clay Wilson, Diego Rivera, Pat Stall, Rembrandt, Gordon Carleton, Salvador Dali and Ralph Fowler—to name only a few that I can think of offhand."

Leslie has read a lot of STAR TREK fan fiction, but when asked to list her favorite sub-genres, she finds that a tough question to answer. She replied, "I have a collection of Trekzines which fills up six large bookshelves, and I've found at least one story to like in almost every one of them. I don't think I could begin to put them in order of favorites. It would be easier to list the authors I generally enjoy and I don't think I can recall all of them quickly, either. There's Gayle Feyrer and Paula Smith, of course, and Jane Aumerle/Penny Warren, and Jean Lorrah, and Diane Steiner and Gerry Downes. I would read the blurb on a cereal box if Connie Faddis wrote it. That's the tip of the iceberg."

THE MANY POSSIBILITIES

Fan fiction includes a wide variety of approaches to the subject of STAR TREK. Leslie has her own particular likes and dislikes.

She noted, "What I'd like to see less of in STAR TREK fiction are the dreary old cliché's of shoot-outs with stereotyped bad guys, and love stories with stereotyped good girls. As a general rule I can't abide romances, in both the historical and modern sense. Strangely enough, the only ST love stories I've usually liked have been the K/S ones, probably because the lovers involved are perfect equals, neither of whom can be reduced to the dithering hysterical idiocy required of the girl in most romances.

"Why is it, I wonder," she continued, "that love has become so tightly linked to female stupidity and subservience in our culture? Could it be that that's what this culture uses love for, to brainwash women into keeping their place? If so, would women be obliged to renounce love in order to gain freedom? There could be quite a story in that.

"What I'd like to see STAR TREK fiction do more of is examine alien societies, and with more imagination. The Kraith and Nu Ormenel series have examined the cultures of Vulcans and Klingons, and a few writers have played with Romulan and Andorian society, as I've done. But there's so much more that could be done here. For example, why are Tholians so famously punctual and territorial, and why do they glow like that? Do they live at the temperature of molten iron? What happened to Platonian society after Kirk broke its chief illusion and exposed its decadence? What happened to the society of the Cloud-Minders after the Trogs found that they could sell Zeenite directly to the Federation and cut their former masters out of the trade completely?"

EXPLORING
ALIEN CULTURES

Leslie feels that just looking at aired TREK opens up numerous story possibilities. She asked, "What kind of culture could have produced the Gorn? How do the Melkotians feel about Organians? For that matter, why didn't the Organians just tell Kirk right at the start, 'Thanks for your offer, but we are incredibly powerful super-beings who can take care of ourselves, so bug off and go squabble with the Klingons elsewhere'? I think it's not enough to look at an alien culture and note how different it is. There's much more to be learned (and written about) by asking how did it get this way? STAR TREK has always geared less toward science fiction hardware stories (such as 'The Doomsday Machine' or 'Immunity Syndrome,' good as they were) than toward examinations of alien cultures and what we can learn from them.

"The tremendous appeal of Spock is an indication of this. Perhaps this is also why most Trek-fen who write stories are women. In this culture males are encouraged (pushed) toward the hard sciences and control of the technology, often to the detriment of their own social and psychological awareness, while females are steered into the soft or social sciences, such as anthropology, sociology and psychology, not to mention the arts."

She continued, "Well, for whatever reason, if the main sciences in STAR TREK's science fiction format are social ones, by all means, let's apply them thoroughly. Whatever you're given, use the fullest. At the very least we'd get lots of thwacking good stories out of such a trend. At the most. . . imagine what would happen if a lot of tomorrow's (and today's) social scientists were Trek-fen. Hoo-hah! Think of their influence! We might even get the future that STAR TREK showed us. I can think of far worse tomorrows."

Chapter 10

IS FAN FICTION LEGAL?

This chapter is about one of those largely unasked and rarely speculated upon questions. When it is asked, the assumptions arrived at are usually wrong. Throughout the discussion, it is important to remember that this refers only to fiction and not to commentary or review.

STAR TREK fan-generated fiction has existed since Trek Classic premiered back in 1966. Oddly enough, it didn't start growing and becoming more widespread until after the series was canceled.

The '70s saw a boom in fan fiction which continued into the '80s. While the zines usually printed less than 500 copies, it was still a hotbed of activity, complete with cliques, claques, awards (which had as much to do with whether the editor was well-liked as it did with the quality of the work produced) and in-fighting. Which is to say that fan fiction fandom is just like real life, only scaled down and more intense.

The question sometimes hesitatingly speculated on is how legal is all this STAR TREK fan fiction? There is no question that were these fan fiction stories published in a wide circulation magazine, and available nationwide, they would have to be done with the express permission of Paramount or face legal action. Paramount licenses the rights to STAR TREK fiction and at present Pocket Books are the only ones who can legally publish new STAR TREK novels. D.C. Comics has the license for comic books based on STAR TREK and THE NEXT GENERATION while Malibu has the comic book rights to DEEP SPACE NINE.

Yet the STAR TREK fan fiction continues in an unabated stream. Old 'zines cease publishing and new ones arrive to take their place. The stories which Bantam Books published in the two anthologies called STAR TREK: THE NEW VOYAGES were not only drawn almost exclusively from the pages of fanzines, but they acknowledge it in the book! So it hasn't been a well kept secret.

BY JAMES VAN HISE

THE FAN POINT OF VIEW

Why does STAR TREK fan fiction continue to be published unchallenged? In the late '70s, Paula Smith, the editor of the well-known fanzine MENAGERIE, made the following observation, "Had strict legality been followed by the fans, no one could have used ST characters' names or references in fan fiction; however such strictness was not observed, and in the last ten years, Paramount has never tried to stop the fanzines, which it knew existed for many editors sent in copies. In so doing it ceded rights to the ST characters and their names, I believe, at least for use in fanzines. Paramount does enforce licensing on merchandise, and consequently retains their rights there.

"Therefore I'd say fanfic, published in fanzines, is 99% legal. Paramount never objected to it there, and is not doing so currently. Fiction printed in professional publications, on the other hand, is regulated by Paramount. The question becomes then, what is fan and what is pro? Personally, I'd set the dividing line on the number of copies printed: 10,000, because that's what SFWA (Science Fiction Writers of America) uses to determine professional sale and qualification for membership."

A COTTAGE INDUSTRY

There are holes in that argument, of course. Whether someone makes 100 copies of something which infringes on copyright or a thousand, it's all the same. But since that statement was made in MENAGERIE some 15 years ago, nothing has changed. Fanzines are still published and sold openly at conventions and Paramount has yet to hassle anyone. Paramount probably wouldn't agree they had ceded the rights to the STAR TREK characters by inaction, and unless the publisher has several million dollars with which to challenge them in court, the issue will never be settled.

STAR TREK 'zines are left alone because they are small and in more than 20 years none have ever threatened to become a big business operation. The reduced costs and easy availability of photocopying has put 'zine publishing in the reach of more people, but there are not really any more 'zines being done today than there were 15 years ago; just different ones.

Fans write and publish in order to explore the STAR TREK universe in their own ways. In some cases, the stories published are novels which the author failed to sell to Pocket Books. More often they are just stories which the fans wrote for the sheer enjoyment.

There is another reason fan fiction is allowed to exist. It helps keep STAR TREK alive. In the '70s, fan fiction was one of the only things which kept the memory of STAR TREK active in-between the infrequently published books issued by Bantam.

In fan fiction, the reader doesn't have to hope someone else will do what they want to see. They can do it.

Concepts and approaches forbidden in the professional books can be explored in fan fiction in an endless variety of ways. Spock was killed frequently in fan fiction back in the '70s, but that didn't mean that the fans were any less shocked when Paramount did it.

IS IT LEGAL?

Gene Roddenberry reportedly once insisted that Paramount leave the fanzines alone back in the '70s, and apparently this policy continued until it became the accepted thing to do. Paramount undoubtedly looks upon fan fiction as a harmless excursion engaged in by a relatively small number of people. It's not a big business and it has helped maintain a continued interest in STAR TREK, so why bother them?

Paramount tolerates fan fiction because they want to, not because they have to. But is it legal? Strictly speaking, no. Not even a little bit.

But what about "fair use" of copyrighted material? People have heard the term and they easily misapply it.

Fair use involves quoting from copyrighted material, not using the original characters somebody owns in a completely new fiction. Misunderstanding that can get you into trouble.

In 1991 a fan contacted author Chelsea Quinn Yarbro about using her vampire character Count St. Germaine in a fan fiction story. Yarbro refused to give the fan permission. The fan did it anyway, and Yarbro hired an attorney. Some people felt that Yarbro was swatting a gnat with a sledgehammer, but copyright law is a tricky thing. If Yarbro hadn't taken visible steps to protect her character, then some publisher or film maker could have argued that the character had fallen into the public domain.

THE REAL THREAT

There is another threat facing fanzines which has to do with the fact that they aren't strictly legal. That same ease in getting things photocopied has resulted in the wholesale copying of 'zines by fans. One fan will publish a zine at some expense, including getting covers professionally printed, only to discover that other fans are buying one copy and making multiple photocopies for their friends. If fanzines don't sell enough copies, the editor usually cannot afford to publish the next issue. If a zine is worth making bootleg copies of, why not just pay full price so that you can insure that the next issue will be published? Unfortunately the pirates don't care.

Some fans supplement their income by copying 'zines and selling them at conventions. This has worked particularly well for them by choosing British fanzines so that it would be highly unlikely that an editor would catch them at it. One bootlegger who was caught by a fan editor watched as the editor seized all the bootlegs of her particular 'zine and carried them off. The angry editor would have been more than willing to fight over the incident, but the bootlegger wasn't.

Bootlegging has changed the face of fan fiction because when the 'zines being copied are STAR TREK 'zines or BLAKES 7, then the 'zine editor technically has no copyright protection. She's already using someone else's copyrighted characters without their permission.

The bootleggers take advantage of this. But how many fanzines will survive if it continues? We may currently be witnessing the slow decline of the fan fiction market until very few new 'zines will be produced because the editors/publishers won't be able to afford them.

The future of fan fiction may well be up to all of you reading this page right now. If you like fan fiction, support the editors, not the bootleggers. Don't be a pirate yourself. Fan fiction is a fragile enterprise which can very easily be crippled and fall by the wayside due to thoughtlessness and greed.

This problem is by no means being exaggerated. I've talked to zine editors who used to have no trouble selling 300 copies of the new issue of their 'zine. Now they can barely sell 100 copies, and they know it's because people are copying them for their friends. They've seen it brazenly done at conventions in which 5 fans will approach a table, buy one each of several 'zines and discuss how they can go down the block and make photocopies so that they will all have copies. Multiply that by the dozens of fans who buy 'zines and the problem becomes evident.

IMAGINARY LINES

A K/S NOVEL BY

ALEXIS FEGAN BLACK

SPECIAL SECTION
DIRECTORY OF FANZINES

Appendix

FANZINE DIRECTORY

Fandom is a place so large that it literally encompasses the globe. The following chapter is a comprehensive guide to most of the fanzines published today.

When contacting editors and publishers, please always include a self-addressed stamped envelope in order to receive current information from them. Each listing contains the address of that 'zine and write only to that address to receive information about the 'zine in question.

Abode of Strife
#19—A short story collection featuring dozens of contributors.
#20—A 500 page novel in which a Romulan plot traps Spock in Earth's past.
Bill Hupe
916 Lamb Road
Mason, MI 48854-9554

Accumulated Leave
(R & R Collected)
YEOMAN PRESS
5465 Valles Ave.,
Bronx, NY 10471

Aehallh
Club Newsletter
Lisa Hartjes
3468 Mulcaster Road
Mississauga, ON
L5L 5B3 CANADA

The Agonizer
Klingon info-'zine
Sue Frank
2508 Pine St
Philadelphia, PA 19103

Alexi
K/S-Alexi, the infamous galactic criminal, has finally been hunted down to a possible location. It's up to

Kirk, Spock, and McCoy to find and apprehend him. They start by teaching Spock to play poker. . .!
MKASHEF Enterprises
PO Box 688
Yucca Valley, CA 92286-0688

Alkarin Warlord
NuOrmene (Klingon) universe
POISON PEN PRESS,
627 E. 8th Street,
Brooklyn, NY 11218

Alnitah
#12, #13,. #14 and OMNIBUS 2. Reprints of #1-4
Joyce Cluett
40 Lordsfield Gardens,
Overton, Basingstroke
Hampshire RG25 3EW
England

Alpha Centura Communications.
Club 'zine.
ALPHA CENTURA, INC., SF 3 SUB Box 120, University of New Mexico,
Albuquerque, NM 87131

Alternate Universe Four
VOL I - Written by Virginia Tilley, Shirley Maiewski, Anna Mary Hall, Illustrated by Virginia Tilley. James Kirk is court martialed for an error in judgement and is forced out of Starfleet. While working for a freight line at the edge of the Federation, he is recognized by a member of Lightfleet, an undercover organization dedicated to preserving peace in the Galaxy. Kirk is persuaded to join Lightfleet and has an encounter with the Enterprise and its new captain, Spock.
VOL II - Written by Virginia Tilley, Shirley Maiewski, Anne Mary Hall, Daphne Hamilton. Illustrated by Virginia Tilley. James Kirk, now an agent for Lightfleet, is rescued by the Enterprise and held prisoner by Captain Spock. Kirk escapes by a ruse that McCoy thinks kills him.
VOL III - Written by Virginia Tilley and Anna Mary Hall. Illustrated by Virginia Tilley and Daphane Hamilton. Spock, who has been told by McCoy that Kirk is alive, sets out to find for himself where Kirk has gone and who or what he is involved with. He, too, must make a decision that could affect both his and Kirk's future. This concludes the serial started in VOL. I. Two other stories are included, one relating a Lightfleet mission Kirk and Malon undertake and another that tells of an encounter between aliens from another galaxy and Lightfleet.
Shirley S. Maiewski
481 Main St
Hatfield, MA 01038

Alternaties
Reprints available. Send an SASE for prices. ST/Adult Age Statement required.
Bill Hupe
916 Lamb Road
Mason, MI 48854-9554

And Starry Skies
Ruth Berman
2809 Drew Ave. S.
Minneapolis, MN 55117

Arakenyo
By Fern Marder and Carol Walske.
POISON PEN PRESS
627 E. 8th Street
Brooklyn, NY 11218

Archives
Reprint 'zine.
YEOMAN PRESS
5465 Vallas Ave.,
Bronx, NY 10471.

As I Do Thee
MKASHEF Enterprises
PO Box 688
Yucca Valley, CA 92286-0688

A-to-Zine
A how-to-publish-your-own-fanzine booklet.
Paula Smith
507 Locust St.
Kalamazoo, MI 49007.

Attulac
A novel by David Gomm.
Why have Federation, Klingon and Romulan ships
been disappearing in one area?
Bill Hupe
916 Lamb Road
Mason, MI 48854-9554

Azimuth to Zenith
Scotty is dying, and only an impossible trip into
an unknown, unchartable future can save him.
McCoy is driven so close to the edge that they
might both be lost. Yet only McCoy has the
answers in this time travel and medical story.
Threading through the frantic drama is a
poignant McCoy love story.
Mary Case
21115 Devonshire St #167
Chatsworth, CA 91311

Before the Glory
K/S (adult) Age statement required.
Kathleen Resch
PO Box 1766
Temple City, CA 91780

Best of "Berengaria"
Star Trek fan fiction.
Vicki Rogers
13018 Emiline
Omaha, NE 68137

Better Late Than Never
NEXT GEN fan fiction
Mia Shapiro
3132 Colcester
Brook Lane, Fairfax, VA 22031

Beyond Antares
Australian zine, available from American repre-
sentative
United States: Bill Hupe, 916 Lamb Road,
Mason, MI 48854-9554
Australia: Joanne Keating, 64 4th Street,
Asbury NSW 213 Australia

Beyond Diplomacy
A Novel of Klingon custom, duty, and honor by
Ann K. Schwader.
Wendy Rathbone
PO Box 2556
Yucca Valley, CA 92286-2556

Beyond Shattered Illusions
Star Trek fiction zine.
Vicki Rogers
13108 Emiline
Omaha, NE 68137

Beyond The Farthest Star
Both Classic Trek and Next Generation fanfic.
Bill Hupe
916 Lamb Road
Mason, MI 48854-9554

Bonds of the Matriarch
ST—TNG adult novel
Taerie Bryant
30075 Rose Lane
Wilsonville, OR 97070

The Bewilderbeast
Commentary zine
Dennis Fischer
6820 E. Alondra Blvd.
Paramount, CA 90723

Beyond the Farthest Star
Bill Hupe
916 Lamb Road
Mason, MI 48854-9554

Beyond Diplomacy
A Star Trek fiction zine.
Wendy Rathbone
PO Box 2556
Yucca Valley, CA 92286-2556

Captain's Log
Club zine.
AUSTREK
GPO Box 5206 AA,
Melbourne, VIC 3001
Australia.

Captain's Log
ST, TNG, Dr. Who, Blakes 7, James Bond.
Quarterly.
Beth Wesley
817 N. 9th
Petersburg, IL 62675

Castaways
ST novel
Vicki Rogers
13018 Emiline
Omaha, NE 68137

Charisma
A Star Trek fiction zine.
Wendy Rathbone
PO Box 2556
Yucca Valley, CA 92286-2556

Chosen Brother
ST novel
Sheila Clark
6 Craigmill Cottages
Strathmartine by Dundee
DD3 OPH
Scotland

"City on the Edge of Whatever"
Humorous coloring book.
T'KHUTIAN PRESS,
200 E. Thomas
Lansing, MI 48909

The Clipper Trade Ship
Multi-media zine; includes ads
Jim & Melody Rondeau
1853 Fallbrook Ave.
San Jose, CA 91530

Collection of Dreams
ST adult
Pon Farr Press
PO Box 2556
Yucca Valley, CA 92286

Coming Of Age
ST: TNG fanfic
Starlite Press
PO Box 2455
Danville, CA 94526

Comlink
The Letterzine of Media Opinion. This quarterly,
double-columned, reduced, 20 page letterzine
features letters of comment from our readers,
occasional feature articles and reader classified
ads (free with any current subscription).
Allyson M.W. Dyar
PSC 1013, Box 73
APO AE, 09725-0073

The Complete Faulwell
Written by Paula Block.
T'KHUTIAN PRESS
200 E Thomas
Lansing, MI 48906

Complete "Dirty Nelly"
By Roberta Rogow.
Bill Hupe
916 Lamb Road
Mason, MI 48854-9554

Complete Kershu Fighter
By Devra Langsam
Marking my 20th anniversery as a fan publisher,
I'm issuing this collection of my stories of a
Terran practitioner of a Klingon martial art.
Includes A.W.O.L., a new story by Langsam and
Crites.
Poison Pen Press
627 E 8th St.
Brooklyn, NY 11218

Continum
ST novel
Lois Welling
1518 Winston Dr.
Champaign, IL 61820

Contrast
Spotlight on Leonard Nimoy. Stories about the
characters he has played.
Carol Davies
77 The Ridings
Ealing London
W5 3DP England

Cosmic Diversities
ST, sf publication of USS Aurora Vulcanus.
Barbara & Charlie Brown
18531 Dearborn St. #3
Northridge, CA 91324

Counterpoint
Adult ST zine
Marian Flanders
3510 La Habra Way
Sacramento, CA 95864

A Crucible for Courage
A Trilogy by J. Richard Laredo, illustrated by
Christine Meyers. It is the compelling story of
Kirk's encounter with a doomsday machine, an
alien named Kilroy, a Klingon named Koloth, a girl
that appears to be almost angelic in appearance
and power, and a thing which calls itself Satan.
178 pages.
Bill Hupe
916 Lamb Road
Mason, MI 48854-9554

Data Entries
A Brent Spiner Newsletter inspired by ST: TNG.
Jim and Melody Rondeau
1853 Fallbrook Ave
San Jose, CA 95130

The Daystrom Project
The exciting novel by Rick Endres set after ST:
TMP. The Klingons have kidnapped Dr. Daystrom.
Their goal: To construct a multitronic computer
with engrams of a Klingon imprinted upon it
which they could use to conquer the galaxy. 174
pages.
Bill Hupe
916 Lamb Road
Mason, MI 48854-9554

DEFOREST KELLEY COMPENDIUM
Non-fiction
Laura Jones Guyer
7959 W. Portland Ave
Littleton, CO 80123

Displaced
ST novel
Lois Welling
1518 Winston Dr.
Champaign, IL 61820

The Disruptor
Club zine
Kag/Kanada
John Gannon
3962 Dundonald Dr.
Petawawa, ON
K8H 2W2 Canada

Dreadnought Explorations (Collected)
Set at the end of the original 5-year mission, Kirk, Spock, McCoy and the rest of the crew take a new mission aboard a new starship: USS Federation, the only dreadnought constructed by Starfleet. Together they face a menace as it advances through Romulan and Klingon territories. 396 pages. $25.00
Randall Landers
3211 Saddleleaf Dr.
Albany, GA 31707-2952

Dr. McCoy's Medical Log
Various issues. A Dr. McCoy fan fiction zine.
Ruth Ann Hepner
4700 Smith St.
Harrisburg, PA 17109

Duty And Honor
Club zine for Denise Crosby Information Society. On Denise Crosby and Romulans.
Laura Schoeffel
306 Walthery Ave.
Ridgewood, NJ 07450

Echerni: The Lightfleet Letters
Story told in letter form concerning a crises that strikes Lightfleet characters first met in the Alternate Universe Four series. While no mention is made of ST characters, readers will learn more about Lightfleet, Klingons, Federation, etc. Contains appendices of the Velonian language and history. Written by Virginia Tilley, Anna Mary Hall and Daphne Hamilton. Illustrated by Virginia Tilley.
Shirley Maiewski
481 Main St.
Hatfield, MA 01038

Eclipse
A novel by Wendy Rathbone. Captain Kirk must face his past or lose command of the Enterprise because of recurring blackouts which threaten his ability to command.
Wendy Rathbone
PO Box 2556
Yucca Valley, CA 92286-2556

Elysia
Star Trek fan fiction. Various issues.
Bill Hupe
916 Lamb Road
Mason, MI 48854-9554

Enterprise Incidents
The Star Trek 'zine of the '70s and '80s! Edited by James Van Hise. Largely non-fiction. No longer being published but misc. back issues still in stock. Features extensive articles and interviews dealing with the world of Star Trek, both yesterday and today. Issues 6-8 have fan fiction. Various back issues available from:
James Van Hise
PO Box 2546
Yucca Valley, CA 92286-2546

Enterprise Incidents
Star Trek genzine
Sheila Clark, Scotpress
6 Craigmill Cottages
Strathmartine by Dundee
DD3 OPH Scotland

The Enterprise Mission Review
Star Trek short stories.
Bill Hupe
916 Lamb Road
Mason, MI 48854-9554

Epilogue
ST novel
Empire Books
PO Box 625
Muray, KY 42071-0625

The Exhibit
Star Trek novel
Keith Jackson
The Upper Mount
Glebe Lane, Knottingly
West Yorkshire
WF11 BET England

Explorations
A compilation of Carol Davis' Next Generation
fiction.
The Fandom Press
Tim Perdue
412 Second Avenue South
Humboldt, IA 50548

Fan's "Little Golden Guide" to Throwing
Your Own Con
STW Booklet on convention-giving by Lori
Chapek.
T'KHUTIAN PRESS
200 E. Thomas St.
E. Lansing, MI 48906

Fantasy
General Star Trek zine.
Bonnie Guyan
323 Fordhook Ave
Johnstown, PA 15904.

Filkindex
Non-fiction filksong book
Robert Rogow
PO Box 1124
Fairlawn, NJ 07410

First Light
ST—TNG & multi-media zine
Elisa Tobler
8782 Allison Dr., Unit E
Westminster, CO 80005

FOLN
Newsletter
Laura Jones Guyer
PO Box 620503
Littleton, CO 80123

Free Fall One
A Star Trek anthology
Peg Kennedy & Bill Hupe
916 Lamb Road
Mason, MI 48854

From One Generation to the Next
ST novel
Judith Brandy
1326 Walnut Street
Philadelphia, PA 19105

Full Moon Rising
ST novel
Yeoman Press
5465 Valles Ave
Bronx, NY 10471

Future Tense Affair
Star Trek/Man From UNCLE novel
Jim & Melody Rondeau
1853 Fallbrook Ave
San Jose, CA 95130

ONE BLADE, ONE BLOOD

ANN K. SCHWADER

FANTASIA no. 2

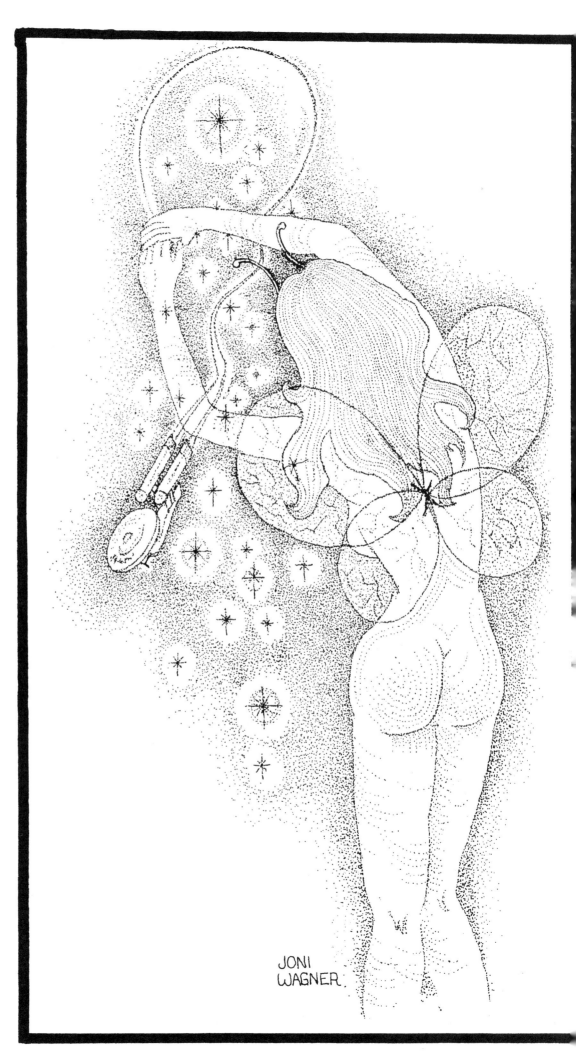

JONI
WAGNER.

Galactic Discourse
Characters interaction genzine.
Laurie Huff
29881 Green Ct.
Menifee, CA 92584.

Galaxy Class
Fanzine based on STAR TREK: THE NEXT GENERA-
TION. Fiction and nonfiction.
Several issues available.
Christopher Laird Simmons
P.O. Box 700-822
Redondo Beach, CA 90277

Garden Spot
Multi-media zine.
Bill Hupe
916 Lamb Road
Mason, MI 48854-9554

A Gathering Of Blaque
Includes the never-before printed stories "And
Everyone In Their Time" (a sequel to "A Time For
Everyone", originally printed "Twin Destiny
1983", reprinted here) and "Love and Logic".
Plus the previously printed "A Strange and
Beautiful Flower" ("Progressions 1985"). Age
statement required.
MKASHEF Enterprises
PO Box 688
Yucca Valley, CA 92286-0688

Gateways: Past, Future, Sideways
SF, fantasy literary magazine.
Adrienne Reynolds
1206 Konrad Pl.
Philadelphia, PA 19116

Gemini Lynx
by Mary Schmidt.
T'KHUTIAN PRESS
200 E. Thomas St.
Lansing, MI 48906

General Quarters
ST publication.
USS Alliance
PO Box 25277
W. Los Angeles, CA 90025

Generation Gap
Stories, poems and artwork based on the original
and the Next Generation
STAR TREK series.
Page's Press
2611 Silverside Road
Wilmington, DE 19810

The Genesis Aftermath
Alternate-universe ST III novel by Joan Verba.
Bill Hupe
916 Lamb Road
Mason, MI 48854-9554

Gigawats
ST: TNG genzine
Page Lewis
2611 Silverside Road
Wilmington, DE 19810

Glory Project
Kirk and Spock must Team up with Romulans,
Klingons and mystics to save their galaxy from
oblivion but not before universal laws are turned
inside out, rendering their ship powerless. At the
mercy of a scientist/mystic, they must listen to
her strange advice, no matter how illogical, in
order to survive.
Wendy Rathbone
PO Box 2556
Yucca Valley, CA 92286-2556

Grip
Star Trek & multi-media genzine.
Roberta Rogow
P.O. Box 1124
FairLawn, NJ 07410.

Grup
Reprints of the classic '70s adult Star Trek zine.
Bill Hupe
916 Lamb Road
Mason, MI 48854-9554

Hailing Frequencies
Next Generation genzine
Natasha Mohr
It Never Happened Press
PO Box 8247
Gainesville, FL 32605

Hailing Frequencies Open
Newsletter of Starfleet Idaho
John Pettigrew
100 Village Lane
Boise, ID 83702

A Handful of Snowflakes.
Short ST stories by M.O. Barnes.
Caro Hedge
6109 Road HH 7
Lamar, Co 81052.

Hellguard Social Register
Club newsletter focusing on Saavik and Romulans.
HELLGUARD SOCIAL REGISTER,
c/o Bill Hupe
916 Lamb Road
Mason, MI 48854-9554

The Hive
A Next Generation story by Roberta Denono. Riker, Data and Worf find themselves trapped on a dangerous planet ruled by beautiful women. On the Enterprise, Captain Picard faces a mysterious, deadly illness that strikes down every woman an board including Dr. Beverly Crusher. 40 pages. Cover and illos by Thena MacArther.

ANKH PRESS
P.O. Box 4020
Alameda CA 94501

Holonotes
ST: TNG zine.
M. Lark Underwood
2470 University Ave
Dubuque, IA 52001

Ice Fire
Wendy Rathbone
PO Box 2556
Yucca Valley, CA 92286-2556

IDIC
ST: TNG zine
Michael Ruff
110 Cedargrove
Rochester, NY 14617

Idylls
#2 - A relationship-oriented 'zine (no K/S) with R-rated material. Features stories by Linda Baker and Ann Zewen. 60 pages.
#1 - The human-interest/romance publication which includes drama hurt-comfort, romance, and the like. Printed in digest format. 36 pages.
Bill Hupe
916 Lamb Road
Mason, MI 48854-9554
I

mzadi: The Marina Sirtis Newsletter
Official Marina Sirtis newsletter. Provides readers with info on the actress, on the character of Deanna Troi, on other ST: TNG cast members and their fictional counterparts. It also includes classic Trek info, convention reports, ST: TNG book reviews and more, including synopsis of episodes of ST: TNG.
William S. McCullars
3084 Chastain Park Ct.
Atlanta, GA 30342

In A Different Reality
Genzine.
Bill Hupe
916 Lamb Road
Mason, MI 48854-9554

In a Different Reality
Authorized reprints of classic Trek 'zine.
Bill Hupe
916 Lamb Road
Mason, MI 48854-9554

In The Wilderness
Special 'zine with substantial stories, original plots, mainly established relationships. Work by: Stallings & Ferris, Rivers, Resch, Gates, Fine, Post, Stuart, Daniels, Kobriń, Rowes. Art by Sibbert and A.H.. Winner of five Surak awards. K/S age statement.
Rosemary Wild
"CWM Croesor" Struckton
Fordingbridge, Hants,
SP6 2HG England

Innomina
Walter Koenig International actor's club annual newsletter available to members only.
WALTER KOENIG INTERNATIONAL
c/o Carolyn Atkinson and Tish A. Kuntz
PO Box 15546
N. Hollywood, CA 91615-5546

Interlude
A novel by Celeste Sefraned, Illustrated by Christine Meyers. A romance for Spock was just what the doctor had ordered . . . Literally! 114 Pages.
Bill Hupe
916 Lamb Road
Mason, MI 48854-9554

Interphase
Sf & fantasy newsletter. Publication of STAR San Diego.
Jefferson Swycaffer
PO Box 15373
San Diego, CA 92175

Jean Lorrah's Sarek Collection
Short stories by Lorrah.
EMPIRE BOOKS
Box 625
Murray, KY 42091.

Katra
Star Trek Genzine
Lana Brown
P.O. Box 30-905
Lower Hutt,
New Zealand

Kefrendar
An Uhura novel. Uhura has made a decision to take leave from Starfleet to serve on board another race's starship. It's a decision which may cost her her friend, career, and possibly life, as she ventures far beyond the borders of the Romulan Empire into territories never before seen by Federation Humans.
Bill Hupe
916 Lamb Road
Mason, MI 48854-9554

Khan Reports
Artwork by: Christine Myers, Sylvia Liske and Anja Gruber. Writers are: John Mills, Sylvia Liske and Mimi English, plus many, many more. Each Khan reports is a limited quantity, numbered inside the first page. This is a family oriented fanzine.
Page Lewis
2611 Silverside Road
Wilmington, DE 19810

Killing Time
By Della Van Hise. The original manuscript as it was first sent to Pocketbooks. Limited edition, signed by the author. $25 US; $27 Canada; $32 Air Europe; $37 Air Pacific
Pon Farr Press
PO Box 2556
Yucca Valley, CA 92286

Klindex
Klingon Index, non-fiction.
Sue Frank
2508 Pine St.
Philadelphia, PA 19103

Kirk
Shatner yearbook by Sonni Cooper.
Sonni Cooper
76 Santa Ana Ave.
Long Beach, CA 90803

Kraith Collected
Short Stories.
Bill Hupe
916 Lamb Road
Mason, MI 48854-9554

Laff Trek
#2 - THE WRATH OF DIJON — Contributors so far include Jan, Williams, Ambassador, Apryl Showyrs and more. Send us your tricks and treats just as long as they tickle the funny bone.
#1 - THE HUMOR ADVENTURE BEGINS — Features 120 pages of ST humor (predominantly ST4), including "Star Trek IV: The Wrath of the Voyage Home"; a Pern/ST crossover, poetry, filks, cartoons and lots more fiction, Contributors include Howard, Summers, Carleton, Williams, Cargill, Erickson, Cloud and 25 others!
Bill Hupe
916 Lamb Road
Mason, MI 48854-9554

Legacy
A 188 page adult Star Trek novel-length 'zine by Lynda L. Roper. Kirk and Spock investigate the planet Meer where women dominate and males are controlled and protected.
Lynda K. Roper
PO Box 34922
Richmond, VA 23234

Legends from the Oracle
Star Trek genzine
Shelley Kelsheimer
948 S. 5th Street
Clinton, IN 4784

Leonard Nimoy Compendium
Non-fiction
Jim & Melody Rondeau
1853 Fallbrook Ave
San Jose, CA 95130

Living In Spite Of Logic
A full length novel sequel to "Mirror, Mirror." In the full 8 1/2 x 11 format, 130 pages. Written by Ellen O'Neil. Price is $16.00
Ellen O'Neil
135 Hamilton Park
Lexington, Kentucky 40504

Locus
Science Fiction and Fantasy in literature and media. Convention listings and reports. Books/magazines reviewed. Published monthly. An important guide to the world of Science Fiction.
Locus Publications
P.O. Box 13305
Oakland, CA 94661

Logbook Of The Galactic Engineers Concordance
Star Trek and SF technology.
Roy Firestone
11400 Abby Lane SE
Clackamas, OR 97015

Lonestar Trek
ST: TNG genzine
Laurie Haynes
PO Box 189
DeRidder, LA 70634

Long and Winding Road
K/S Star Trek novel
Wendy Rathbone
PO Box 2556
Yucca Valley, CA 92286-2556

Lost
A complete set of this series to date by editor Ruth Ann Hepner. A series of 10 stories set to a timewarp theme where Dr. McCoy, Kirk, and Spock find themselves in a civil war period that is difficult to get out of because of their own mistrust for each other. Full series sent to you in a box. How can you not take this opportunity? Only a few left.
DR. MCCOY'S MEDICAL LOG
c/o Ruth Ann Hepner
4700 Smith St.
Harrisberg, PA 17109.

Lyret Dedreen
Club newsletter
Susan Eisenhour
210 W. Jackson
Charleston, IL 61920

Mark of Cain
A novel by Pam Baddely. A story where there has been an explosion in a nuclear plant on a colony planet. Mostly about the colonists. Not many left.
Bill Hupe
916 Lamb Road
Mason, MI 48854-9554

Masiform D
Genzine, both current and back issues.
POISON PEN PRESS
627 E. 8th St.
Brooklyn NY 11218

A Matter of Honor
A collection of ST: TNG stories and poetry.
Peg Kennedy & Bill Hupe
916 Lamb Road
Mason, MI 48854

McCoy—Examined!
Genzine
Bill Hupe
916 Lamb Road
Mason, MI 48854-9554

McCoy's Toy
Multi-media 'zine
Bonnie Guyan
323 Fordhook Ave
Johnstown, PA 15904

Medtrek Convention Fanzine
Multi-media Australian Convention zine
Bill Hupe
916 Lamb Road
Mason, MI 48854-9554

Menagerie
Star Trek Genzine.
Paula Smith
507 Locust St.
Kalamazoo, MI 49007

Minara Nova
Zine honoring EMPATH.
Ruth Berman
2809 Drew Ave. South
Minneapolis, MN 55416

Mind Meld
#IV - A general ST 'zine focusing on the Kirk-Spock-McCoy friendship. Stories and poetry by Cummins, English, Fern, Fisher, LaCrois, Martin, Morris, Resch, Rottler & Syck & Ridener, Sylvester, Wetson, C. Zier, and S. Zier. Art by Decker, Forsell, Godwin, Graves, Hedge, Kunz, Mills, Myers, Soto, Stacy-MacDonald, Summers, Veltkamp, and Caren Parnes and Steve Saunders. Appr. 220 pages. Offset, perfect bound. Flyer available.
#I - Reprint of first issue, includes work by Fine, Werson, Cross, Stallings, Barr, Bounds, Gilbert, LaCroix, Ridener and Syck, Volker, Decker, Forsell, Hedge, Kunz, Lovett, Myers, Parnes and more. Reprint will be in spiral bound and offset. Approx. 224 pgs.
Sandy Zier
6656 Aspern Dr.
Elkridge, MD 21227

Mindset
ST: TNG 'zine
Ankh Press
PO Box 4020
Alameda, CA 94501

The Monthly (Zine Listing)
Newsletter
Lynda Roper
PO Box 34922
Richmond, VA 23234

More Missions, More Myths
Below are samples of past issues. Many more issues are available. Star Trek genzine.

#8 - Stories by Body, Pierce, Santos, Schutter, Schnirch, Trimble and more. Plus lots of poetry and artwork. Appr. 110 pages. SASE for flyer.
#7 - Stories by Santos, Pierce, Cummins and more. Artwork by Howard, Veltkamp, Dragon and more.
#6 - In a sequel to The Voyage Home, McCoy becomes lost on a hostile world and Kirk and Spock have little hope of ever finding him alive, plus five more exciting stories by these authors: Cupp, Pierce, Santos, Schnirch, and Wray. Excellent artwork by Dragon, Howard, Veltkamp, Zoost and more! 100 pages, reduced type, available now.
#5 - Kirk goes into pon farr! Sulu falls in love with a mysterious woman. Spock is stranded an a primitive planet Exciting poetry and art. 108 pages, reduced, comb, bound.
#4 - Stranded in time, Kirk and Spock again meet Captain Christopher, only to learn of the tragic changes his life has taken since their first meeting. Many more stories, poems, art. 132 pages, reduced, comb bound.
#1-3 - Adventure and characterization stories with the feel of the old series. Wide variety of art and poetry. Detailed flyers available, send SASE. Each copy is 90 (+-) pages, reduced, comb bound.
Wendy Rathbone
PO Box 2556
Yucca Valley, CA 92286-2556

The Mouth of Fear
Club newsletter, 23rd Klingon Assault Fleet
T. Woolman
1454 Woodview Rd.
Yardley, PA 19067-5776

My Soul To Sleep
By Della Van Hise. A Star Trek novel in manuscript form. Signed by the author. $25 US; $27 Canada; $32 Air Europe; $37 Air Pacific.
Pon Farr Press
PO Box 2556
Yucca Valley, CA 92286-2556

MORE MISSIONS, MORE MYTHS

MORE MISSIONS MORE MYTHS

16

The Neofan's Guide To Star Trek Fandom
A useful guide for the new fan; includes information about clubs, conventions, fanzines. $1.00.
Joan Verba
PO Box 1363
Minnetonka, MN 55345

Newsletter at the End of of the Universe
Club newsletter on ST and TNG.
BOSTON STAR TREK ASSN.
P.O. Box 1108
Boston, MA 02103.

Niatrek/Sci-Fi Bulletin Board
A Star Trek, Doctor Who, science fiction fantasy and space newsletter with six objectives: 1) To provide information on conventions, special events and contests. 2) To provide information on clubs, organizations and services. 3) To provide information on merchandise for sale and/or trade. 4) To provide information on stores and mail order outlets. 5) To Provide information on books, magazines, fanzines and newsletters. And 6) to provide any other information which may be of interest to the reader. Those wishing single copy rates, subscription rates and back issue rates should send a self-addressed stamped envelope (SASE) or international reply coupon (IRC) to:
NIATREK/SCI-FI BULLETIN BOARD
30-"E" Packard Court
Niagara Falls, New York 14301

Night of the Twin Moons
Famous fan fiction novel about Sarek and Amanda
Empire Books
PO Box 625
Murray, KY 42071-0625

No Peaceful Roads Lead Home
By Susan Crites, art by Reitz. Sequel to "Games of Love & Duty." When does "happily ever after" start? Can a Klingon arms master and a Terran doctor, thrown together by circumstances, make a marriage work? 260 pages.
POISON PEN PRESS
627 E. 8th St.
Brooklyn, NY 11218

Nova Trek
All new "classic" Trek stories. Perfect bound. 300 pages.
Helena Seabright
PO Box 5026
Evanston, IL 60204

Nu Ormenel Collected
Klingons universe, by Fern Marderm Carol Walske.
POISON PEN PRESS
627 E. 8th St
Brooklyn, NY 11218

Off The Wall
K/S Star Trek zine
Jean Hinson
7830 DePalma St.
Downey, CA 90241

One Night Stand
Wendy Rathbone
PO Box 2556
Yucca Valley, CA 92286-2556

One Small Bite for Man
ST: TNG
S.L. Schneider
19043 SE Caruthers
Portland, OR 97233

One Way Mirror
By Barbara Wenk - humor.
Poison Pen Press
627 E. 8th St.
Brooklyn, NY 11218

Ongoing Voyages
Classic Trek, films, TNG. Published annually.
1117 N. Randolph St. #403
Arlington, VA 22201

Orion Incident
Many issues available. For example:
#25 - Features "The Day They All Came Home" -
a special novella set after ST III and a prior to ST
IV about the crew's flight to Vulcan; "Alis Volat
Propriis" - after the tragedy of Serenidad,
Admiral James T. Kirk, now assistant dean at
Starfleet Training Command, learns to deal with
a young cadet who reminds him of himself;
"Vanguard," and more. Illustrations by Hawkins,
Kyle, Summers and Williams. Articles by Landers.
Reviews by Brady. Perfect-bound, wrap-around
cover. 110 pages.
#24 - Features the exciting conclusion to
"Serecidad: The Costs fo Freedom" by Rick
Endres; "Ad Astra Per Aspera" - a Sulu Stry;
"Parts is Parts" - A humorous Scotty story; and
an exclusive interview with David Gerrold. Does
contain some violence, rough language, adult sit-
uations and nudity, but no age statement is
required. 200 pages.
#23 - Features the ST comic strip "Star Trip III:
The Search for Spock" by Summers; plus
"Shadows of Tomorrow" by Santos; "The 'I Win'
Scenario" by Petersion; by Endres, plus more.
Art by Endres, Kilmer and Summers. Cover by
Endres. 136 pages.
#22 - (Formerly Stardate) Features fiction from
Mary Cress and Chris Hamann, Steven K. Dixon
("Runner"), Rick Endres ("Screnidad: The Cost
of Freedom II") Linda Goodman ("The
Wounding"). This is a solid action-adventure
issue featuring ST fiction set during the series
and some after ST III. 86 pages.

Bill Hupe
916 Lamb Road
Mason, MI 48854-9554

Our Favorite Things
Multi-media genzine.
Elan Press
P.O. Box 615
Macedon NY 14502-0615

Perchance to Dream
TNG zine.
Ankh Press
PO Box 4020
Alameda, CA 94501

Perfect Object
Novel by Mindy Glazer.
Yeoman Press
5465 Valles Ave
Bronx, NY 10471

The Picardian
TNG newsletter
Marilyn Wilkerson
829 SE Riverside Dr.
Evansville, IN 47713

The Pillage Voice
Next Generation Club Newsletter
Lewis Murphy
1367 Orchard Ave
Winter Park, FL 32789

Plak Tow
ST genzine
Bonnie Guyan
323 Fordhook Ave.
Johnstown, PA 15904

Precessional
Adventure/character relationship novel
Laurie Huff
29881 Greens Ct.
Menifee, CA 92584

Protocols
Information booklet for new fanzine readers.
$2.75 per copy.
Judy Segal
PO Box 414
Pawling, NY 12564

Queen's Herald
Club newsletter.
QUEEN TO QUEEN'S THREE
P.O. Box 87331
Chicago, IL 60680.

Random Encounters
Multi-media zine.
Lynn Tucker
5809 Robin Lane
Las Vegas, NV 89108-4775

Ready And Will-ing
Jonathan Frakes zine, published by Friends, Fans
& Followers of Jonathan Frakes
Marianne Morici
Suite#214
145A Danbury Road
New Milford, CT 06776

Rec-Room Rhymes
THE TAPES: You've read the lyrics, now hear the
tunes! #1 is Star Trek Filk; #2 covers every-
thing else!
Roberta Rogow
P.O. Box 1124
Fair Lawn, NJ 07410.

The Rekindling
ST novel
Jim & Melody Rondeau
1853 Fallbrook Ave
San Jose, CA 95130

Rendezvous, and Renegades
Two ST novels.
Mary Case
2115 Devonshire St. #167
Chatsworth, CA 91311

Revenge of the Vulcan Kartune Book
Genzine
H. Roll
2419 Greensburg Pike
Pittsburg, PA 15221

Revenge of the Wind Rider
Ankh Press
P.O. Box 4020
Alameda, CA 94501

Ring of Deceit
ST novel
Empire Books
PO Box 625
Murray, KY 42071-0625

A Russian Inwention/Security Check
The only fanzine devoted entirely to the life and
times of ST's Pavel Chekov. All issues are beauti-
fully illustrated and over 100 pages.
C. Atkinson/T. Kuntz
PO Box 15546
North Hollywood, CA 91615-5546

1701-D
Newsletter
Natasha Mohr
It Never Happened Press
PO Box 8247
Gainesville, FL 32605

Science Fiction Chronicle
Science Fiction news magazine for both fans and
professionals. Published monthly.
Science Fiction Chronicle
P.O. Box 2730
Brooklyn, New York 11202-0056

Sensor Readings 1
This 'zine features articles on the warp factor
cubed theory (by Tim Farley), shuttle craft land-
ing approach methods (by Steven K. Dixon), the
electronic printing methods available to fanzine
editors today (by Randall Landers, a former
Kinko's manager). Also, a spoof of "Wolf in the
Fold" by by Kiel Stuart, and an interview with
Robert Bloch and David Gerrold. 53 pages.
Bill Hupe
916 Lamb Road
Mason, MI 48854-9554

Ship's Log
Star Trek genzine
Lee S. Pennell
227 Clydesdale Ln.
Mableton, GA 30059.

Ship's Log Supplemental
ST: TNG zine.
Tim Perdue
Box 285
Swea City, IA 50590-0285

Ship's Log, USS Defiance
Club newsletter.
STARFLEET, USS DEFIANCE, NCC 1717
c/o Janis Moore
P.O. Box 188993
Sacramento, CA 95818

Sing A Song
Filk song book
Roberta Rogow
PO Box 1124
Fair Lawn, NJ 07410

Sojourns
Winner of 1988 Surak Award. K/S novel by Jean
Hinson. An adventure of discovery never before
fully explored; a new perspective on the K/S
relationship. 300 pgs. Age statement required.
Jean Hinson
7830 DePalma St
Downey, CA 90241

Solar Archives
Club 'zine,
SOLAR ARCHIVES
c/o Luther Yee
P.O. Box 2207
Daly City, CA 94017.

The Sound Of Rain
Adult ST novel
Wendy Rathbone
PO Box 2556
Yucca Valley, CA 92286-2556

Spinner of Nightmares
A novel by Pam Braddeley - sequel to her earlier
novel Weaver of Dreams (now unfortunately
O/P). Who are the hostile aliens on Sigma
Orionsis IV?
Peg Kennedy & Bill Hupe
916 Lamb Road
Mason, MI 48854

Spock
Club 'zine.
AUSTREK
P.O. Box 5206 AA
Melbourne, VIC 3001
Australia.

Spockanalia
Reprints of the FIRST Trek zine.
POISON PEN PRESS
627 E. 8th St.
Brooklyn, NY 11218.

Squired Again
Trelane, The Squire of Gothos, is back again. All Grown up and spoiling for a rematch. Is the Enterprise up to dealing with a grown up Trelane? And now he has a yen for Uhura!
Mary Case
21115 Devonshire St #167
Chatsworth, CA 91311

STCOGR News and Views
Club Newsletter.
Star Trek Club of Grand Rapids
PO Box 8883
Kentwood, MI 49518-8883

Starfleet Communique
Publications of the club Starfleet. (12-16 pages offset)
Starfleet Communique
PO Box 430
Burnsville, NC 28714

ST: TNG The Complete Encyclopedia
Peg Kennedy & Bill Hupe
916 Lamb Road
Mason, MI 48854

Star Trek Credits
The complete credit listing from the series, compiled by Janey Quarton. A very useful reference manual.
Peg Kennedy & Bill Hupe
916 Lamb Road
Mason, MI 48854

Star Trek Songbook
Ruth Berman
2809 Drew Ave. South
Minneapolis, MN 55416

Star Trek Welcommittee
Newsletter. Judy Segal, P.O. Box 414, Pawling, N.Y. 12564 - An up to date listing of current clubs (national and international), fanzines and related information. Send $3.00 for current Directory of STAR TREK organizations.

Star Trip 1
This is the third printing of the collection of "Star Trip" cartoons from Stardate 3-19, featuring "Star Trip: The Plotless Cartoon," "Star Trip: The Wrath of Dhon." 58 pages.
Bill Hupe
916 Lamb Road
Mason, MI 48854-9554

Starbound: Nichelle/Nyota
A new all-Uhura 'zine by Friends of Nichelle Nichols, her official fan club. Published by Black Coffee Press, edited by Florence Butler. Orginal stories, poems, art, plus one reprint from Destiny's Children I. Cover by Chuck Frazier. Offset appr. 80 pages. G-PG rated.
Friends of Nichelle Nichols
PO Box 1051
Silver Spring, MD 20910

Stardate
Authorized reprints of the fanzine STARDATE.
Bill Hupe
916 Lamb Road
Mason, MI 48854-9554

Starlines 1
A collection af Star Trek stories, STARLINES 1: A MIDSUMMER'S NIGHT ZINE features a Marie Willams cover. Contents include a humorous piece by Williams, Sorenson & Czetli; a Who/ST crossover, and more stories by Marshall and Sorenson, Artists include Willams, Sorenson, Emelander and Haley. Edited by Amie Herick. 85 pages.
Bil Hupe
6273 Balfour
Lansing, MI 48911

Steady As She Goes
An ST: TNG anthology
Peg Kennedy & Bill Hupe
916 Lamb Road
Mason, MI 48854

Stellar Gas
Genzine.
#2 A THOUSAND WINGED UNICORNS Xerox.
$10 US and Canada; $12 Air Europe; $14 Air
Pacific.
#1 Two short Novellas. LOST IN THOUGHT and
THE GIFT. $8 US; $8.50 Canada; $12 Air Europe;
$14 Air Pacific.
Pon Farr Press
PO Box 2556
Yucca Valley, CA 92286-2556

Syndazine
Multi-media fanzine.
T'KHUTIAN PRESS
5132 Jo-Don Dr.
E. Lansing, MI 48823.

T-Negative
Reprints only.
Ruth Berman
2809 Drew Ave.
Minneapolis, MN 55416

The Third Verdict
A Scott adventure novel.
Bev Zuk
2 South 041 Lloyd
Lombard, IL 60148

T'hy'la
K/S zine.
Kathy Resch
PO Box 1766
Temple City, CA 91780

Time and Time Again
ST: TNG 'zine.
Michael Ruff
110 Cedargrove
Rochester, NY 14617

Timeshift
With his crew, Kirk is summoned to Earth's 27th
Century, to a Federation wracked by an extra-
galactic menace. To save the galaxy, Kirk undertakes a bizarre journey while Spock gains forbidden knowledge which presages surprising events
in his life. McCoy glimpses a love that can never
be, and other officers are caught up in the social
and technological changes of their own distant
future. 72 pages, no interior art.
BLACK COFFEE PRESS
c/o Florence Butler
8030 14 St. NW
Washington, DC 20012.

To Boldly Go
Adult ST: TNG 'zine.
Starlite Press
PO Box 2455
Dabville, CA 94526

Too Near to Tomorrow
Star Trek fan fiction zine.
Ruth Ann Hepner
4700 Smith St.
Harrisburg, PA 17109

Touchstone
Star Trek novel.
Ankh Press
PO Box 4020
Alameda, CA 94501

Transition
Star Trek novel.
Lois Welling
1518 Winston Dr.
Champaign, IL 61820

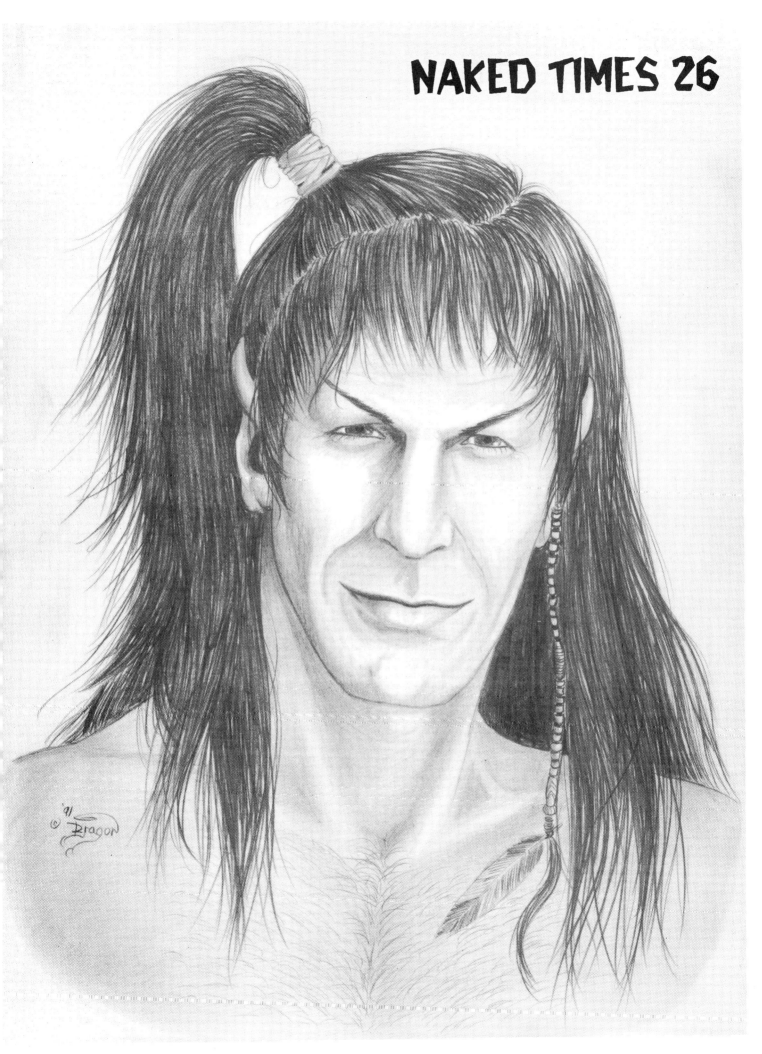

Trek Connections
Star Trek novel.
Ankh Press
PO Box 4020
Alameda, CA 94501

Trek Encore
Star Trek genzine.
Vel Jaeger
1324 Stratford Dr.
Clearwater, FL 34616

TREKisM at Length
Star Trek Genzine.
Vel Jaeger
1324 Stratford Dr.
Clearwater, FL 34616

Trek Memorabilia Price Guide II
The definitive 'zine for the Trek collector.
Emily Lazzio
434 Belmont Ave.
Niles, OH 44446.

The Trek Monitor
Newsletter
The Trek Monitor
PO Box 305
Anthon, IA 51004-0305

Trek Talk
Newsletter
Deena Brooks
PO Box 2522
Renton, WA 98056

Trekville Gazette
Club newsletter.
TREKVILLE USA
Jay Hastings
1021 S. 9th Avenue
Scranton, PA 18504

Trekzine Times
ST newsletter
Forever Productions
PO Box 75
New York, NY 10276

Trexindex
A complete and comprehansive index to Star Trek fanzines. Each volume contains listings as indicated, a selection of fannish art and an introduction.
FOURTH SUPPLEMENT, VOLUME I:
Stories and articles, Author/title/subject listings, 1983-1986.
FOURTH SUPPLEMENT, VOLUME II:
Poetry/art listings, 1983-1986.
THIRD SUPPLEMENT, VOLUME I:
Stories and articles, Author/title/subject listings, 1980-1984.
THIRD SUPPLEMENT, VOLUME II:
Portry/art listings, 1980-1984.
SECOND SUPPLEMENT, VOLUME I:
Stories and articles, Author/title/subject listings, 1979-1981.
SUPPLEMENT, VOLUME I: Stories and articles, author/title/subject listings, 1977-1979.
SUPPLEMENT, VOLUME II: Poetry/art listings, 1977 1979.
"ORIGINAL", VOLUME I: Titles of fanzines, titles of stories and articles, 1966-1976 (reprints).
"ORIGINAL", VOLUME II/III: Stories and articles, authors/subject listings, 1966-1976.
"ORIGINAL", VOLUME IV/V: Poetry/ art listings, 1966-1976.
Roberta Rogow
P.O. Box 1124
Fair Lawn, NJ 07410-1124.

Trinary Star
Star Trek Genzine.
Diana King
4901 Montgomery St.
Annandale, VA 22003

Trojan Angel
A Star Trek novel by Barbara Lenore Snowberger.
Peg Kennedy & Bill Hupe
916 Lamb Road
Mason, MI 48854

True Vulcan Confessions
Star Trek Genzine.
Dusty Jones
1009 East-West Highway
Takoma Park, MD 20912

The Twenty-Fith Year
A K/S anthology celebrating 25 years of Star Trek.
Pon Farr Press
PO Box 2556
Yucca Valley, CA 92286-2556

Twilight Trek
K/S 'zine. Adult.
Jean Hinson
7830 DePalma Street
Downey, CA 90241

Understanding Kraith
Reference dictionary.
Judith Segal
PO Box 414
Pawling, NY 12564

Ultimate Mary Sue
Multi-media 'zine.
Peg Kennedy & Bill Hupe
916 Lamb Road
Mason, MI 48854

Unholy Alliances
K/S zine. Adult.
Pon Farr Press
PO Box 2556
Yucca Valley, CA 92286-2556

Vaeya
Star Trek novel.
Lee S. Pennell
277 Clydesdale Lane
Mableton, GA 30059

Variations on a Theme
Star Trek genzine from England.
Peg Kennedy & Bill Hupe
916 Lamb Road
Mason, MI 48854

The Voice
THE VOICE 1-5 is a series of K/S zines about the established relationship; the lives of Kirk and Spock as told by Sheak, Rivers, Daniels and Rowes. (No A/U of death) K/S - age statement please. #1 - 88 pages, #22 - 90 pages, #3 - 95 pages #4 - 110c pages, #5 - 96 pages.
Rosemary Wild
"Cwm Croesor" Stuckton
Fordingbridge Hants, SP6 2HG
England.

Vulcan Kartune Book
Satirical cartoons
H. Roll
2419 Greensburg Pike
Pittsburg, PA 15221.

Warped Space
Genzine. Fan fiction based on many different shows besides Star Trek. This 'zine has been around since the '70s. Many issues published in the past 20 years.
T'Khutian Press
200 E. Thomas Street
Lansing, MI 48909

Way Home
K/S novel. Adults.
Pon Farr Press
PO Box 2556
Yucca Valley, CA 92286-2556

Sacrifices

When Le'matyas Sleep

Way of the Warrior
K/S fiction; adult.
Jean Hinson
7830 DePalma St.
Downey, CA 90241

Weaver of Dreams
Star Trek novel.
Peg Kennedy & Bill Hupe
916 Lamb Road
Mason, MI 48854

The "Web" Novels
Four novels from Tholian Web.
Sylvia Stanczyk
1953 E. 18th St
Erie PA 16510.

The Weight Collected
This 520 page zine reprints the STAR TREK time travel story, "The Weight" by Leslie Fish, which was serialized in the 'zine WARPED SPACE in the '70s. It also contains three related short stories. This is one of the most famous fan fiction stories. Highly recommended. This collection was published in 1988 and may be out of print. Write for availability.
T'Kuhtian Press
200 E. Thomas Street
Lansing, Michigan 48909

We The People
Star Trek newsletter, publication of USS Constitution.
Cynthia Temple
6247 Fulton Ave #4
Van Nuys, CA 91401

Wheel of Fate
Star Trek novel.
Peg Kennedy & Bill Hupe
916 Lamb Road
Mason, MI 48854

The Wheel Turns
Star Trek novel.
Peg Kennedy & Bill Hupe
916 Lamb Road
Mason, MI 48854

When Heroes Die
A McCoy Novel.
Joyce Tulloch
12528 Cate Ave.
Baton Rouge, LA 70815.

When Le'Matyas Sleep
Shore leave with humans is not Spock's idea of fun; Spock returns to Vulcan to take a wife; Spock and Chapel stranded on a hostile planet, plus poetry and art. 75% of this is Spock /Christine. 75 pages, reduced, comb-bound. Rated PG-13.
Wendy Rathbone
PO Box 2556
Yucca Valley, CA 92286-2556

When the Sun Shines
Star Trek novel.
Peg Kennedy & Bill Hupe
916 Lamb Road
Mason, MI 48854

When Two Worlds Collide
Star Trek novel.
Peg Kennedy & Bill Hupe
916 Lamb Road
Mason, MI 48854

Where Do We Go From Here?
A post-SEARCH FOR SPOCK story. Did you ever wonder what happens after Spock's fal-tor-pan? Can Spock survive it? How does Jim Kirk bear up under the fal-tor-pan?
Lee S. Penell
227 Clydesdale Lane
Mableton, GA 30059.

Where None Have Gone Before
ST: TNG newsletter; articles, features.
Publication of Enterprise America.
Enterprise America
PO Box 3273
Costa Mesa, CA 92628

Will What Was Ever Be?
Written by Carolyn Huston. What happens when a typical 1986 Star Trek fan gets cought in a Romulan time-tampering, history-changing scheme? Sarah finds herself in 1846 England, where she is befriended by Jane Eyre. Later, when the crew of the Enterprise shows up to foil the Romulan plot, she meets her heroes. Between all the action, adventure, emotion and often hilarious by-play, one wonders if Sarah will get home. Appr. 30,000 words. Cover art by Rosemary Comings Tole.
Carolyn Huston
46 Mar Vista Dr.
Monterey, CA 93940

Wine of Colvoro
Star Trek novel
Peg Kennedy & Bill Hupe
916 Lamb Road
Mason, MI 48854

World of Difference
Star Trek novel.
Peg Kennedy & Bill Hupe
916 Lamb Road
Mason, MI 48854

The Year In Review
ST: TNG guide/lexicon for each season. Summer annual publication of Enterprise America.
Enterprise America
PO Box 3273
Costa Mesa, CA 92628

The Zine Connection
Published 6 times a year. Lengthy lists of available fanzines supplied by various fan publishers. Pamphlet size. Average 40 pages.
Jean Hinson
7830 DePalma Street
Downey, CA 90241

Zine Publishing Information
Allyson M.W. Dyar
Forty-A Cecil Lane,
Montgomery, Alabama 36109-2872
"I can answer questions on how to put together a fanzine as well as technical answers as I hold a BA in Communications, worked for an off-set printer as well as hold a certificate in off-set printing."

Zottly's Zine
Star Trek genzine.
 Barb Krause
104 Clariton St.
Pittsburgh, PA 15250.

The Zumbooruk Hyperflash
A newsletter for fans of all aspects of Trek.
Zumbooruk Hyperflash
POBox 165026
Irving, TX 75016
And so ends the listings of STAR TREK fanzines. Write for information directly to the zines listed only, not to Pioneer Books.

Opposite page: The cover of SEHLAT'S RAOR #5 (December 1977) which features the article by Leslie Fish on her concept for the outworlds.

THE MAN WHO CREATED STAR TREK: GENE RODDENBERRY

James Van Hise

The complete life story of the man who created STAR TREK, reveals the man and his work.

$14.95 in stores ONLY $12.95 to Couch Potato Catalog Customers
160 Pages
ISBN # 1-55698-318-2

TWENTY-FIFTH ANNIVERSARY TREK TRIBUTE

James Van Hise

Taking a close up look at the amazing Star Trek stroy, this book traces the history of the show that has become an enduring legend. James Van Hise chronicles the series from 1966 to its cancellation in 1969, through the years when only the fans kept it alive, and on to its unprecedented revival. He offers a look at its latter-day blossoming into an animated series, a sequence of five movies (with a sixth in preparation) that has grossed over $700 million, and the offshoot "The Next Generation" TV series.

The author gives readers a tour of the memorials at the Smithsonian and the Movieland Wax Museums, lets them witness Leonard Nimoy get his star on the Hollywood Walk Of Fame in 1985, and takes them behind the scenes of the motion-picture series and TV's "The Next Generation." The concluding section examines the future of Star Trek beyond its 25th Anniversary.

$14.95.....196 Pages
ISBN # 1-55698-290-9

THE TREK FAN'S HANDBOOK
Written by James Van Hise

STAR TREK inspired its millions of loyal fans to put pen to paper, in order to discuss the various themes and issues being raised by the show's scripts, explore the characters in minute detail and ponder where both STAR TREK and humanity are headed in the future. THE TREK FAN'S HANDBOOK offers a guide on who to write to, what products are available, information on the various STAR TREK fanclubs, addresses, membership information nad details on the fanzines they publish.

THE TREK FAN'S HANDBOOK allows the reader to tap into the basic backbone of what has allowed STAR TREK to thrive over the past quarter century.

$9.95.....109 Pages
ISBN # 1-55698-271-2

TREK: THE NEXT GENERATION
James Van Hise

They said it would not last, and after its cancellation in 1969, it looked as if it wouldn't. But the fans refused to let it die and now *Star Trek* is thriving as never before. The *Next Generation* television series continues the adventure. This book reveals the complete story behind the new series, the development of each major character, presents a complete episode guide, and gives plans for the future.

$14.95.....164 Pages
ISBN # 1-55698-305-0

COUCH POTATO INC.   5715 N. Balsam Rd   Las Vegas, NV 89130   (702)658-2090

Use Your Credit Card 24 HRS — Order toll Free From: **(800)444-2524** Ext 67

TREK: THE MAKING OF THE MOVIES
James Van Hise

TREK: THE MAKING OF THE MOVIES tells the complete story both on-screen and behind the scenes of the biggest STAR TREK adventures of all. Plus the story of the STAR TREK II that never happened and the aborted STAR TREK VI: STARFLEET ACADEMY.

$14.95.....160 Pages
ISBN # 1-55698-313-1

TREK: THE LOST YEARS
Edward Gross

The tumultouos, behind-the-scenes saga of this modern day myth between the cancellation of the original series in 1969 and the announcement of the first movie ten years later. In addition, the text explores the scripts and treatments written throughout the 1970's, including every proposed theatrical feature and an episode guide for STAR TREK II, with comments from the writers whose efforts would ultimately never reach the screen.

This volume came together after years of research, wherein the author interviewed a wide variety of people involved with every aborted attempt at revival, from story editors to production designers to David Gautreaux, the actor signed to replace Leonard Nimoy; and had access to exclusive resource material, including memos and correspondences, as well as teleplays and script outlines.

$12.95.....132 Pages
ISBN # 1-55698-220-8

COUCH POTATO INC.   5715 N. Balsam Rd   Las Vegas, NV 89130   (702)658-2090

THE HISTORY OF TREK

James Van Hise

The complete story of Star Trek from Original conception to its effects on millions of Lives across the world. This book celebrates the 25th anniversary of the first "Star Trek" television episode and traces the history of the show that has become an enduring legend—even the non-Trekkies can quote specific lines and characters from the original television series. The History of Trek chronicles "Star Trek" from its start in 1966 to its cancellation in 1969; discusses the lean years when "Star Trek" wasn't shown on television but legions of die hard fans kept interest in it still alive; covers the sequence of five successful movies (and includes the upcoming sixth one); and reviews "The Next Generation" television series, now entering its sixth season. Complete with Photographs, The History of Trek reveals the origins of the first series in interviews with the original cast and creative staff. It also takes readers behind the scenes of all six Star Trek movies, offers a wealth of Star Trek Trivia, and speculates on what the future may hold.

$14.95.....160 Pages
ISBN # 1-55698-309-3

THE MAN BETWEEN THE EARS:
STAR TREKS LEONARD NIMOY

James Van Hise

Based on his numerous interviews with Leonard Nimoy, Van Hise tells the story of the man as well as the entertainer.

This book chronicles the many talents of Leonard Nimoy from the beginning of his career in Boston to his latest starring work in the movie, Never Forget. His 25-year association with Star Trek is the centerpiece, but his work outside the Starship Enterprise is also covered, from such early efforts as Zombies of the Stratosphere to his latest directorial and acting work, and his stage debut in Vermont.

$14.95.....160 Pages
ISBN # 1-55698-304-2

COUCH POTATO INC.   5715 N. Balsam Rd   Las Vegas, NV 89130   (702)658-2090

Use Your Credit Card 24 HRS — Order toll Free From: **(800)444-2524** Ext 67

BORING, BUT NECESSARY ORDERING INFORMATION

Payment:

Use our new 800 # and pay with your credit card or send check or money order directly to our address. All payments must be made in U.S. funds and please do not send cash.

Shipping:

We offer several methods of shipment. Sometimes a book can be delayed if we are temporarily out of stock. You should note whether you prefer us to ship the book as soon as available, send you a merchandise credit good for other goodies, or send your money back immediately.

Normal Post Office: $3.75 for the first book and $1.50 for each additional book. These orders are filled as quickly as possible. Shipments normally take 5 to 10 days, but allow up to 12 weeks for delivery.

Special UPS 2 Day Blue Label Service or Priority Mail: Special service is available for desperate Couch Potatoes. These books are shipped within 24 hours of when we receive the order and normally take 2 to 3 three days to get to you. The cost is $10.00 for the first book and $4.00 each additional book .

Overnight Rush Service: $20.00 for the first book and $10.00 each additional book.

U.s. Priority Mail: $6.00 for the first book and $3.00.each additional book.

Canada And Mexico: $5.00 for the first book and $3.00 each additional book.

Foreign: $6.00 for the first book and $3.00 each additional book.

Please list alternatives when available and please state if you would like a refund or for us to backorder an item if it is not in stock.

COUCH POTATO INC.   5715 N. Balsam Rd   Las Vegas, NV 89130   (702)658-2090

Use Your Credit Card 24 HRS — Order toll Free From: **(800)444-2524** Ext 67

ORDER FORM

_____ Trek Crew Book $9.95
_____ Best Of Enterprise Incidents $9.95
_____ Trek Fans Handbook $9.95
_____ Trek: The Next Generation $14.95
_____ The Man Who Created Star Trek: $12.95
_____ 25th Anniversary Trek Tribute $14.95
_____ History Of Trek $14.95
_____ The Man Between The Ears $14.95
_____ Trek: The Making Of The Movies $14.95
_____ Trek: The Lost Years $12.95
_____ Trek: The Unauthorized Next Generation $14.95
_____ New Trek Encyclopedia $19.95
_____ Making A Quantum Leap $14.95
_____ The Unofficial Tale Of Beauty And The Beast $14.95
_____ Complete Lost In Space $19.95
_____ ..doctor Who Encyclopedia: Baker $19.95
_____ Lost In Space Tribute Book $14.95
_____ Lost In Space With Irwin Allen $14.95
_____ Doctor Who: Baker Years $19.95
_____ Doctor Who: Pertwee Years $19.95
_____ Batmania Ii $14.95
_____ The Green Hornet $14.95 _____ Special Edition $16.95

_____ Number Six: The Prisoner Book $14.95
_____ Gerry Anderson: Supermarionation $17.95
_____ Addams Family Revealed $14.95
_____ Bloodsucker: Vampires At The Movies $14.95
_____ Dark Shadows Tribute $14.95
_____ Monsterland Fear Book $14.95
_____ The Films Of Elvis $14.95
_____ The Woody Allen Encyclopedia $14.95
_____ Paul Mccartney: 20 Years On His Own $9.95
_____ Yesterday: My Life With The Beatles $14.95
_____ Fab Films Of The Beatles $14.95
_____ 40 Years At Night: The Tonight Show $14.95
_____ Exposing Northern Exposure $14.95
_____ The La Lawbook $14.95
_____ Cheers: Where Everybody Knows Your Name $14.95
_____ SNL! The World Of Saturday Night Live $14.95
_____ The Rockford Phile $14.95
_____ Encyclopedia Of Cartoon Superstars $14.95
_____ How To Create Animation $14.95
_____ How To Draw Art For Comic Books $14.95
_____ King And Barker:an Illustrated Guide $14.95
_____ King And Barker: An Illustrated Guide II $14.95

100% Satisfaction Guaranteed.

We value your support. You will receive a full refund as long as the copy of the book you are not happy with is received back by us in reasonable condition. No questions asked, except we would like to know how we failed you. Refunds and credits are given as soon as we receive back the item you do not want.

NAME:_____

STREET:_____

CITY:_____

STATE:_____

ZIP:_____

TOTAL:_____ SHIPPING_____

SEND TO: Pioneer Books, Inc. 5715 N. Balsam Rd., Las Vegas, NV 89130